Rotting Trees

Bezzina's Emporium of Magical Artefacts & Antiquities Book I

ROTTING TREES

First edition. January 31, 2025.

Copyright © 2025 Francesca Astraea.

ISBN: 978-1838204662

Written by Francesca Astraea.

Table of Contents

Prologue

Why do people go shopping? Your answer might depend on whether you incline towards philosophy or marketing consultancy. Why do people sell their belongings? Here, your response may vary depending on your perspective on dusting, or your experiences of moving house. A third question, as we're beginning a trilogy: in what ways do the people and their reasons change when the shop is steeped in magic?

A more interesting question: what sort of person is best suited to working in a shop steeped in magic?

To imagine this particular shop, you need to think of a supermarket, with flickering strip lighting and enormous humming fridges and queues all the way to an overcrowded car park. Now picture the entire monstrosity fizzling into nonexistence and try not to think of it again. *Our* shop is small and old, and smells like a restaurant where the owner knows you, or a cosy old library, or a hug from a trusted adult when you were seven. Note: this is not necessarily somewhere you consciously decide to visit. Your brain, when it notices you stepping over the threshold, hisses, *you won't be staying long, you're just popping in, you don't really* need *anything*. All the while, your heart has a feeling you'll find exactly what you've been needing for months. Years. A lifetime.

As established, you might be selling an unwanted item—this is the sort of business where two-way transactions are encouraged, as long as everyone involved has metaphorically and actually washed their hands. In which case, you let the shop door close behind you knowing that you also got what you've been needing for months, even if what you've been needing is to not own that little vintage ashtray you picked up for pennies and quite liked until you realised it was haunted, or sentient, or vocally judged your smoking habits.

It is a very reasonable assumption that the people who work in our shop must be up to their eyeballs in what's best referred to, even in polite company, as *weird shit*. Magic. Death. Magic-and-death. Probably they steal your breath as you say hello and steal your hair as they stand next to you at a cabinet. Your star sign is probably entered into a ledger as soon as you set foot inside, next to your height and the colour of your aura, and on weekends they use your soul energy to keep themselves young, or rich, or free always from insect bites.

Probably.

Or, possibly, they came looking because they were as lost as you were.

Or they needed a job and the hours were good.

2015.

Spring

Chapter One

Ariel Scarlet arrived in Southend-on-Sea on a train so early it felt like it was still yesterday. It was a gloomy April and she had left her home in Bath when it was still dark, reaching Essex as dawn gave way to an overcast, chilly morning. Officially, Ariel was in Southend to visit her older brother, a student at one of the local universities. It was unlikely he would be awake to meet her before midday. Not because he was a student, but because Ariel had told him she wouldn't leave the family home until mid-morning.

He wasn't the reason she made the trip across the country.

A cold wind greeted Ariel as she stepped out of Southend Central train station, and she gripped her little shoulder bag instinctively. She was wearing it cross-body, the strap clipped to a belt loop, but checked it was secure every five minutes nevertheless. Her duffel bag, containing clothes and a gift for her brother, was an afterthought slung over one shoulder. She dug a piece of paper from her pocket, crumpled from obsessive re-folding. She reread the address and her scribbled directions for the hundredth time, took a deep breath and strode away from the station, into Southend high street.

Having never visited Southend before—the previous autumn, their father ferried Seb to his student house in a rented van—Ariel's first impression was of a recently-liberated Soviet state. According to a perfunctory internet search, Southend in its heyday was a busy seaside town, beloved by tourists for its dry climate and proximity to London.

Now it just needed a good wash.

Concrete buildings looked rather as though they were bleeding their grey into everything else: sky, metal benches, bundled-up commuters. A few planters held depressed shrubs. When Ariel looked upwards, she could see the signage of long-gone businesses painted on shop fronts. They were faded and grimy, like no one wanted to remember that life once thrived here.

Buffeted by wind, Ariel battled down Southend high street towards the seafront, wind whipping through her pixie crop. She could vaguely see the Thames Estuary ahead, and the outline of a theme park and a pier (Seb promised a trip to both) but she focussed on finding the correct side street. Mercifully, when she turned a corner, the wind died down enough for her to consult her notes and triple-check she had the right road. Two doors down, one door down...

She did not need to check the address to know she was at the right place. A small, worn shop front with a large glass window displaying vases and pots full of hyacinths and forget-me-nots, so confidently blue against the dull day that they hurt to look at. The flowers surrounded a cheery kitchen scene; a wooden table and cushioned chairs with patterned tablecloths and gleaming crockery. A handwritten label explained, *Table and chairs are self-cleaning. Please enquire for price.* Above the window, worn hand-painted signage declared:

Bezzina's Emporium of Magical Artefacts and Antiquities.

Ariel took a deep breath, touched her shoulder bag once more and pushed the frosted-glass door.

It was locked.

Ariel blinked and checked her watch. It was gone nine o'clock. The shop, behind the window display, was dark. An old cardboard sign, hanging in the door, read 'Closed.'

There was no visible list of opening times.

Ariel exhaled a soft swear. *Why* had she assumed they would open at nine? For all her research, Ariel couldn't find an online presence for Bezzina's Emporium, not even a clunky online directory listing. There were a few posts on social media by customers, geo-tagging the shop's location, but the earliest upload Ariel could find was time stamped mid-morning. A nine o'clock opening was her best guess, and it was convenient. She wanted plenty of time to conclude her visit before she met Seb.

Ariel shrugged off her duffel bag, took a plastic bag from a side pocket, and smoothed it out on the pavement. She pulled her jacket hood over her head and sat down carefully on the plastic. She leant against the shop window, duffel pulled against her for warmth. She hadn't arrived planning to wait, but she had once queued outside of the Pandora shop in Bath before a launch for a new bracelet charm and had learnt the hard way to always carry something to put between your designer jeans and the ground.

Minutes ticked by. Ariel pulled some reading material out of her bag—only some leaflets she picked up last time she was in the pharmacy—but she was too nervous to focus, so she just turned them over in her hands.

Maybe Bezzina's Emporium didn't open on a Monday.

'All right there, love?' a man asked. Ariel glanced at him for a split second, long enough to ascertain that he was grizzled, stooped and possibly using the sort of drugs one did not buy from a chemist.

Statistically, this man wasn't going to be the thing that killed Ariel.

She stared unblinking at her phone, texting her dad: *Don't forget to take Rocket out, don't forget she needs half a can of wet food with the biscuits.* The old guy muttered to himself and shuffled away.

Maybe Bezzina's Emporium wouldn't be able to help her anyway.

Across the road, a woman wearing platform heels and a mini dress stumbled out of a front door. 'AND DON'T TRY THAT AGAIN!' she shouted in the general direction of an upstairs window. Ariel watched as the woman lit a cigarette and tottered around the corner. Her retreating figure, adorned with a fluffy black jacket and laddered tights, would have made a brilliant photograph in the grey light.

Maybe, if Bezzina's Emporium couldn't help, she would have to find something to think about other than the contents of her shoulder bag.

Ariel was trying to push the thought to the back of her mind when a voice said, 'Can I help you?'

Ariel pulled off her hood and stood, shaking out pins and needles. The girl in front of her was small and stout, with olive skin and reams of dark hair underneath a cheap woollen beanie. She was around Ariel's age, fifteen or so, and on one shoulder hung a tote bag depicting an illustrated cat. In one hand was a door key and in the other, a Malorie Blackman paperback.

'What time do you open?' Ariel asked.

'We're ten until two today.'

'Today? *Just* today?'

'It's the school holidays.' Ariel waited, but the girl did not elaborate. Instead she unlocked the shop door and flicked a light switch. 'Would you like a coffee?'

Chapter Two

Bezzina's Emporium of Magical Artefacts and Antiquities was everything like Ariel expected and nothing like Ariel expected. Once, on holiday in Crete, her family stumbled across an antiques shop stuffed full of curiosities stretching back decades if not centuries. It was the sort of place small children shouldn't enter unless wearing a harness, because every surface contained something breakable: ornaments, vinyl records, glassware. Wallpaper disappeared under pictures or shelving, and there wasn't a surface without a dozen objects all waiting to be purchased or knocked over. Ariel had loved it even as she was afraid to move too quickly.

Bezzina's Emporium reminded her of that, except it was more... bizarre. *Bizarre* was the best word, she decided. As the assistant disappeared into a back room and the bubbling sounds of a kettle floated out, Ariel loitered on an empty rectangle of carpet and felt like she was inside a catacomb, except instead of bones she was surrounded by *stuff*. She could indeed see ornaments and records and glassware, organised on side tables and shelves, inside cabinets and cases. Neat, joined-up handwriting on little card labels indicated a variety of price ranges. The air smelt of degradable materials when they've been degrading quite some time: paper, cotton, wood. But it also smelt like furniture polish and fresh air, like a much airier, larger space. Lamps threw yellow light into every corner, which Ariel was grateful for in the gloom of the day. If you weren't paying attention, Bezzina's Emporium could pass as a regular antiques shop.

But Ariel was paying attention, so *bizarre* was her only adjective. Her gaze snagged on another handwritten sign, attached to a sparkling jewellery cabinet. *Top shelf: mundane. Middle shelf: charmed. Bottom shelf: dangerous. Please ask for assistance.* Then the clothing rack: *Left to right: Vintage: mundane. Vintage: magical. Contemporary: magical.* A pink silk dress, in the mid-

9

dle of the rack, smouldered gently. Smoke seemed to touch nothing except for the dress, which was on fire but not disintegrating. Ariel could smell neither smoke nor burning silk. She *could* hear ticking, quietly beating against the outside sounds of traffic and seagulls. She searched for the source and found it after several seconds of peering through the shop's collection. Between a sideboard displaying bone china and side table holding a tape recorder, a freestanding dark wood clock kept time perfectly. Ariel squinted at the label: *Granddaughter clock, circa 1930s. Haunted.*

'You don't have to worry about that.'

The shop assistant had returned. Without her coat and jumper, she was bony and sallow and wearing a burgundy pinafore Ariel thought made her look like a grungy primary school teacher. The girl handed Ariel a large mug and pulled a folding chair out from behind the counter.

'Would you like to sit?'

Although Ariel had done a yoga routine before she left the house to stop her legs going dead while she spent the morning sitting on several trains, she found her knees were a little weak. Maybe because she'd slept badly the night before—well, worse than normal. A dream about an old tree, of all things, woke her up. She could even smell the dead wood as she hauled herself out of bed and headed downstairs to let Rocket into the garden. But she shook her head at the chair. The assistant wasn't sitting, so neither would she. Ariel sipped her coffee. It wasn't burned, which surprised her. It contained oat milk, which surprised her more. She hadn't asked for it.

'Thanks.'

'Welcome.' The assistant leant against the counter. 'How can we help you?'

Ariel touched her bag. 'Are you the only person here?'

'I am today, yes.'

'What about Mr... Bezzina?'

The assistant's eyes, which were dark brown and deep set under eyebrows that needed a good tweeze, darkened further. 'Bold assumption he's a mister.'

Fair. Ariel drank some coffee. The assistant kept talking.

'He is a mister, as it happens. Ernest. He's on a retreat until tomorrow. I'm holding the fort.'

'You're my age,' Ariel said before she could stop herself.

'And yet we've both managed to arrive here independently and fully dressed.' The girl's eyebrows knotted. 'You're welcome to return when Ernie's back.'

'No, it's fine.' Ariel was due to meet Seb soon. She had to get this over with. She reached into her shoulder bag and eased out a velvet case. She placed it on the counter, careful to ensure her coffee was well out of the way, and undid the clasp. Inside nestled a very old, very heavy necklace, glinting in the lamplight.

'Would you like it valued?' the assistant asked.

'No.' Ariel's father had it insured and kept in the family safe. Ariel didn't know its precise monetary value, but knew she would be grounded until graduation if anyone found out she had taken it on a trip across the south of England. *University* graduation, not secondary school graduation.

'Is it for sale?'

'No.'

The assistant waited, arms crossed. She glanced at Ariel's coffee. Ariel knew she was thinking her hospitality had been a waste of time. But now she was here, Ariel was having trouble forming the words. She looked around the shop as she tried to steady her thoughts, taking in an old camera, a trunk of shoes and a 1970s' pride flag with singed corners.

'I need to know if the necklace is cursed. And who cursed it and why. And how to break it.'

The assistant's eyebrows moved again, but Ariel thought she had her interest. She looked down at the necklace, then produced a small eyeglass from behind the counter.

'Is it safe to handle?' she asked, hands hovering over the necklace. 'We've had a few cursed items that can't come into contact with anything other than air.'

'You're fine to touch it.'

For the next five minutes, neither of them spoke. Ariel watched steam rise from their mugs and looked around the shop a little more. She itched to go and inspect the camera she'd noticed, but didn't want to distract the assistant's attention from the necklace.

For her part, the assistant was completely absorbed in her task, turning over the chain and getting so close to the necklace that her nose was almost touching it. Occasionally she would refer to a dogeared sheet of paper. It was handwritten and spidery, but Ariel recognised vocabulary pertaining to jewellery: shape, transparency, species.

Now she was looking at the necklace in the company of a stranger, Ariel could appreciate with fresh eyes why her father kept it locked away. Its chain and casings were gold, with seven pear-shaped gems hanging from the chain in pleasing intervals. A ruby, an emerald, a marcasite, a second emerald, another marcasite, a bloodstone, a third emerald and finally another ruby. The central gems hung a little lower, so the effect when worn was one of a heavy, dark, sparkling collar. At least, Ariel assumed it was. She had never wanted to try it on.

Eventually the assistant tucked away her eyeglass. 'This necklace is extremely valuable,' she said, as though she needed to say it for the record. 'I think it's magical. I'm almost sure.'

'Almost?'

'Curses are hard to pin down. Ernie says it's because they're so personal. And as you pointed out, I'm not an expert. Ernie will know for sure what the deal is. Can you come back tomorrow?'

'I think so. Can you—can you store this here?' Ariel's stomach churned at the thought of handing over a family heirloom, but she had made the trip expecting that she would have to. She didn't want it going to her brother's shared house if she could help it. Her plan hadn't been to leave it in the care of someone who hadn't finished their GCSEs, though.

'You can put it in our safe yourself and I'll give you mine and Ernie's phone numbers,' the assistant said, clearly sensing Ariel's hesitance.

'All right.'

The girl carefully placed the necklace back into its case and handed it back. 'I'm Sophey, by the way.'

'Ariel.'

Sophey guided Ariel into a back room, to a large iron safe, and began turning the combination. With the necklace installed alongside some money bags and cardboard boxes, they returned to the shop floor and Sophey produced scrap paper from beneath the counter. She wrote down a set of names and phone numbers and handed it to Ariel, then watched as Ariel wrote her own number. 'I forgot to ask, what is the nature of the curse? I'll make a note for Ernie.'

'It kills all the women in my family before the age of forty.'

With that, Ariel walked back out into the grey.

Chapter Three

The next morning, Ariel got a text from Sophey's number, at eight o'clock:

Hi Ariel. Ernie's opening at eight thirty. He's expecting you. -Sophey

As Ariel had anticipated, Seb was still asleep. His Easter holiday coincided with Ariel's—even if she hadn't wanted to visit the local magical antiques shop he'd told her about in phone calls, she would have come up to see him. The previous evening she left him in his shabby living room at ten o'clock, playing cards with flatmates whose names she could not remember. Several glass bottles crowded the kitchen table. While Ariel was in no way allowed to consume alcohol, her presence was apparently enough to warrant an impromptu gathering of Seb's closest new friends, mostly so she could tell stories about their childhood while they drank cheap mixers. Ariel half-exaggerated her tiredness and retreated upstairs to an air mattress and sleeping bag earlier than she normally would, to call their dad and check on Rocket... and to remind Dad that she'd left three plastic tubs of chilli in the freezer so he wouldn't die of scurvy while she was away. She hoped the quiet of the evening would let her collect her thoughts. All that happened was that she tried and failed not to fret about the necklace. She wasn't sure if leaving it at Bezzina's Emporium was the safest option, after all. She wasn't sure if going to the shop was the sensible option, after all. Mostly she wasn't sure if she really wanted to know about the curse, after all.

Her phone vibrated as Seb texted her from downstairs: *I checked the front and back doors are locked and told everyone to check their windows are closed/on the latch.*

She texted back a thumbs up and a smiley emoji.

When Ariel wasn't asleep after half an hour, she got up and did a yoga flow routine in her pyjamas and socks.

When she wasn't asleep after one hour, she picked up her phone to check her notifications, even though her wellness app told her off for unlocking the phone more than the number of times she had pre-set as acceptable after nine o'clock in the evening.

Not even group messages from her best friends, Chloe and Madge, could lift her mood. They had gone into central Bath for the day and sent multiple selfies of themselves in the changing rooms of various stores, pulling faces while they tried on high heels and cute jackets and the sort of garments Ariel would usually ban them from buying if she had seen them first. She sent back a selfie of her own, in the low light of Seb's desk lamp, pulling the best grimace she could, and captioned it *gone back in time eighty years send help.*

When she was not asleep after two hours and the phone had given up telling her not to look at it, she tried scrolling through her old messages deleting all the crap she didn't need. She smiled at badly spelt texts from her grandfather, and long family WhatsApp threads from various aunts and uncles. Most of these old messages could be deleted, she decided, except for the ones from her nearest and dearest. Text from the school on a snow day, gone. Text from fashion retailers when her item was about to be delivered, gone. Appointment reminders from the nail bar, gone. Her finger hovered over one long-dormant thread of texts. Grace's messages. Ariel had last texted in... God, in December. Ariel had messaged 'Happy Christmas!' then followed it up a few days later on New Year's Eve. No response. Their last real text conversation was the previous October, probably around the last time they had spoken in person.

Ariel did not delete the message thread.

She stared at the posters on Seb's ceiling until long after she heard him come to bed. When she nodded off, as dawn began to break, she dreamt of old wooden cabinets, all stacked on top of each other. A breeze rattled through the dream, and the cabinets fell in on themselves, burying her. She was trying to figure out why the cabinets smelt like fresh, living wood when someone outside the house slammed a car door and she sat bolt upright.

So when Sophey's text buzzed on her phone, Ariel was already awake, doing push ups in Seb's living room amongst last night's detritus.

Unwilling to risk a shower in the shared bathroom, she pulled on her clothes, cleaned her teeth and washed her face, then left a note for Seb next to a doodle of a coffee cup: YOU DIDN'T BUY THE RIGHT MILK. BRUNCH?

Statistically, dairy would not be the thing that killed Ariel.

Seb's student house, thankfully, was a short walk from Southend high street. The wind was still bitter today, but the sky was a clear blue and the shops looked slightly friendlier in sunlight than they did under cloud cover, although the general effect was still of somewhere pigeons came to die. Bezzina's Emporium of Magical Artefacts and Antiquities looked identical to the previous day, but as she went to push the door, it opened from the inside.

'Ariel? It's a pleasure to meet you. I'm Ernest Bezzina.' Before Ariel's eyes had a chance to adjust, before she was quite over the threshold, she was on the receiving end of a firm handshake.

The man in front of her did not look like an antiques dealer. He was old, which did seem on brand—she couldn't imagine an antiques dealer under the age of forty—but where she had anticipated red corduroy trousers and polished leather brogues, she got a linen kaftan and sturdy boots. Where she'd imagined a bow tie and halitosis, she got a sprinkling of hand and neck tattoos, and a not unpleasant smell of jasmine. His accent was smoother than Sophey's—not posh, but with fewer dropped consonants. Ariel wondered where he was from originally. Somewhere that made kaftans.

'Come in,' Ernest was saying. 'We were about to put the kettle on. Coffee?'

'Okay.' The shop was no less strange today. In fact, seeing it for a second time highlighted just how utterly weird it was. Somehow, yesterday she had looked right past a framed photograph of the Dalai Lama, whose eyes literally followed her across the room.

'Sophey!' Ernest called into the depths of the shop. 'We are three of us. Now, Ms...'

'Scarlet.'

'This necklace of yours, Ms Scarlet.' Ernest motioned to a couple of armchairs Ariel had assumed were for sale, and gestured at her to sit. 'I've had a look.' He took the necklace case from a neatly pressed trouser pocket and handed it to Ariel. She was glad to feel the weight of it again.

'And?'

'It's definitely magical.'

Ariel expected him to say something else, but Sophey arrived with a tea tray. Her cardigan was mustard coloured, over the same burgundy pinafore, and Ariel suspected she had knitted it herself.

'Apologies I couldn't be here yesterday—I tend to take Mondays off these days, and Sophey isn't allowed to work more than a certain number of hours... something to do with child labour laws.' Ernest's hazel eyes twinkled. 'So that's why you had a bit of a wait. I must say, though,' he added, 'you have quite the piece of jewellery. Even if it wasn't magical, it would be worth more than a lot of our other items.'

'It's not mine to sell,' Ariel said stiffly. Her eyes hurt from lack of sleep, and she could feel a headache creeping into her right temple. She was so tired she could have sworn that the rune-like tattoos on Ernest's knuckles moved as he poured his tea, but it was just the light. 'I just want to know about the curse.'

'Would you mind telling us more about the necklace and its story? Sophey gave me the basics, but it's helpful to hear the history of an item directly.'

Ariel glanced at Sophey, who was balancing a notebook on her knee, pencil poised. 'Do you mind?' Ariel asked. 'I'd rather you didn't take minutes.'

Sophey flushed and put the pencil down. 'Sorry. I'm learning on the job. I was just going to write down anything that might come in useful later.'

'Then you can write it down later.'

Sophey nodded and fidgeted with a cheap plastic beaded bracelet. Ariel turned to Ernest. 'The necklace was my mother's. I was told it's been passed down in the family since the nineteenth century.'

Ernest nodded. 'I'm confident it's early-mid Victorian. The Early Victorian period was...' He looked at Sophey, who straightened up.

'1837 to 1860. The death of Prince Albert in 1861 was the start of the Grand Period.'

'Excellent.' Sophey beamed and Ariel felt a stab of irritation that even if Sophey wasn't taking notes, this visit was a teachable moment.

'I don't c—that's not relevant,' Ariel said. 'I'm not interested in the antique aspect of it. The story has always been that someone in the family was gifted the necklace by a friend, but the friend had cursed it because of a falling out.' She sipped coffee. It was as delicious as yesterday's. 'Ever since, every woman in the family has died young. No one's made it past their late thirties. I need you to confirm if that's really because the necklace is cursed.'

'I wouldn't normally ask such personal questions on a first meeting...' Ernest said. Sophey's eyebrows moved as though she disagreed. 'Are you intent on finding out because you think you'll be next?' His voice was gentle. Ariel wondered how many people had visited the shop with similar questions. Maybe thousands. Maybe everyone's family had a curse.

She shifted in her seat. Sophey was looking down at her closed notebook and Ariel wondered if she had been rude, before. She would also have liked something to do with her hands, now she thought about it, so she turned the cup around as she spoke. 'I'm here because it's a stupid curse. I want to find out what the deal is and I want to break it.' Because she was looking at the cup, Ariel couldn't see Sophey or Ernest's reaction to her words, but she could imagine them. Her answer was a non-answer, and everyone in the room knew it.

For several long seconds, all Ariel could hear was the ticking of the grand-daughter clock, and the outside sounds of the working day. Ernest sipped tea, and Ariel thought that it was the sort of silence she shouldn't interrupt, like when her father was reading a dusty textbook for a piece of research.

Eventually Ernest set down his teacup. 'As I said, it is definitely magical. I can feel that a mile off. But curses, well. I decided a long time ago that I wasn't interested in pursuing the dark or dangerous.' Ariel thought this was a bit rich coming from a man with neck tattoos, but she nodded.

'Do you know anyone who can help?'

'Of course. Sophey.'

'What?'

Both girls had spoken at once. Ariel suspected that Sophey's indignant, irritated expression perfectly mirrored her own. She thought Sophey also looked a little betrayed.

Ernest continued as though they hadn't spoken. 'This is the perfect opportunity to learn the industry, Sophey. You can help Ms Scarlet find out if this necklace is cursed or if her family is merely afflicted by bad luck.'

Before either Ariel or Sophey could protest, the door tinged. A woman in her mid-thirties stepped through, carefully manoeuvring a pram containing a blanket-swaddled infant.

'Svetlana! Alexei! How are you both?' Sophey stood immediately, tucking her notebook into her pinafore, no sign on her face that she had just been upset with her boss.

'We are very well, thank you.' The woman's accent was heavily Eastern European. 'We came to thank you for the teething charm. We are both sleeping *much* better.' The baby gurgled in agreement. 'This is a thank you,' Svetlana continued. She held out a small piece of sketch paper, placed carefully between cardboard and cellophane. 'Since you do not charge enough.'

Ernest took the sketch and smiled. 'You really didn't have to. Thank you. And thank *you*, little one,' he added to the baby. He passed the paper to Sophey and Ariel caught a glimpse of a surprisingly competent pencil illustration of the front of the shop.

'Now we are both resting more, I have the energy to draw again,' Svetlana smiled. 'I will not forget this.'

Ariel was glad she had not asked for sugar in her coffee. If the atmosphere in here got any more saccharine, she would need dental work.

She waited while the staff exchanged pleasantries with Svetlana and the child for a few more minutes, and was glad when the door closed after them.

'Investigating the curse—' she began. But the door was opening again.

'Bezzina!' This customer was the sort of man you saw playing the cheeky, not-totally-bad bad guy in a film. Small and round, with a red face, he reminded Ariel immediately of one of those little Father Christmas baubles. Following behind him was a pre-teen boy, awkward and hunched.

'Hello,' Ernest said mildly. 'How can we help you, sir?'

'I'm going to sue.'

'For what?' Ernest asked.

'For *what*? For selling me a dangerous object.' From his coat he produced a small, clothbound book. 'This *thing* gave my son nightmares! And this girl—' he jabbed a finger in Sophey's direction, 'sold me it under false pretences.'

Sophey stood taller, which was not remotely tall, and said firmly, 'You asked me if we had anything your son might like and after browsing my suggestions, you decided on this. I read you the label.'

'The label?' the man blinked. The boy, presumably the traumatised son, was flushed pink with his hands deep in his pockets, staring at the floor.

'The same information is printed on your receipt. It's also written up on the wall.' Sophey pointed. Ariel followed her finger and indeed, on the wall above the till was a computer-typed sign in bold:

Bezzina's Emporium of Magical Artefacts and Antiquities bears no responsibility for any unpleasant or unsettling experiences induced by our products, as the origin and intended effects of each product is clearly indicated on the label.

You have thirty days to return anything, unused, with the receipt and in the correct packaging, as long as it is not damaged. This does not impact your statutory rights.

'My rights *have* been impacted!'

Sophey blinked several times and took a deep breath, like she had rehearsed this. 'Sir, you asked for something exciting for your son's birthday. You told me he likes fantasy novels. You chose to purchase this copy of *Percy Jackson and the Lightning Thief*. I explained to you, as did the label, that this particular copy is multisensory. You read a few paragraphs, remember, and you nearly vomited at the sensation of falling from the St Louis arch.'

'That's one thing. My son has had screaming nightmares from reading the scenes set in hell!'

'The label did warn you. As did I, when you told me he was only twelve. You *insisted* he was mature for his age and had already read a mundane copy several times. I distinctly remember you saying, "he won't find it scary, he's not a girl."'

The man puffed up. Ariel realised that, like Sophey, she was bristling. The child, now blushing down to his neck, risked a glance at his father, and then at Ernest and Sophey. Ernest watched the scene with a slight crease in his forehead but did not move to intervene.

'You're within your thirty days, so we're happy to refund you,' Sophey suggested, 'although the product has clearly been used.'

'Dad, I don't mind,' mumbled the boy. 'I knew it was going to be scarier than my other copy of the book. The normal book isn't that scary,' he said seriously to Sophey. 'I love the whole series.'

Sophey smiled. 'So do I.'

The child smiled back, standing upright for the first time. 'Have you read the other books he wrote?'

'I love them!' Sophey looked as though she wanted to say more, but glanced at the father. He was turning puce.

'Fine. *Fine.* I won't be coming back here, and I'll be leaving you a bad review. Come on, Jameson.'

The man strode away as fast as he entered. Jameson took a last look around and ducked his shoulders apologetically, shutting the door gently behind him.

Sophey and Ernest turned to each other. 'Well handled,' Ernest said. 'Calm, professional...'

'I've been practising reciting the returns policy,' Sophey said. She was a little pink in the face herself, her hands clasped into fists. 'I *did* do my best to show him it wasn't a soft little gift.'

'You did everything correctly. Ah, Ms Scarlet, thank you for waiting in the corner there.'

'Welcome to a normal day,' Sophey said lightly. 'Where were we?'

'Finding out about the curse,' Ariel said. She was still unconvinced that the person to help her uncover the mystery of her family's cursed necklace was a teenage girl, but she was willing to take what she could get. 'When do we start?'

'I have this afternoon off. There are a few things it would be useful to have a look through before we meet, so I can get some notes down. Do you have a family tree I can look at?'

'No.'

Sophey looked disappointed. 'Um, the first thing I thought we could do is check who in your family is most likely to have been cursed versus who might have died from natural causes. And a family tree would help find out who was the first cursed person. Do you know if the curse impacts women who married into the family? That might be important.'

Ariel felt stupid. Why hadn't she thought of that? 'I have a few names in my recent family. I wouldn't know how to research anyone from a long time ago.' Sophey handed Ariel her notebook and pencil, and Ariel printed the names she knew: her grandma's, her Aunt Katie's, her second-or-third cousin, Jenna. Her mother's. 'Our—the surname is McLean. The surname of the side of the family... with the curse.'

'This is a good start. I have some ideas we could look into. I can meet you any time after one?'

'I'm meeting my brother for brunch,' Ariel said, 'but I'll text you when I know I can get away.'

Chapter Four

As she found her way to the café Seb had texted her to meet at, Ariel considered not messaging Sophey. She didn't want to waste hours of her precious few days with her brother. And it probably would be a waste of both their time. Sophey wouldn't really have a clue who to ask or what to research to find out about the necklace, any more than Ariel had. She was just a teenager with an interesting part time job. Ariel must have been preoccupied, because Seb put down his fork during their meal and said, 'Ariel. What's up?'

Seb Scarlet was taller than his little sister, but not by much. He was politer than his little sister, by quite a lot. Otherwise the only important difference between the two of them was that, being four years older, he had more memories of their mother. He never made a big deal out of it, though.

'Nothing,' she said immediately. 'Nothing's up. Except this café's interior design. You know I don't trust places that put photographs of food on their menu.'

'And yet you are eating,' Seb said drily. He opened his mouth to say something, but changed his mind and closed it again. He picked his fork back up. 'How's Dad?' he asked.

'He's fine. Conference in Swindon today until Thursday. Rocket's going to have to stay with Grandpa and Uncle James, God help all of them. Then Dad's up in Manchester again for another conference in a few weeks' time. He's talking about hosting Grandpa and Uncle James for Christmas.'

'Really? After last year?' Seb grinned. 'Are Uncle Chris and Aunt June coming with the girls?'

'Maybe. They might be taking Em and Lottie to Hong Kong for the holidays to see Aunt June's parents.'

Uncle Chris met Aunt June on a trip to Hong Kong in the nineteen eighties. Several thousand air miles, two weddings on two continents and

Grandpa making some very awkward mispronunciations in Cantonese later, Chris and June lived in Bath but spent most holidays with June's family in Hong Kong. Em and Lottie regaled the McLean cousin group chat with anecdotes about aeroplane food and baggage allowance on a regular basis, and Seb and Ariel missed them when they were away. 'Do you want another coffee?' Seb asked.

'No thanks. This one tastes of sadness.'

When she suggested brunch to her brother, Ariel pictured somewhere pretty and wallpapered, offering shakshuka in ceramic pans and pancakes served with dinky jugs of syrup, possibly overlooking the beach. Instead he'd suggested this greasy spoon—sorry, a pie and mash shop—in another of Southend high street's side roads. Seb tried to convince her to try pie and mash—'it's the food of the gods, I promise,'—but Ariel did not know what liquor was in a culinary context and did not want to find out. The café was cosy enough, she supposed, if you liked metal chairs and assumed that only accepting cash was a practical decision and had absolutely nothing to do with tax dodging.

'Ariel. I didn't expect you to love it here but I didn't expect you to turn your nose up at everything.' Seb frowned into his own mug. Ariel wasn't sure if by *here* he meant the café or *here* the town of Southend-on-Sea. 'You've been weird ever since you arrived at the house yesterday.' *Here* as in Southend, then.

'I am not *turning my nose up*. I'm just tired from the journey. I hate the London Underground.' Ariel looked over at the other customers to avoid her brother's eye. Several pensioners worked their way through plates of pies, while small children slurped fizzy drinks as their mothers nursed mugs of tea. There were more tracksuit bottoms in this room than Ariel had ever seen outside of a gym. She looked back at Seb. 'Tell me how your course is going.'

Seb gave her a look that meant he knew she was changing the subject but was happy to indulge her. 'The course is going fine. I passed first semester. I like Southend a lot. Actually... there might be a job here for me over the summer.'

'You won't come back home?' Ariel put down her fork. 'Why not? There are jobs in Bath.'

'I know. But this is a paid internship with a local start up, and it will be great for my CV, and it's relevant for my modules next year. And...' He stared down at his plate. Ariel resumed her scrambled eggs and mentally said a small prayer that he wasn't about to announce he'd got a girl pregnant.

'I don't really want to go back to Bath, Ariel. You know I couldn't wait to leave.'

'Is this because of Dad?' Ariel demanded. 'Because I can't think of a single other reason you'd want to swap a clean, historic World Heritage City for a town full of concrete and Ugg boots.'

'It's not just because of Dad. And you're being unfair. Did you know that Southend has the longest pleasure pier in the world? I said I'd take you there. The locals say you should walk out and take the train back.'

The pier was long enough for a train? Wait, no, Ariel refused to be side tracked. 'Why were you so desperate to move away after your gap year? Home isn't that bad.'

Seb stared at Ariel for so long that she felt uncomfortable. The Scarlet siblings looked similar enough, both embarrassingly pale with large blue eyes and dark hair. Seb began adding jewellery to his face in his early teens and preferred boxy band t-shirts and live music to Ariel's carefully curated designer clothes and shopping trips. But they were used to seeing their own face reflected in the other person.

So it was disconcerting that now, Ariel had no idea what Seb was thinking. She wondered if she should tell him about the necklace.

'It's complicated,' Seb said eventually. 'Look. This is meant to be a fun trip. Want to go down the beach when we're done here? There's a cliff lift that might be working. We can do the pier. I'll be up earlier tomorrow for more sightseeing, I promise.'

'No, don't change your routine for me. I was thinking I could hit the shops sometime this week if you've got stuff to do,' Ariel said vaguely, as though it had just occurred to her. 'Not that there are many here. I might go for a wander this afternoon, take some photos of the beach.' She paused, like she'd just remembered something. 'Didn't you say you have boxing this afternoon? If we go to the beach after lunch, I could stay while you go to training. I know you find it boring when I'm messing around with my camera.'

'Really? If you're sure. Don't go further than the casino on one side of the pier or the Sea Life Centre on the other. Southend is secretly massive. And a bit dodgy in the wrong areas.'

'I'll stay safe,' Ariel promised. 'I just want to get some pictures for my GCSE portfolio. Seagulls and boats and that.'

Seb paid their bill and they walked down the high street to the seafront. It *was* larger than Ariel expected. Or rather, it was longer: miles of beach and the Thames Estuary in both directions. Seb led her along to a quiet-ish spot with fewer families enjoying the school holiday, where she could stand on the stones, inhale the sea salt smell and listen to gulls shouting at each other as they flew above. If Ariel turned to her right she could see along the coast towards London, and if she turned to her left, she could see along to the open Estuary, where it began to look more like the proper sea. Just a few miles across the water was Kent, a grey-green landscape with indistinct buildings. The tide was in, and little boats bobbed happily in their moorings. Further out, Ariel could see windsurfers gliding across the water's surface, and further out still vast container ships, bright metal containers stacked like patchwork.

'They're going to Tilbury or somewhere up London,' Seb said as Ariel watched the ships. They were so huge Ariel wondered how the water was deep enough to hold them. Seb bent down to pick up a pretty shell and examined it. 'Want to take a photo?'

Ariel produced her mobile from her pocket and snapped a few photos. They weren't great but she could see the potential of capturing somewhere like this. The lines of the Kent coast on the horizon, wee boats near the shore, layers of sand and shells and kelp on the beach at her feet. She stood experimentally on a pile of kelp. When was it called kelp and when was it seaweed? Either way, these black-green tendrils, in clumps with bits of grass and twigs like they'd been washed up by the tide, were sort of bouncy and lifelike. Ariel crouched down to inspect closer and found the seaweed looked a little like tagliatelle, or green beans. While she was down there, she peered at the sand. It wasn't a sandy beach like you get in photos of tropical holidays: this was sand and shells and stones and bits of flotsam, all mixed together like someone had started packing sand into an ideal beachy scene and then knocked over a jar of 'assorted beach objects' and not bothered to tidy it up.

Ariel looked back out to sea. When the sun reflected off the water it sparkled like the gems in the cursed necklace. Gazing up into the blue sky, high and wide with a breeze ruffling her hair, cleared Ariel's headache, like cobwebs blowing away. She imagined that sunrise and sunset, especially on cloudy or misty days, must be something worth seeing.

She supposed she could see why Seb liked it here, just a little.

'I'll take some proper photos with my camera later,' she lied. Ariel had not brought her camera. A slick little digital model that she received the previous Christmas, it came everywhere with her... except here. She hadn't wanted to worry about keeping it safe while she focussed on the necklace, and hadn't wanted a distraction from the job. Besides, *her* hobby wasn't the one she was thinking about as she planned the trip. Seb had been boxing since they were in primary school and she'd known that she would get an hour or two to herself if she made sure her trip aligned with the days he had training sessions at his club.

'Want to go down the pier today after all?' Seb asked. He was looking troubled. Possibly Ariel wasn't excited enough by all this kelp. 'We have loads of time before my boxing starts.' Ariel followed his gaze to the Southend Pier. It was quite some landmark: bleak, but quietly impressive. A sort of criss-crossed wood-and-metal structure sticking out into the Thames for miles and miles in an L shape, buildings hunched on the bit at the end, too far out to sea to look real. A train made its way seabound from the shore. Ariel wondered who had looked out at this particular bit of water and thought 'I know what will improve this: trains.' It was hard to tell if the pier had emerged from the sea or was being slowly consumed by it.

Ariel glanced back at Seb. He still looked worried. 'When does your boxing start?'

'Four o'clock, I have to be back on the shore at about ten to. I can cancel—'

'No, we've got time.' Ariel said. 'Let's do the pier. I came all this way.' She did her best to rearrange her face, so she looked more cheerful. 'The train looks fun.'

While they were queuing to buy tickets, she texted Sophey.

Is four o'clock okay?

Meet me at the main entrance of Southend Central train station. S.

It would probably be a wasted trip, meeting Sophey, but she'd come all this way.

Chapter Five

'There's someone I think we should speak to before we get into your family history,' Sophey said when Ariel found her waiting by the steps outside the train station. She'd been reading a creased paperback as she waited, but she shoved it into her tote bag when she saw Ariel. 'His name's David, he makes and trades jewellery that we sometimes sell. He knows gemstones better than Ernie or I, and I want to start with the necklace itself. Who made it, where, that sort of thing.' She held out the necklace case and Ariel took it, glad to have it back.

'Where does David work?' Ariel asked.

'In Shoebury. A couple of train stops away on this line. David works out of an industrial unit.' Ariel squinted into the train station foyer, at the LED display showing train times. Next train to Shoeburyness, five minutes.

'Shoe...bury...ness.' Ariel tried the word out.

'It's pronounced Shoe-bree. Not *bury*.'

'Shoeburyness.' Ariel tried again. 'Like the Loch Ness Monster.'

'I suppose.' Sophey did not look as though she had ever given it much thought. 'I phoned David earlier and he's willing to meet us this afternoon. He has some stock for Ernie anyway, I can drop it off at the shop when we're done.'

Ariel checked the time. 'Okay. But I have to be back by seven.' She wondered if she should be worried about taking a train to a different part of town with someone she'd just met. But she'd taken self-defence classes for years and was reasonably confident that if it came to it, she could outrun Sophey.

Sophey was looking at Ariel as though she too was thinking about the best way to take her down in a fight. 'Ticket office is over here.'

S hoeburyness was uglier than Southend. Ariel wasn't sure if it was its own town or a suburb because it was just a few stops on the train, but the houses felt even closer together, the roads narrower and the streets somehow even dirtier. Or maybe it felt claustrophobic to Ariel because she'd recently been standing on the end of an extremely long pier. Sophey, who had said precisely nothing since they bought their train tickets, led her on a short walk from the station to a sprawling industrial estate. Or rather, one huge industrial estate full of little industrial estates, each one signposted and hidden behind hulking gates or walls. Enormous lorries rumbled by, full of concrete and steel, and Ariel felt that if she took a wrong turn she would be stuck here forever, walking in circles past car mechanics and ambiguous commercial construction warehouses until time ended, marking distance with burger vans.

Eventually Sophey led her around a corner, then another corner, then another corner, until they were in a brown brick estate, standing in front of a huge steel door reading 'D. BORDEN, JEWELLERY & RESTORATIONS.' Sophey used both hands to push it open.

Inside, the warehouse was a vast workshop, full of benches and boxes. Bright industrial lamps at intervals on the benches illuminated a well-used but neat treasure trove of jewellery-making tools, reams of wire and bottles of chemicals. Little glass boxes held gemstones and lobster claw fastenings and plush velvet boxes. Away from the lamps it was cold, with too many corners hidden in shadow, the perfect hidey spaces for large spiders. A radio, somewhere in the workshop's depths, played Radio Four. It was *The Archers*. The pleasant conversations of the soap opera were at odds with the man who sat at a workbench, folded over some sort of metal work with a pair of pliers in each hand. A steaming mug of tea sat next to him, alongside a packet of cigarettes and some chewing gum. He was the sort of thin that usually accompanies serious illness, his hair shorn right to his skull, and his pale skin was almost completely hidden beneath a baggy jumper, his long fingers nestled in knitted gloves. As Sophey heaved the door shut behind them, Ariel and the man took one another in. He did not stop turning the pliers over in his bony fingers as he stared at her.

His eyes were as hungry as the rest of him.

'Hello, David,' Sophey said. 'Thanks for meeting us.'

'Hello, Sophey.' He did not get up, but Sophey did not seem to expect him to and approached his bench. Ariel followed.

'Gemstones and a curse?' David said when they reached the bench, although he did not sound exactly as though he was asking a question. 'How delicious.' Ariel handed him the case and the girls stood back as he examined the necklace in much the same way Sophey had the day before, except he also put it onto a set of scales.

'It's got aesthetic value to an extent, but not in a particularly commercial way,' David said eventually. He picked up his wire again. 'This isn't something you'd find in a shop to buy your sweetheart. Too many different stones. It's well made, but I'd expect diamond or sapphire in work of this quality, not marcasite or bloodstone.'

'That's what I thought,' Sophey said.

David clicked his tongue. 'Ernest Bezzina can be a thorn in my side, but he's right about a lot of things, and one of them is that you need to have more confidence in yourself. What can we deduce from the gem choice?'

'Aesthetics weren't important.'

Sophey and Ariel looked at each other. Again, they had spoken simultaneously.

David raised an eyebrow at Ariel. 'This is your little trinket?'

'My family's,' Ariel said stiffly. She didn't know why she wanted to defend the necklace. She'd already known what the gems were, already known they were a strange choice, unevenly placed with no symmetry.

'Do you know who made it?' David spoke directly to Ariel. Maybe it was just the light, but Ariel thought his eyes had no whites to them, like a shark's.

'It doesn't have a proper hallmark and there's no paperwork in my family that I can find. So, no.'

'Well observed.' He angled the light more closely toward a section of the necklace, then slid a gold ring off one of his fingers and held it into the light for comparison. 'We'd usually have a full hallmark like this one, see?' Ariel knew a little about this already: proper jewellery, like David's ring, should have a hallmark made of tiny stamps indicating who made it and the type and quality of the metal used, plus where the hallmark was granted.

'This necklace has only got a standard mark,' David continued. 'So we know it's made from top quality gold, but there's no maker's mark and no assay office mark. Assay offices are where the piece is hallmarked and signed off, as it were, and usually we'd see a date mark on a piece of this age.'

The gold standard mark on Ariel's necklace was a rectangle missing its corners with *916* stamped onto the inside, and it was hidden away near the clasp. It was teeny tiny and easy to miss unless you knew what you were look-ing for—or unless you were Ariel and had spent hours staring at it through a magnifying glass while your dad's back was turned.

'Someone wanted to hide where and when they got it made and paid the jeweller to not get it hallmarked in an assay office,' Ariel said.

'Or the creator didn't want to be associated with it,' Sophey suggested.

'Ten out of ten.' David smiled and that, too, seemed sharky. 'Either way, what can we surmise?'

'The necklace was a custom job,' Ariel said. 'It wasn't cursed after it was made. The necklace was crafted with the curse in mind.'

'Curse is a strong word,' David said mildly. 'One person's curse is another person's charm!' He chuckled. Ariel felt the hairs on the back of her neck stand up.

Statistically, this man and his workshop would not be the thing that killed Ariel.

'Thanks, David,' Sophey said. She did not seem perturbed by his creepy smile, but did look ready to move on. 'Where's this stock for Ernie?'

'Oh, over there.' David waved a languid hand in the direction of a few small cardboard boxes. 'A couple of antique pieces I bought from an Italian gentleman and restored, plus those enchanted bangles Ernie asked for and a pair of gold earrings. *Fully* hallmarked.'

'Thanks. Mail us your invoice.'

'I already have. Knock it down to three thousand. Since you picked it up in person. By the way,' he said suddenly. 'I had another of our mutual friends come calling.'

'Really?' Sophey balanced the boxes carefully inside her cat tote bag, found they didn't fit, then dug out her paperback and put all the items back in, heaviest-first. The book stuck out of the top. *The Colour Purple*. Ariel re-membered Seb reading it for school. 'Were they one of our noisy friends or one of the creepy ones?' Sophey asked David, and Ariel thought, *isn't every-*

one who associates with Bezzina's Emporium creepy? Then she remembered that she, too, now associated with Bezzina's Emporium.

'One of the noisy ones,' David was saying. 'Big bloke, lots of toxic masculinity and repressed sexual urges. Told me he was in touch with a priest. Or an imam. I forget. His group would be praying for us, he explained, and he hoped that we found salvation before our souls were truly doomed.'

'That's what they all say,' Sophey shrugged. 'I'll tell Ernie to look out for him, though.'

'It was *charming* to meet you,' David said to Ariel as Sophey headed out the door. Ariel looked back and saw him watching the necklace case with that same hungry gaze. She stuffed the box in her shoulder bag and ran after Sophey.

'Where next?' Ariel asked when she and Sophey were back on the pavement. She could see five different shades of brown in this industrial estate, and four different shades of grey. The only pop of colour was an unforgivably pink Fiat, parked by a door advertising wedding events. Sophey, bag on her arm, looked for all the world like she was carrying art supplies or groceries, not three grand's worth of valuables.

'Back to the shop, to get rid of these and put the necklace in the safe,' Sophey said. 'Then, if there's time, the library. I want to show you how we can find out about your family history.'

Chapter Six

Once upon a time, Ariel had watched films like *National Treasure* and *The Mummy* and thought that history was cool. As a child, she considered Indiana Jones the most glamourous fictional character going.

School cured her of such romantic notions. Researching her family history with Sophey did nothing to inspire a return to them.

This might have been because Southend library was, like every public library in existence, chronically underfunded and hovering on the just the right side of functioning. This particular concrete-and-glass building seemed to be home to various colleges and an art gallery as well as the library, as though someone had decided all the town's culture should fit under one ugly roof. The library had the sort of square, boxy layout that sent Ariel one way when she meant to go another, then forced her to walk an enormous circle to find the correct section. Sophey and Ariel managed to find an available and working computer, so Sophey could log into the terminally slow machine to access a genealogy site, but Ariel was frustrated within fifteen minutes of Sophey showing her how the genealogy system worked.

She didn't know enough details about her family to input the right information. Sophey, looking over her shoulder, made her feel extra stupid for not knowing Aunt Katie's precise year of birth. Ariel's phone wouldn't connect to the Wi-Fi so she could look back through family messages to see if anyone had mentioned it on an anniversary. The assorted customers did not help either; a man sat at the neighbouring computer blared music loud enough that Ariel could follow the lyrics through his earbuds. He caught her eye occasionally and smirked every time. A handful of teenagers crowded the YA section, loudly debating the merits of a new series. Sometimes Sophey would seek out a member of staff for a reference, but there was always a queue behind a pensioner asking for help to access their email.

Ariel wished she had had more than thirty minutes sleep the night before.

Sophey, for her part, was not as annoying as Ariel anticipated. Sure, she had a habit of tapping a pencil against her notebook and refused to speak at a normal volume once they were inside the library, but she knew her way around a family tree. It would not have occurred to Ariel to work backwards through the generations until they reached the 1860s, or to consider the men in the family.

'They had daughters and sisters and mothers,' Sophey pointed out when Ariel asked why they needed to bother with her male relatives. 'Their lives have been impacted too. We should look at the whole McLean family.'

Ariel wished she was smart enough to have thought of that.

'I think I've got this,' Ariel said after half an hour of inputting names and jotting down notes of things to look up when she was back in Bath and could speak to her grandfather. Her legs were dead, her headache was back and she was ready to fling the mouse at a wall. 'Can we please call it a day?'

They walked down to a café on the ground floor. Sophey bought an overpriced bottle of water and Ariel a slightly different overpriced bottle of water.

'Your brother doesn't know why you're really here, does he?' Sophey asked. The question caught Ariel off guard, although she had at that minute been checking her watch to make sure she had time before Seb finished his boxing session.

'No,' Ariel admitted. 'I don't know how he would react. He and our dad have a... complicated relationship. Especially about the curse.'

'Neither of them are going to be killed by it,' Sophey observed. Ariel's gut twisted a little, hearing the truth stated so calmly. Sophey sipped water. 'I'll tell Ernie what we've learnt when I'm back at work tomorrow. Can you come to the shop?'

'Not tomorrow. We're going to London—my brother and I. Meet you in the shop on Thursday morning?'

'I'll text you to confirm opening times.'

'Where are you going in London?' Sophey asked as they walked back to the high street.

'Camden Lock.'

'It's nice there. I go with my grandmother sometimes. I like seeing a proper market.'

'Yeah.' They were back by some shops; Ariel knew where Seb's house was from here, and Sophey looked ready to walk in the opposite direction. Ariel did not know the correct way to say goodbye to someone with whom you have just researched cursed jewellery, so she said, 'See you Thursday.' Sophey nodded in response and strode towards a side street.

Ariel hurried through the commuting crowds towards Seb's house, digging the spare key he had given her out of her purse. She really hoped the bathroom was clean enough to shower in. She wanted to wash off the dust of David's workshop and think about how she could use the Bath library to access a genealogy programme.

Her phone buzzed with a text from Seb as she got dressed in something nice enough to go for dinner in: *Any good photos?* She texted back: *A couple. Nothing to shout about.* She added a skull and crossbones emoji and went to comb her hair.

Chapter Seven

Seb treated Ariel to dinner in a nice restaurant on the seafront. Anywhere she could see the sea, Ariel decided, was her favourite part of Southend. Bonus points that this place was genuinely nice, with glass windows looking directly onto the beach. As it got darker the Thames Estuary turned a stormy slate colour, but the water was calm and the view as the sun set was pleasantly pink-tinged.

'How are Chloe and Madge?' Seb asked over food. As the only potentially attainable older brother in Ariel's friendship group, Seb had been the subject of many adoring gazes and excited whispers from Ariel's friends on sleepovers for years.

Ariel spoke around a mouthful of salad. 'Good. Chloe is spelling it C-H-L-O-umlaut-over-the-E now. Madge wants to go to Kenya on her gap year.'

'I thought Chloe was spelling C-H-L-O-forward dash over the E.'

'That's very last year. Well, she went to France last year and Germany this year.'

Seb unsuccessfully hid a smile. 'How's Grace?' he asked.

Ariel swished some lettuce around her plate. 'We don't really talk anymore.'

Seb looked surprised. 'Grace and you fell out? Why? You've known her since you were five.'

'I think that might be the problem.' She thought about telling Seb about the last argument she'd had with Grace, but the meal was going well. She swallowed. 'How are *your* friends? The emo one, the other emo one...'

'If you are referring to Janie and Cal, they are both fine. They came to visit the other week. We went to that weird old antiques shop in town. You'd like it,' Seb said. 'We should go.'

Ariel tried to keep her face neutral. 'The occulty one? I popped inside to-day, actually.'

'Anything take your interest?'

'Maybe. There was a nice old camera.'

'You'd like the old guy who runs the place. He's a bit strange, but he always finds you what you're looking for. I was thinking of asking for a summer job there, actually, if my internship falls through.'

'No,' Ariel said sharply.

'What? Why not?' Seb frowned.

'It looks like the sort of place to close down any minute.' Ariel shrugged, trying to look nonchalant. 'They're probably trading human remains on the side or something.'

Seb didn't look like he would be bothered by this. 'I'm not sure I need to worry too much about that if I just get a part time job.' He studied Ariel. 'Is this your death thing again?'

'I do not have a *death thing*,' Ariel protested. 'You're the one who only wears black and has too many piercings.'

'It would be okay if it was,' Seb said, unperturbed by her assessment of his aesthetic choices. 'I knew it might get worse after I left for uni.'

'Nothing's got worse! I am fine!'

'So you haven't been obsessing over that necklace? Or visiting Mum at night? Or memorising health information leaflets?'

'I went to visit Mum *once*. And they opened the cemetery gates eventual-ly.'

'Talk me through your average day,' Seb said. 'I meant to ask you to do that when I last rang, but I had that bloody essay due.'

Ariel scowled. 'Up at six. Coffee, walk Rocket, breakfast for me and Rocket, school, walk Rocket, homework, yoga or my street dance class or self-defence, hang out with Chloe and Madge and Rocket. Bed at ten. Sleep... after ten. On weekends it's less school and more yoga. Or food shopping with Dad. You know he can't go on his own, he just buys crisps and spare note-books. Is that an acceptable teenage lifestyle? Or would you prefer me to be holding seances to talk to Mum's ghost and going through Grandpa's paper-work trying to find evidence of what killed Grandma? Would that fit better with your picture of your weird obsessive baby sister?'

Before Ariel could continue ranting and set the whole visit on fire, a waiter asked if they wanted dessert.

'Look,' Seb said as he started on ice cream and Ariel sipped herbal tea. 'I'm sorry I sound like a second parent. But I know Dad's away a lot and I know you found the last couple of years really hard. I'm glad Rocket's giving you some structure.'

'She's the best thing about home,' Ariel said, and meant it. 'I'm doing okay.' Seb still looked unconvinced, so she said, 'ask about my grades.'

He raised a metal-adorned eyebrow and jabbed a spoon into his ice cream. 'What are your grades?'

'As and Bs. I can't be getting a As if I'm having a breakdown.'

'I'm not sure that's how that works.'

'Seb. I promise I will tell you when I'm not okay. How are *you*?'

'Like I said,' Seb said, and Ariel detected a slither of ice in his tone. 'I'm really enjoying it here. I needed a change.'

'Because of you and Dad fighting.'

'We weren't fighting. We were....'

'Discussing loudly the exact timeline of Mum's illness. Don't pretend I'm the only sibling with parent shit,' Ariel said over her teacup. 'We're both allowed parent shit, remember? That's what Thingy said. The therapy lady.'

'You should probably do some more therapy,' Seb said absently. 'So should I,' he said after a moment.

'So should Dad,' Ariel said. Seb inclined his head in her direction. On their father's interesting coping mechanisms, at least, the siblings would always agree.

'So, we're both doing okay,' Seb said. 'And we agree we'll tell each other when we're not.'

'Precisely. So where is Camden Lock Market?'

That night, Ariel dreamt of Southend Pier. At first she didn't realise she was asleep and thought it was a memory of today's sojourn. She had liked the trip, actually. It took a good half hour to walk down the pier, and she was surprised by how nice the view was from the end. Sea in all directions, but two sets of coastline. Buildings she recognised from the Southend coast became tiny boxes, windows reflecting the sunshine, and she could see fishing boats and kite surfers up close. Clos*er*. If she looked east, towards the sea, she could see wind turbines, and cargo ships making their way to and from the English Channel. If she turned west towards London, she could see the buildings and cranes of the huge port Seb had mentioned. It was strange to be this far from shore but surrounded by so much activity.

Wandering around the end of the pier was a peculiar experience. There were proper buildings there, selling food and advertising seasonal events. It was busy with holiday visitors and locals fishing. But all the time Ariel was conscious that just a few metres beneath her feet was a churning, cold body of water. The boards of the pier weren't perfectly aligned, and sometimes she looked down into a gap that would definitely eat her keys or her mobile.

Part of her wanted to test the theory.

After a cup of tea, Ariel and Seb took the train back to the seafront. It reminded Ariel of a toy town train: extremely rickety and simultaneously too small to be taken seriously but too heavy to so cheerfully ferry people over a mile to and from the middle of the sea.

'Estuary,' Seb kept correcting her. 'River's that way, sea's the other way.'

'It's salt water,' Ariel retorted.

So vivid were her memories of their trip that now it took Ariel quite a while to realise she was in a dream.

This wasn't the harsh, lovely view or the lively breeze Ariel had enjoyed leaning on the railings next to the lifeguard station. The dream focussed on a set of stairs leading directly down into the sea. In real life it was closed off, presumably used for lifeboat access. Now, Ariel stood on the last step before the sea swallowed the staircase, and water lapped at her boots. She stared down, down, down and listened to the sea sloshing around her. How far out was the end of the pier? One-and-something miles. How deep was the sea at one-and-something miles out from shore? As Ariel stared down at her feet, trying to figure out if the tide was coming in, she became aware of something watching her. She looked up to see a seal, head bobbing above the surface. She'd never seen a seal before this afternoon. They looked a little like dogs, with their whiskers and wet noses. She wanted to get closer, but she was right, the tide *was* coming in and her feet and ankles were soaked.

She looked back up, but the seal was gone.
She woke up.

Chapter Eight

On Wednesday morning, Seb indeed took Ariel to Camden Lock Market. The siblings had visited London a couple of times on family trips, but never Camden. Ariel did not like the London Underground (statistically, falling in front of a train or down the escalators would not be the thing that killed her, but an airborne disease from another passenger might be) but she did like spotting dogs on the Tube. She also liked the grungy artisan feel of Camden Lock and sent a handful of photos to her group chat with Chloe and Madge, who demanded a video call that evening. She almost bought an antique camera—the sort that would never work, even with careful restoration, and was good only for hanging on a wall to tell visitors that you took photography Very Seriously—but she remembered the one in Bezzina's Emporium and found herself thinking, *they need the business more than this place does.* Just as she shook her head at the vendor, who was hovering like a buzzard, her phone vibrated. She expected it to be one of her friends, but it was Sophey:

Necklace breakthrough. Is tomorrow still good for you?

A moment later:

Ernie's baking biscuits.

Ariel wasn't sure if that was meant to improve the prospect, but she texted her agreement nonetheless.

After dinner, she video called Chloe. She hoped it wouldn't be a long conversation; she was exhausted. Tonight she was determined to catch up on some rest. Or at least lie in bed with her eyes closed listening to a podcast, which was the same thing.

'Where are you two?' she asked when the screen opened to her friends' blurry faces. 'Are you... in Bristol?'

'Yep!' Chloe's blonde head bobbed up and down as she jiggled the phone. 'We came vintage shopping!'

'You inspired us with your Camden trip,' Madge smiled. Or at least, Ariel thought she was smiling. The connection was appalling. Possibly her friends were wandering a late-night market, possibly they were in one of those vintage stores, possibly they were just hanging out in Madge's kitchen.

'Bristol is *way* better than Camden,' Chloe said, although Ariel couldn't remember Chloe ever having visited Camden Lock.

'Who are you with?' Ariel asked.

'My mum brought us in,' Madge said. 'She had a work thing here anyway, so she's doing whatever and we're looking at overpriced trousers. I bought this pearl Alice band, look!'

'Suits you,' Ariel said.

'I got this top,' Chloe said. She waved fabric in front of the camera. Ariel thought it was possibly pink and probably sequinned, but it was hard to tell.

'Perfect for parties.'

'Miss you, A,' Madge said.

'Miss you too,' Ariel said. 'We'll go into Bristol for the day when I'm back.'

When the call ended, she phoned her dad to check in on Rocket and ensure he hadn't forgotten that Rocket liked playing tug in the evening. Whenever Ariel forgot or was busy, Rocket tended to play by herself, with Ariel's shoes. Peter Scarlet's leather Oxford brogues, Ariel suspected, would be an acceptable plaything to Rocket, but not to Peter. But Dad always went time blind when he was in his study working through research papers.

After they hung up—'don't forget tomorrow's bin day!'—Ariel showered off the feel of London, put headphones on and turned up her podcast to block out the sound of Seb's flatmates playing Xbox, then curled up in her sleeping bag.

Sleep would come soon.

Sleep would come soon.

Statistically, exhaustion wouldn't be the thing that killed Ariel.

Statistically, not looking before she crossed the street because she was too tired to focus properly—

Statistically, losing her grip on a pan of boiling water as she made dinner—

She got up and did push ups for twenty minutes. Then she pulled a medical leaflet out of her backpack. This one was on cervical cancer. Ariel had her HPV jabs at school, of course, but it made her feel better to know what she might be dealing with.

The leaflet did not lull her to sleep. When she eventually nodded off, she dreamt of Rocket escaping out of the front door and running into traffic.

Chapter Nine

At Bezzina's Emporium on Thursday morning, Seb safely cocooned in his boxing club doing something called circuit training and under the impression his sister was shopping for cosmetics, Ariel waited and nursed a coffee as Sophey and Ernest dealt with a morning rush. There wasn't really enough space for her to linger while other customers did actual shopping, but she did not want to invite herself behind the counter. She pored over the jewellery cabinet instead, hoping to avoid getting underfoot. A mosaic glass set caught her eye: earrings, a bracelet and a pendant. Ernest's neat handwriting explained it was from the eighteenth century, made in Rome from ancient Roman glass. Price on enquiry.

Ariel assumed 'price on enquiry' meant it was too expensive for anyone who wasn't aristocracy or head of a social media company.

She studied the jewellery and reread the description. The pieces were beautiful, the glass mosaic multicoloured and shot through with silver. The glass had been ancient when the pieces were made, Ariel realised. Something old had become something new back in the seventeen hundreds and now, in 2015, it was old again.

She decided to stop leaning on the cabinet, and to put her mug in the sink in the back rooms before she could knock coffee dregs onto something older than this building.

Back on the shop floor and manoeuvring between a couple looking for something magical for the top table of their wedding reception, Ariel found the vintage camera from before, and picked it up absentmindedly. It was in good condition, and she was fairly sure it would work. She held the lens up to her face and clicked randomly.

'Do you like photography?' Ernest asked. Ariel jumped. She had not realised he had been watching.

She nodded. 'I'd like to do something with it one day.' There was, in fact, a student exhibition back in Bath that she had applied to be a part of. It was just in a café in a few months' time, nothing fancy, but Ariel knew that it would be something to work towards.

'There's money in photography,' piped up one of the customers, the one after wedding decorations. 'We're paying a small fortune for our wedding photos. It'll be worth it if we don't have to think about capturing all those moments ourselves.'

'You should be busy enjoying your day,' Ernest agreed. He looked at the camera Ariel held. 'That one's safe to use,' he assured her. His eyes twinkled and Ariel wondered how he'd known if she was wondering what it might do. 'What does the label say?'

Ariel had a look. *Vintage camera, estimated early 1900s. Described by previous owner as 'extremely illuminating.' Bezzina's Emporium of Magical Artefacts and Antiquities bears no responsibility for any unpleasant or unsettling experiences induced by our products, as the origin and intended effects of each product is clearly indicated on the label.*

You have thirty days to return anything, unused, with the receipt and in the correct packaging, as long as it is not damaged. This does not impact your statutory rights.

She found the price: thirty pounds.

'If you help out with this next batch of customers,' Ernest said, 'you can have it on the house.'

'What batch of—'

The door opened. Through it stepped a middle-aged woman and teen girl, between them an elderly lady using a walker.

'This is Bezzina's Emporium of Magical... something?' asked the middle-aged woman. Ernest stepped forward and offered his hand.

'Ernest Bezzina, ma'am. How may we help you today?'

'It's my mother-in-law.' She indicated the lady with the walker. 'We'd like something to help with her balance.'

'Would you like to sit down?' Sophey asked quickly. She shoved one of the ever-present armchairs as far into the room as she could manage, and the teen guided the older lady into it. Her feet dragged along the ground at angles. She was clearly unable to move without the walker. Ariel shifted a few chairs, too, into a rough circle. When everyone was seated Sophey said to the elderly lady, 'What's your name, ma'am?'

'She doesn't talk,' the middle woman said quickly. 'I'm Lise. This is my daughter, Jade.'

'Gran's name is Petunia,' Jade mumbled.

'My mother-in-law has trouble with her balance and movement, as you can see.' Lise continued as though Jade hadn't spoken. 'We'd like to get her back to health as soon as possible. No more walker or wheelchair!'

Ariel watched as Sophey and Ernest surveyed the three of them. Sophey was looking between grandmother and granddaughter, while Ernest kept his gaze on Lise.

'Let us make you a tea,' he said after a moment. 'Sophey, would you do the honours? Kettle's just boiled.'

'Do we have to pay for it?' Lise asked. 'We have a strict budget.'

'Tea is on the house. So are pastries and biscuits.' He winked at Jade, whose mouth quirked. 'We find it's often easier to match the customer to the object over a cup of tea then it is just standing around. Ms Scarlet, what do you think Miss Petunia might benefit from?'

Sophey disappeared into the back of the shop as Ariel thought, *please don't leave me.* She swallowed and looked at the three women like she would if she were trying to figure out how best to take a photograph. She took in the way Lise sat as far from her mother-in-law as she could, but Jade had moved her chair as close to her grandmother's chair as possible. Ariel worked up to looking fully at Petunia.

Normally, old people gave Ariel the heebie-jeebies. Especially old, sick people. They were too hard to understand because their teeth weren't working, they were too much work to accommodate when a wheelchair or mobility aid wouldn't fit into a shop, they were too hard to talk to because they were all deaf. Ariel's family contained fifty percent fewer old people than the average, for obvious reasons. Ariel wondered now if she would be less terrified of Petunia if she had nursed a grandmother. Or known a grandmother. Jade, after all, was Sophey and Ariel's age.

Petunia was old. Properly old. And ill. One side of her face moved differently to the other, and one of her arms seemed in near-constant movement.

A stroke, maybe, or Parkinson's. Another curse side effect: Ariel never bothered learning about inflictions that came with age.

But Petunia was well dressed, wearing pressed trousers and a clean blouse underneath her quilted jacket. She wore a wedding ring and a gold necklace; her thinning hair was clean and combed. Her eyes, when they met Ariel's, were bright green and alert. When Sophey returned with a tray and Jade passed her grandmother a teacup, she ensured it was firmly in Petunia's grip before letting go. They clinked cups then grinned at each other, like toasting was a tradition.

Lise was clearly unimpressed with Ariel's silence. 'My mother-in-law needs to walk again—'

'I think we should ask Petunia what she wants,' Ariel said, eyes on the old lady. She knew it was a cardinal sin to interrupt a customer—if she had been shopping and been interrupted by a salesperson, she would have asked to see the manager—but she had a feeling she would get away with it. Lise broke off, startled. Ariel did not break eye contact with Petunia. 'Ma'am, what do you think could help you?' Petunia looked about to open her mouth when—

'My mother-in-law—'

'*Mum.*' Jade had not raised her voice, but her tone was clear. She bit into one of Ernest's biscuits and passed the plate to her mother with a pointed look.

It took Petunia a few more seconds to form words than it would have for anyone else in the room. But when she spoke, although her words were stilted and a little slurred, she was understandable.

'Standing... and moving... are difficult now. My body is...' another pause. Ariel was unsure if this was an effect of her illness or if she was just searching for the right vocabulary. 'Not my own anymore. I would like to feel more... comfortable.'

'Okay.' Ariel thought hard. What had she seen in the shop that might genuinely be of use? She turned her mug around in her hands. The tea was jasmine, and she found it calming. Wait, tea. 'First of all, I recommend some herbal teas. We have a blend that helps with rest and sleep, so you'll be more comfortable when you aren't moving and can better build your energy back up. We have another blend that can help with aches and pains, too.'

'I have plenty of those,' Petunia smiled. Galvanised, Ariel stood.

'I think this scarf might help you.' She grabbed one from the box under the clothing rail. 'It imbues the wearer with physical strength.' She checked the label. 'It says not to wear for longer than eight hours, so don't get any ideas about running marathons.'

A beat of silence. Ariel wondered if she'd gone too far and offended all three of them, until Petunia laughed.

'Finally, this cutlery set.' Ariel picked her way over to the window display, praying she had remembered its label correctly. 'Everyone who uses it reports a better dining experience. Their food goes down more easily, they don't make a mess, they're fuller for longer... It has a couple of decent steak knives and teaspoons which you could always use for preparing food,' she added. She did not want to say, 'so you can make a cup of tea and a sandwich without having to talk to your daughter-in-law,' but she hoped it was implied.

'I'll take them all,' Petunia said.

'But the budget—' Lise, again. Jade, just outside of her mother's line of sight, rolled her eyes.

'*I* am paying,' Petunia interrupted. Ariel wondered how much energy it took to effectively interrupt someone when your speech had stopped working properly. 'How much?' Petunia asked.

Ariel looked at Ernest. This part, surely, was beyond her.

Ernest said, 'Twenty-five.'

In the corner, Sophey raised one eyebrow very slightly. Ariel didn't blame her: the scarf alone was labelled as more than that.

'Then there is some left...' Petunia said, 'For Jade to get something.'

'Really?' Jade asked. 'Are you sure?'

Petunia nodded vigorously.

'Take your time browsing,' Sophey said. 'If there's anything you're particularly interested in, just ask. Miss Petunia, Ariel will check out your items.'

Will I? Ariel thought. She went behind the counter anyway, finding shelves beneath stocked with paper bags and wrapping paper, alongside thick Bezzina's Emporium business cards. Taking up a large chunk of the counter was a handwritten ledger. Ariel added Petunia's items, made a note of the price and was very grateful when Petunia handed over exactly the right cash. She wasn't sure she was up to working out change. She deposited the cash into the ancient till and wrote out a receipt, as she had seen Sophey do, then wrapped everything carefully, double-bagging the items and adding twine to the bag's handles so it could hang from Petunia's walker without the weight ripping the paper.

'Thank you,' Petunia said, and when Ariel said, 'you're welcome,' she meant it.

Ten minutes later the family departed, Jade hugging a Jane Austen novel. That too, Ariel suspected, had been heavily discounted.

'How did I do?' Ariel asked when the door closed.

Ernest walked to the shelf containing the camera and handed it to her. 'You fit right in here, you know.'

'I'm just good at shopping,' Ariel said. She tried to look nonchalant, but she felt strangely triumphant at having helped Petunia find her items. She turned away from the counter. 'Sophey, what have you learnt about the necklace?'

Chapter Ten

'I think this could be big,' Sophey said ten minutes later. She was sitting cross legged on the floorboards of the stock room, a fresh cup of tea next to one knee and a stack of books next to the other. Ariel sat across from her, uncomfortably aware that her skirt was getting creased and, more awkwardly, was not quite long enough to reach her knees as she sat. Sophey, thankfully, was focussed on the task at hand. Ernie's biscuits sat between them, and next to the plate sat Ariel's necklace. This was about as private as they could manage; Ariel didn't want a customer interrupting them.

'I was thinking about the gemstones used in the necklace and if they might mean anything.' Sophey held up her notebook. 'I was doodling the names of the gems and I noticed something.' Ariel leaned closer. Sophey's notes were cramped and busy, with words circled and crossed out and underlined. Ariel could make out the phrases 'friends falling out?' and 'why all the women?' Then, on the middle of a page, so obvious Ariel couldn't believe that she had never noticed:

RUBY
EMERALD
MARCASITE
EMERALD
MARCASITE
BLOODSTONE
EMERALD
RUBY

'Remember.' Ariel pronounced the word carefully, as though she had never said it before. 'David confirmed the necklace was probably made with the curse in mind.'

'Or it was cursed as part of the construction process,' Sophey agreed. 'The design and the curse could be one and the same.'

'Someone commissioned the necklace knowing exactly what they wanted.' Ariel tried a biscuit while she thought about that. The biscuit was soft and buttery, with just a hint of lemon. She did her best to eat it in more than two bites. 'The falling out between those two friends was about something important.'

'The acrostic is subtle,' Sophey mused. She rolled her beaded bracelet up and down her wrist as she spoke. 'I wonder if the friend who received it ever joined the dots.'

'Depends on how soon after they got the necklace that the curse kicked in,' Ariel said. 'Do you think the first victim *knew* they were the first victim of a cursed necklace? Or as they were dying did they just think, *I'm really unlucky to have been killed by XYZ.*'

Sophey picked up one of the books. 'I think I know how to start finding out. How do you feel about doing some magic?'

Chapter Eleven

Magic, it turned out, was not nearly as exciting as Ariel thought it would be. She envisioned smoke, potions, chanting and possibly a crystal ball.

What she got was Sophey, still sat on the floor, frowning over a book that smelt like mould, as Ariel held the necklace and felt like an idiot. She sat there for ages, while Sophey found the right book from the shelves lining the stock room. Ariel wondered if anything in the back of the shop was actually for sale, or if the staff just kept things they thought might come in handy. Like this mouldy book, which was in Olde Englishe and quite ugly.

'Okay, so if you're sure about this...' Ariel said. Ariel was not, now she thought about it, sure about this.

'I am.' Sophey took a deep breath. 'You need to hold the necklace and focus on all your memories of it. Everything curse-related you can think of. Then I'll say this line here—wait, no, *this* line—' Ariel briefly wondered if Sophey would get the incantation wrong and send Ariel to another dimension. 'And then we should both... the book says "understand."' She looked at Ariel doubtfully. 'I'm not sure if that's a visual thing or if we'll hear a voice or something.'

'In my experience,' Ernest said, 'It's more an *experience*.' Both girls jumped.

'How long have you been standing there?' Sophey demanded.

'Long enough that I think you're on the right track,' he replied. 'Ms Scarlet, are *you* sure about this?'

Ariel swallowed. 'Yes. Do I need to sign a waiver in case your work experience girl zaps me into the apocalypse?'

'Actually, that's not a bad idea.' Sophey took her notebook and scribbled some words. '*I, Ariel Scarlet, confirm that I am of sound mind and consent to partaking in magic with Sophey Cartwright to establish the nature of my necklace's curse.* Sign and date here please.'

Ariel did so. She wondered after if she should have thought about it more, but she wasn't sure if consenting to a ritual performed by a teenager was any worse than consenting to the terms and conditions of an ecommerce site. Ernest chuckled as she set down her pen. He had pulled up a chair and was taking in the scene with the air of someone watching amateur theatre with high hopes and low expectations. 'Waivers. In my day, we just took a deep breath and went for it.'

'In your day, people thought the earth was flat,' Sophey mumbled. She was tapping her pen against her leg, visibly nervous. 'Full disclosure, Ariel, I've never tried a spell before.'

'Full disclosure, Sophey, no one's ever included me in a spell before.' Ariel picked up the necklace. 'Let's do it.'

As Sophey began reciting from her book, Ariel closed her eyes and focussed on the necklace in her hand. It was cold, and heavy. What was her earliest memory of the necklace? That was it: seeing it on her mother's dressing table as a very small child.

'This one's special,' Nicole said as Ariel perched on her lap. They were getting ready for an evening out, Ariel wearing a spangled party dress and her mother in her silk dressing gown, nursing a pre-dinner gin and tonic as she did her make-up. 'We don't wear this one, little miss, we just look at it.'

'Why not? It's the shiniest.' Ariel's mother laughed. She smelt like perfume and lotion.

'Because it's very old, and because it's a little bit different to the others.'

Next, Ariel was older, and retrieving her family's passports from the safe for a holiday to Hong Kong. Aged nine, it was her one important job to help prepare for the trip, and she took rearranging the safe's remaining items very seriously.

'Dad? Why is Mum's necklace in the safe? I thought you kept all her jewellery in her box.'

The Scarlet family had a memorial box for Nicole, a pretty wooden chest she bought on her travels, filled with her most valuable items: the children's hospital bracelets, her wedding ring, handwritten notes from her own mother.

'Not that one, little miss. That one's too valuable for the box. It's a bit differ-ent to the others. It's an heirloom.'

'What's an air loom?'

'It's a very old, very special object. Put it back now, please.'

Aged eleven: Ariel and Seb's paternal grandmother's funeral wake. Drinks and a buffet in a Bath restaurant, Ariel and Seb wearing their best clothes and their best posture.

'Ariel! My darling, you're getting so tall.'

'Hello Auntie Faye. I'm sorry about Nana.' Auntie Faye, Ariel's father's sis-ter, was holding a large glass of red wine and, by the look of her teeth, it was her fourth or fifth. Funerals, Ariel's father had said as they waited for the car to take them to the restaurant from the cemetery, were for paying one's respects to the dead. Wakes were for everyone still living. Auntie Faye, certainly, had cried off her mascara and was now rather cheerful as she cheek-kissed the children and held her wine glass out of the way of turbulence.

'Oh, sweetie, don't be sad. She had a good innings, didn't she? Eighty-three! And to go in her sleep... that's the way to do it.' Ariel nodded politely. 'Not like your poor mother,' Faye continued. 'My heart hurts for her and you children, you know, all the time.'

Ariel, always uncomfortable when someone mentioned something personal, gripped her lemonade glass and looked at the floor.

'That curse,' Aunt Faye was saying. 'I never believed it, you know, it sounded like such nonsense when your mother used to tell the story after a few too many. She used to love telling it to us like her relatives had told it to her. All dramatic pauses and toasting to the dead. But, well...' She trailed off and stared into the bottom of her wine glass.

'What curse?' Ariel asked.

'Oh, sweetie... nothing. It's nothing. Ask your father.'

Ariel had. Or had tried to. On Mum's anniversary, or on her birthday, or when jewellery came up in conversation. She always got the same response: *'Curses aren't real, little miss. Your mother died of cancer. We count our blessings it took her quickly in the end.'*

'But all the women in Mum's family die really—'

'Ariel. I know you miss your mother, but chasing daydreams won't bring her back. Please let's change the subject. How's school going?'

A breeze ruffled Ariel's hair, bringing her back to the present. She became aware of Sophey, still reciting, and the feeling of the smooth wood of the stock room floor.

She could smell wood, too, but this wasn't the treated wood of the Bezzina's floor or shelving: it was the earthy, growing smell of a garden with trees. She opened her eyes—although until she did so, she thought they were already open—and found herself in a garden. It was pretty and manicured with a path and flowerbeds, and a little bench on a patio. It reminded Ariel of the sort of garden you saw on television, the type you needed a full-time gardener to maintain, so any normal person's own efforts to recreate it inevitably seemed scruffy.

Speaking of gardeners. In front of Ariel a small, wiry, brown-skinned man in grubby clothes was digging a hole. Next to the hole stood a tree sapling, ready for planting. This wasn't one of her memories, Ariel thought with a sudden thrill. For the first time since Sophey began chanting, Ariel felt nervous. Revisiting her own past was sad. Stepping into someone else's felt dangerous.

Ariel heard a door open and looked towards the house to see a well-dressed woman in old timey clothing walking down the path, three small children tumbling in her wake like kittens. Ariel didn't know which period the woman's clothes were from. A time when ladies wore hats and gloves as part of their normal daywear. When she spoke, it was with a crisp English accent, the sort Ariel assumed died out decades ago.

'Henrietta,' the woman was saying, 'and Josephine. Which of you will plant this tree, then?'

'I will!' called one of the girls. They looked similar enough to be twins, although the girl talking was a little taller and sturdier. They both wore pretty cotton dresses far too impractical, in Ariel's opinion, for gardening. She'd never thought before that she was grateful for the invention of dungarees. And elasticated waistbands.

'We both can,' said the smaller girl. 'And Bertie.' She tugged the hand of the youngest child, who was really still a toddler.

The gardener put down his spade and crouched down to the children, now crowded around the hole in the ground. 'We'll need all three of you to do this,' he said solemnly. 'It might be a difficult job.'

'We can do it!' insisted the middle girl, Josephine.

'All right then. All three of you take hold of this sapling—mind your fingers, Bertie—and then on three, we lift. One, two—'

On three, the children hefted the tree into its new home. The older girl immediately seized the spade and began pilling earth onto the roots, as the younger girl smoothed the sapling's delicate leaves and their brother plopped down to investigate a worm.

Ariel wondered what type of tree it was. She liked to think it was an oak and would grow big enough to shelter the whole garden from rain. She looked up at the clear sky and back at the house the family came from. It was a huge old house. No, not old. It was the style that seemed old, to Ariel, looking at it from the twenty-first century. This building was quite new. She squinted up at it, but the scene was dissolving around her. She looked back at the family and saw the children and their mother leaning over the sapling, talking animatedly to the gardener.

As the scene faded, Ariel became aware of something... else. A sound? No, that wasn't it. Ariel felt drowsy, her head heavy, like she was car sick. She struggled to put a name to the sensation. Which of her senses was working? She couldn't tell.

Rain on her face. That was it. Drizzle, the sort that clings to your face and neck like walking through a wet flannel, sure to leave your clothes vaguely damp for hours.

Voices. Voices? Yes, she could hear voices, over Sophey's continued murmurs, but it was hard to see. Was it dark out? Yes, she was outside, and it was nighttime. She could hear water and the rustling of trees, like they were in a park. She squinted towards the voices and could just about make out two adult figures, illuminated dimly by a distant lamp.

'I'm sorry we fought,' one voice was saying.'

'So am I. Will you come home? Mother and Father and Bertie miss you. As do I, of course.' Women's voices, as clipped and well-spoken as the lady before. Could these women be the sisters from the garden? This must be two decades, at least, after the scene with the tree. Ariel peered into the gloom, but it was hard to see either of them clearly. She'd never thought about how dark public spaces were at night before electric streetlights.

'I will. Tomorrow morning. I... I bought you this. When we were in Europe, actually. I know how sorry you were to miss the trip.'

'Oh, Josephine, really? You shouldn't have. And you've kept it all this time.'

'Yes, well, I—I saw it and thought of you.'

The necklace grew hot in Ariel's hands. She could smell burning.

A split second later, she realised the burning was coming from *her* and felt a jolt as the park and the women disappeared.

'Ow!' Ariel opened her eyes—again, she hadn't known they were closed—and took in the stock room, now overbright compared with the darkness of the park.

'Oh! Are you okay?' Sophey still held the mouldy book, and she was sweating visibly and shaking a little. She also looked extremely guilty as she gazed at Ariel's hands.

'Christ alive, your spell *burns*.' Ariel blinked down at her blistered hands, red and angry. She looked across at Sophey, still staring at Ariel with wide eyes. The necklace, on the floor, was smoking gently.

'There's a toilet and sink down the hall.' Ernest's voice floated down. 'Rinse your hands under the cold tap and I'll apply a poultice.'

'I'm sorry,' Sophey said a few minutes later, as Ernie applied gunk from a glass jar onto Ariel's hands. It smelt strongly of aloe vera, and helped immensely. 'The book did not say that burning would be a side effect.'

Ariel flexed her fingers. 'I guess your spell worked. Did you... did you see what I saw?'

'Your memories? Yeah. Did you see...?'

'The garden and the park conversation with two sisters? Yep.'

'Their way of speaking fits with the necklace being Victorian,' Sophey said. She eyed the necklace, now snug in its box and showing no signs of just having been red-hot. Now she came to think of it, Ariel wasn't sure if the heat had been quite... real. Like the dress on the rail on the shop floor, it did not emit smoke.

Her fingers definitely hurt, though.

'So we know the necklace was gifted,' Ariel said, to fill the silence. 'Some sort of fake peace offering.'

Sophey winced. 'I don't have siblings, but I can't imagine hurting a sister like that.'

'I do have a sibling, and I can't imagine it.' Seb could be irritating, sure, but Ariel couldn't picture cursing him and all his descendants. Maybe if he sold Rocket to Cruella de Vil to make himself a pair of earmuffs.

'We should keep looking into the family history. What was the name of one of the women?'

'Josephine.' Ariel felt a little cold. 'The woman who gifted the necklace was Josephine.' She thought back to the scene in the garden. 'Her sister was Henrietta and there was a brother, Bertie. Albert, maybe?'

'They're who you have to find in your research. In theory, women before Josephine and Henrietta would have lived past forty if they didn't die of consumption or in childbirth or whatever. If you can find a cause of death for Henrietta and Josephine, that would help.' Sophey looked at Ernest. 'Is there any way we can find out more about Josephine and her family?'

'I have a few thoughts.' He looked pensive. 'I'm not sure I want you doing any more spells, though.'

Sophey looked relieved. 'Any idea who we can ask?'

'Do you remember Alexandria?'

'The lady with all the hair?' Sophey asked. 'Ernie! Why didn't you suggest we go to her in the first place? She's perfect for this sort of thing.'

'I knew you'd get a long way on your own.'

Another magic person? Ariel thought. 'Is she local too?'

'No,' Ernest replied. 'She's based in Barcelona. But I can ask her to come over. She supplies us with artefacts sometimes. We'd like the excuse to meet up, to be honest with you.' He rubbed the compass tattoo on his arm.

'What's the earliest she could get here?' Ariel asked. 'I leave tomorrow.'

'Oh, of course you do.' Sophey rubbed her eyes. 'She's a bit pernickety, Alexandria. She barely uses a telephone. Could you come back to Southend another time?'

Ariel thought about it. 'My brother might be staying here over the summer. I can visit him. I have exams in May, though, so not before then.'

'So do I.'

'What about the May-June half term?' Ariel suggested.

'That would work. Maybe you could put together an actual family tree in the meantime? We could highlight the people we're sure were cursed and then highlight the ones who might have died from natural causes, and build a picture.'

'I'll see what I can do.' Ariel did feel more confident, now she knew how to use the genealogy page on the library computers and had an idea of what to ask Grandpa when she saw him. 'Do I have to leave the necklace here?'

'No, you should take it back,' said Ernest. 'It's your family's, after all.'

They were back in the shop proper now, and a noise caught Ariel's attention. 'Um... Ernest. What are those people doing?'

Half a dozen people brandishing posters, marching up and down on the pavement, chanting something indistinct. 'Are they protesting the shop?' Ariel asked. She felt a little silly, because they were just standing right there on the pavement, and she'd seen protests in Bristol where whole crowds paraded across the city. This group was far smaller but looked as determined as any protest she'd ever seen.

'They have to protest the shop because they hate anyone and anything remotely interested in living in the twenty-first century.' Ariel wasn't looking at Sophey's face, but could feel Sophey rolling her eyes nevertheless.

'Why?' Ariel asked.

'Some people don't have enough going on in their lives,' Ernest said. 'We tend to ignore them. They're like wasps.'

When Ariel left the shop twenty minutes later to meet Seb from boxing, one of the protesters came towards her. She leaned back instinctively. He was built like a rugby player and the wooden sign he was holding ('SAVE OUR CHILDREN FROM THE DEVIL') was equally substantial. 'We'll pray for your soul,' he told her. 'The Lord forgives even the worst sins!'

She turned away quickly, and walked as fast as she could back to the high street.

She wished she had been brave enough to ask which sin he was talking about.

Chapter Twelve

A riel didn't know how to explain her blistered hands to Seb, so she wore fingerless gloves, bought hastily from Primark, for the remainder of her trip. Thankfully, Seb was used to Ariel making strange choices in the name of fashion and didn't comment. True to his promise, Seb insisted on showing her Southend's sights. After Southend Pier, these were limited to rollercoasters and candy floss at Adventure Island amusement park ('the locals call it Peter Pan's,'), a small cliff lift ('this is not a real cliff, Seb.' 'It's a steep hill. Basically it's a cliff. Stop pulling that face and enjoy the view.'), and the local museum ('did you know that a Saxon king was found buried across the road to an Aldi? They built a pub to commemorate it.').

The theme park was fun, and the cliff lift was sweet, and she could sort of see the appeal of the museum, if you liked history. Sophey probably liked it. She probably volunteered here.

Seb dropped Ariel at the train station on Friday morning after a final trip to the pie and mash shop. 'I'll come back at half term,' she said, and she didn't have to feign enthusiasm.

'Say hello to Rocket for me,' he said. 'And Dad and Grandpa and Uncle James and everyone.' He hugged her, smelling like the woody aftershave he'd found at a Christmas fair. 'See you soon, little miss.'

On the journey home, Ariel tried not to think about her upcoming meeting with the mysterious Alexandria, or the exams she knew would happen before then. Instead, she opened her phone and researched 'Saturday jobs in Bath.' After ten minutes of jotting down email addresses, she put her head in her hands and let the train lull her to sleep.

She dreamt of Jane Austen novels, old trees and woke up when she smelt burning.

Nothing was on fire, of course, but her hands were newly blistered.

Chapter Thirteen

'How's your brother?' Ariel's father asked when she stepped through the front door that evening. 'How many piercings has he added since Christmas?'

Ariel couldn't answer, because she was too busy being headbutted by a small, wiry, grey dog. 'Hello monster,' she said happily into Rocket's fur. 'You smell really bad. Yeah you do, you—oh, no, don't lick my mouth—'

Statistically, Rocket was not going to be the thing that killed Ariel, unless she ran into the road and gave Ariel a heart attack. Ariel suspected there was a very real chance that Rocket's eventual death would cause Ariel to die of grief, but she hoped she had a few years before she had to deal with that one.

'She's been really good,' Ariel's father said from the doorway. 'Met a German Shepherd in the park, chased some seagulls, ate almost an entire bag of carrots.'

'You didn't have to give her an entire bag at once. One at a time would do. Do you mean the Shepherd with the red collar and the owner who looks like Princess Anne? That's Sparky. Rocket loves Sparky.' To indicate her agreement, Rocket chased her tail and stood on Ariel's boots. Ariel's family knew neither Rocket's breed nor her history, except that she had been abandoned not long after puppyhood. Ariel's theory was that she was some kind of terrier crossed with a whippet crossed with a firework.

'I worked that out,' her father said drily. 'So, your brother...'

'No more piercings... that I could see.' Ariel hung her jacket on its hook next to the intruder alarm and extracted her boots from Rocket, placing them on their shelf next to her running trainers. She looked over the stack of post by the front door. A couple of letters for her father, presumably from his academic contacts, postmarked Edinburgh and London and Manchester. A fashion magazine for herself, to be consumed in the bath with a biro to mark all the garments she wanted to save up for. 'Can I smell moussaka?' she asked. Her father, prematurely grey haired and perpetually bespectacled, stood in the hall with a tea towel in one hand and a chopping board in the other.

'You made it so well last time that I thought I'd have a go. Ready in fifteen minutes. And there's someone in the kitchen to see you...'

'Grandpa!' Ariel barrelled through and hugged her ancient, rickety grandfather. He smelt badly of cigarette smoke.

'Hello little miss. You're getting taller.'

'*You're* getting smaller. How's Uncle James?'

'Trying to murder me with salads and annoy me to death with Radio Four. He's at a film showing this evening with his yuppie friends. I *told* him they won't like it, but he doesn't want to hear from me. Especially because I made him clean up after Rocket in the garden.'

Ariel's maternal grandfather lived with his son James, an eternal bachelor who spent his weekdays fixing new cars and his weekends fixing old cars. Neither loved the arrangement, but Grandpa had been widowed since his four children were teenagers. After the death of his remaining daughter, Ariel's mother, he suffered what the family delicately called 'a wobbly.' During his wobbly he dedicated his days to bad television, Golden Virginia tobacco and his favourite whisky, occasionally yelling at postal workers and doctors: 'IT'S PRONOUNCED MC-LAIN! NOT MC-LEEN. IT WOULDN'T BE DIFFICULT IF YOU SPOKE THE QUEEN'S ENGLISH.' After a minor stroke on the anniversary of Aunt Katie's death, a succession of carers attempted to persuade him to eat more, drink less and/or stop making comments at foreign people in the high street. All failed, culminating in an evening in which Grandpa threatened to jump off one of Bath's many bridges and into the River Avon. This was followed by a trip to a psychiatric ward and consultations with various doctors, then Uncle James cleared out his spare room and told Grandpa that he could move into James's house or stay in the nut house.

These days, Grandpa took walks around the park with his bereavement group and told everyone who would listen that he had taken his wife's surname in the 1960s. 'I was a very modern man in my time,' he liked to say. His progeny would reply, 'you're a very old-fashioned man now.'

'So, what do you think of Southend-on-Sea?' Ariel's father asked as he served up food. 'Take another portion of salad, Mr McLean.' Ariel did not know why, after all these years, her father insisted on calling his father-in-law Mr McLean instead of Dennis, but Grandpa seemed to like it.

'The town is gross. But I liked the seafront and the pier. Lots of sand and seagulls. Has Seb told you about his internship?'

'He texted me something about a start-up and a summer job,' her father admitted. 'I can never read his texts properly.'

'You just have to learn to speak emoji,' Ariel said. 'I can read them.' She washed her hands, inhaling deeply. The bright, chair-filled kitchen-dining-living-room smelt as it always did: of dinner, apple-scented cleaner, and her father's collection of history books. 'How was your conference?'

'Excellent, unless you count the fact it was in an airless room in Swindon. A few of us snuck out for decent coffee.'

Like father, like daughter, Ariel thought. 'How was the chilli I left?' She asked.

'Good. Lovely. Very... vegetable heavy.'

'It was vegetable chilli.'

'You're like your uncle,' Grandpa observed. 'When I was your age, I was interested in motorbikes and chip butties. Young people now are so health conscious.'

'Uncle James is forty-three. And I made a chilli with some sweet pota-toes, not a spirulina smoothie. I *could* make you a spirulina smoothie.'

'What's spirulina?' Grandpa asked.

'Disgusting,' Ariel's father said cheerfully. 'I've banned Ariel from ever bringing it into the house again. Right, I'm dishing up!'

'I found a cool antiques shop when I was in Southend,' Ariel said when they were all seated and eating. She nibbled some aubergine and wondered why the topic of Bezzina's Emporium always came up over food. 'Got an old camera. It got me thinking about family history.' Ariel had rehearsed this conversation mentally, and knew she had to tread carefully to avoid having the same argument she'd been having with her father for years.

Her father's eyebrows knitted, and Ariel knew he was preparing to repeat himself. Grandpa just shoved another forkful of moussaka into his mouth.

'*Not* the necklace,' Ariel continued quickly. 'Just history. Family trees. On *both* sides of the family,' she added pointedly. 'I don't know much about your and Auntie Faye's family.'

'There's not much to tell. Our dad died when we were teenagers, and you remember Nana. Both my sets of grandparents were from the West Country or Wales.'

'Farming?'

'Mm. Auntie Faye was the first person in the family to go to university. Patricia's—your mother's mother, Ariel—her family was from London, weren't they, Mr McLean?'

'Really?' Ariel asked. 'You've never mentioned that.'

'It was a few generations back,' Grandpa said. 'Moved to Bath back when Bath was affordable for normal people. *More* affordable. Course, it was difficult then,' he added. 'Because they were Scottish before they came down to London. No one liked Scots in those days. No one likes Scots now. It sticks to you, being Scottish in England.'

Grandpa had been saying this for as long as Ariel could remember, as though the whole family smelt like kilts and highland cattle. As he firstly had married into a Scottish family and secondly had only been to Scotland once, on a long weekend to Fife, Ariel was never sure how much of Grandpa's family history was accurate. He did have a piece of family tartan, though. Uncle James had it framed, then put it up in his downstairs loo.

'The McLeans moved down south in the Victorian era.' Grandpa was still talking, fork bobbing as he warmed to his subject. 'Difficult time for Scots, the Victorian era.'

'Victorian?' Ariel had not heard this part before either.

'Oh, very narrow minded, those Victorians. Worse than us.'

'That's not what I... never mind.'

'I'll have to go through our wedding photos with you, point out the names,' her father said. 'You'd like taking the mickey out of all the outfits.'

'That would be lovely,' Ariel said, and meant it. 'Thanks, Dad.'

'By the way,' Grandpa said. His voice was noticeable for how casual he was trying to sound, but his fork twitched in his hand. 'I had a phone call from Patricia's cousin Jamie. Not cousin. Ariel, your grandmother's great-

great-something grandfather and Jamie's great-great-something grandfather were brothers.'

This sort of conversation was common in McLean territory. When all the women in the family died young, the remaining men kept in touch, if just for a familiar face at the next funeral. Jamie and Ariel, who knew each other from family get togethers, were probably so distantly related that their children would have the correct number of toes. The thought would have given Ariel the ick even if they weren't related, though.

'How's he doing?' Ariel's father asked. Jamie, after all, had been to many of the funerals.

'He's well,' Grandpa said. 'He had some news. He and his wife, lovely woman apparently, from... Bhutan. Or Iran. Somewhere that way. They're having a baby.'

Ariel said, 'It's a girl, isn't it.'

'That's not what Jamie said.'

'He just told you to be ready,' Ariel said.

'Well. Yes.'

The clock in the hallway chimed. That's what happened when every girl in the family was born, Ariel thought. Instead of a baby blanket or soft toy, they should have been given a stopwatch.

'Are you going to finish that plate?' Ariel's father asked her.

She pushed it towards him. 'You have it.'

That evening, Grandpa watching a game show and her father in his study with a stack of research books, Ariel snuck the necklace back into the safe. Then, with Rocket curled up on her rug, Ariel unpacked her bag and got out her memory box. It was nothing fancy, just a novelty gift box from Uncle Chris and Aunt June and Em and Lottie, big enough to store knickknacks and mementos. It lived in the back of her wardrobe, so she thought it a good place to keep her research on family history. So far, she had only a few names for her list: Mum's, Aunt Katie's, her cousin Jenna's and Grandma's. Inspired by Sophey, Ariel dug a fresh notebook from a drawer and made a list of the names, adding birth and death dates where she knew them, printing as neatly as she could. Plenty of space for more. She began a rudimentary family tree overleaf, in pencil. Then, on a fresh page and with a pen, she wrote 'JOSEPHINE?' and underlined it. With a ruler.

The rest of the page stayed blank.

She would begin researching tomorrow.

Now, she leafed through the rest of the memory box. Postcards from aunts and uncles on holiday. A handmade Christmas card from Em and Lottie. The last birthday card Ariel's mother had written her: *Happy seventh birthday my darling girl. Lots of love, Mummy, Daddy and Sebby.* It was followed by seven kisses, a blocky signature from Seb and a cartoon of a frog, courtesy of her father. He always drew frogs in cards.

Ariel put the card back inside the box and went to have a shower. She was glad to be back in the house. As much as she loved Seb, there was something extremely satisfying about having a wash in a bathroom you personally had cleaned with apple-scented cleaner. It was something to do with being able to scrub the corners. She felt a new appreciation for her bedroom, too. It was quiet, because her parents had put in double glazing, and it was pretty, because she and Seb and Uncle James had painted it an extremely pale pink and illustrated flowers at pleasing intervals along the picture rails and skirting boards. Cherry blossoms framed the wardrobe, periwinkles peeked out from behind her yoga mat, daffodils grew out from above the desk. The bedside cabinet was neat, containing a drinks coaster, a lucky cat from the summer in Hong Kong, and her medical dictionary, which she read when her insomnia played up. The room wasn't huge, but it was calm, and clean, and hers.

Too bad that it took until five o'clock the next morning to fall asleep (she'd gotten through half of 'H' in the dictionary) and immediately after doing so she dreamt of the entire room catching fire.

She woke up and checked the fire extinguisher was still next to her bed and still in date. She peered up at the fire alarm and made a note on her calendar to check all the house's alarms still worked, and to mention to Dad that she was testing them. She would check the front and back door, while she was at it, and the windows. She was sure that the last time she'd opened the living room window, the latch had felt a bit loose. It might need replacing. Her dad had the number of a locksmith, from the time Seb locked himself out, so at least they knew who to go to if the window did need fixing. Ariel made another note on her calendar.

As she leant over, the paper of the calendar rustled and a photograph fell from between its pages. Ariel had forgotten that she'd stuffed it there when she was cleaning and unsure what to do with it. It was a selfie, taken with her friends in the loo of an ice cream parlour. Even in the dim light, she could make out Chloe's brilliantly blonde hair, Madge's ridiculous plastic flower crown—it was her birthday—and Grace's bright smile, smushed up against Ariel's equally beaming face. They looked like an advert for *young teens of to-day*, with all the bases covered: Ariel and Chloe looking what Grace termed 'Ed Sheeran white,' Madge olive skinned and extra tanned from a recent holiday, Grace herself dark brown. Ariel picked up the photo and squinted. This would have been... Madge's thirteenth birthday. No, fourteenth. They went bowling for her thirteenth, and the guy in the next lane broke his fingers on a bowling ball.

They'd been a gang of four for so long.

Ariel put the photograph in a drawer.

Then she popped to the loo, got back into bed and wondered if she should start switching off all the electrical sockets before she went to bed. She needed the light, though. Maybe she could replace the socket lamp with a battery-powered one.

Statistically, faulty electrics wouldn't be the thing that killed Ariel.

But she wasn't going to risk it.

<u>Scarlet-McLean Family Tree (In Progress)</u>

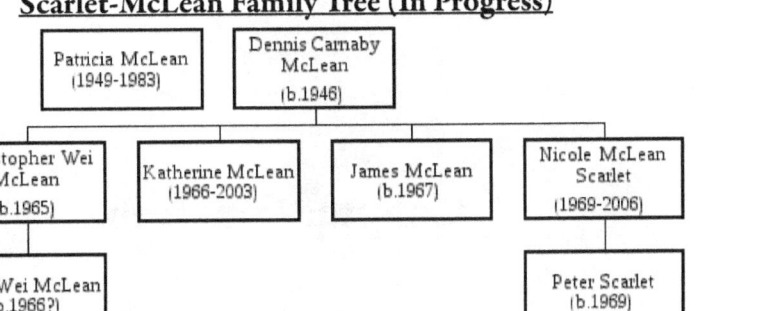

Patricia McLean
(1949-1983)

Dennis Carnaby
McLean
(b.1946)

Christopher Wei
McLean
(b.1965)

Katherine McLean
(1966-2003)

James McLean
(b.1967)

Nicole McLean
Scarlet
(1969-2006)

June Wei McLean
(b.1966?)

Peter Scarlet
(b.1969)

Lottie Wei
McLean
(b.1996)

Emily Wei
McLean
(b.1996)

Seb Scarlet
(b.1995)

Ariel Scarlet
(b.1999)

Chapter Fourteen

The school summer term began; April moved into May; Ariel settled back into the routine she had described to Seb, with added moments snatched at the local library to research her family. Walk Rocket, go to school, walk Rocket, struggle through homework, hang out with Chloe and Madge... Ariel felt like she was in *Groundhog Day*. She wondered if that's why she disliked school: too much repetition. She loved walking Rocket every day, though, so routine itself wasn't the problem.

It was, however, a little harder to wake up early enough to walk Rocket when she was falling asleep as the sun rose. She'd never been a good sleeper, even as a very small child. She remembered her father talking about how she had taken hours to settle as a baby. She usually got five or six hours of sleep over an eight-hour period. But she'd never had insomnia or bad dreams like she experienced since her first visit to Bezzina's Emporium. After a brief internet search informed Ariel that sustained lack of sleep was extremely dangerous, especially for the teenage brain, she stopped drinking coffee after three o'clock in the afternoon and increased the amount of yoga she did every evening. She purchased some lavender bags from a local shop and left them by her pillow. She downloaded a meditation app and deleted all social media from her phone except for messaging apps. She updated the settings to stop the phone from buzzing at her unless she *really* wanted it to and did her best to throw herself into her schoolwork. That would make her tired enough to sleep before midnight, wouldn't it? It should have, the amount of work her teachers bloody gave her.

Ariel did not like school. She did not like arbitrary rules, like asking to use the toilet in class, because they got in the way of rules that made sense, like wearing a uniform so everyone had the same number of pockets. She did not like teenage girls, because she was one and knew what they were like.

She did not like most lessons, because she did not know how to focus on her teacher and not on every other interesting thing in the room, or disappear into a rabbit hole of thoughts hinging on someone's throwaway comment.

But she was willing to immerse herself in it to wear herself out enough to sleep before dawn.

Sophey and Ariel texted infrequently; they both had school commitments, and Sophey had a habit of not responding to a message for several hours, then sending multiple paragraphs at once. Alexandria would probably be coming in May or June, she said, in the meantime keep up with the research. Both in year ten and well into their GCSEs, they occasionally exchanged a message comparing their various teachers and subjects (Ariel, despite her best intentions, continued to resent every subject except Photography and spent two thirds of her study time staring at a textbook waiting for the words to enter her brain. Sophey enjoyed every subject except for obligatory PE and spent two thirds of her study time making colour coordinated flash cards.)

In early May, when Ariel awoke from a dream (a tree branch snapped and landed on her), she forgot what time it was and texted Sophey something about research at five o'clock in the morning, then got up for a coffee. It was getting warm enough that Ariel could rise as dawn broke and not need to immediately apply seventeen layers to her person, for which she was grateful as she traipsed downstairs in her nightie and fluffy socks. The socks, she remembered crossly, were a Christmas present from Grace, years before. Then she wondered why she was feeling cross. *She* wasn't the person who cut off all contact. *She* wasn't the one who'd given up on a decade of friendship.

Anyway, they were just socks.

It was gone seven when Sophey replied *please tell me you nap in the afternoon to make up for being awake all the time.*

Oh. Arial *could* snatch an hour of sleep every afternoon after school and Rocket-walking duties were done. Ariel began napping strategically to make up for her insomnia, giving up on sleeping throughout the night for the time being. She spent the wee small hours studying, or using her laptop to research the mysterious Josephine and Henrietta. On Sophey's advice, she requested files of information from the National Archives, and had them mailed to Bezzina's Emporium. While McLean was a common enough surname, she did her best to narrow down information pertaining to the specific names she had found in her genealogy research. It didn't make her feel any better when she was sitting in Maths so tired she couldn't remember how to write numbers, but it felt more productive than lying in bed staring at the ceiling.

A happier change to her routine was that one of the weekend jobs she'd found responded to her application. Ariel successfully interviewed for a front-of-house role in a local sandwich shop and brought many, many leftovers home to her father. Her boss, Carol, it soon turned out, had a lackadaisical attitude to everything except gossiping with her customers... which Ariel should have seen coming, as her interview consisted of sitting opposite Carol on the plastic seats outside the shop, Carol fidgeting with an e-cigarette. 'Can you clean?' Carol asked.

'Yes, I do most of the household cleaning,' Ariel replied.

'Can you make sandwiches?'

'Um, yes. And I do a lot of the cooking at home.'

'Do you like cooking?'

'It's... it can be quite meditative.'

'You won't need meditation here, my lovely, you'll need to make tuna sweetcorn by the litre. And text me when the health and safety people come round.'

Ariel took the health and safety manual home with her—statistically, food hygiene might be what killed her, or got her fired. At least her dad appreciated the sandwiches. He also noticed she was sleeping less than normal.

'I'm going to take you to the GP,' he said over dinner one evening. Ariel had made pasta and was irritated that she'd left it on the stove for too long, so it went squishy. She wasn't sure she should have made it with regular pasta, now she thought about it. She'd read online about how some people put courgette through a giant pencil sharpener and it became courgette-spaghetti. Courgetti. Her father was still talking. 'It's not healthy for you to be so tired so often. Could be anaemia.'

'Could be,' Ariel agreed. She'd already thought of that and was taking iron supplements, just in case. 'I'll make an appointment. You don't have to come. I know you're teaching late classes this semester.' She tried another forkful of pasta and decided to look into courgetti.

In the end, it was just Ariel who went to the GP, her father's apologies in her wake. She needn't have bothered: the doctor told her to exercise more.

'More?' she asked doubtfully. 'I do a lot of yoga. And I run. And dance—'

'Most people your age are too inactive. Try more cardio. Avoid screens before bed.'

'I usually do—'

'If that doesn't work, come back and we'll put you on medication.' The doctor was already looking at his computer screen; Ariel was dismissed.

She added another run to her schedule.

It made no difference.

When she spoke to Seb about it on the phone, he said, 'what does Dad say?'

'He said he'd take me back to the GP if I'm still tired in two months.'

'He didn't even take you the first time.'

'It's not a bad thing to do more exercise,' Ariel said, feeling she had to stick up for the doctor. She wasn't sure how much public tax money went towards a ten-minute GP appointment, but it was probably loads. 'I *do* need to stay in shape.'

'You're going to damage a ligament,' Seb said darkly. 'Muscle damage bloody hurts.'

'If I do it'll only hurt for a few years,' Ariel said. There was a silence on the other end of the phone. 'Seb. I said, it'll only hurt for—'

'I heard you. I get the joke. The not-joke. Were you joking?'

'Sort of,' Ariel replied. 'Not really.'

'*That* is what Dad should be taking you to the doctor for,' Seb said. 'I told him...'

'Told him what?'

'Nothing. How's your revision going?'

Chloe and Madge noticed Ariel was neglecting them. 'Want to hang out on Sunday?' Chloe asked on Friday afternoon as they changed after PE.

'Can do,' Ariel said. 'Is the library open Sunday? No, it isn't,' she answered her own question. She had been using the library's genealogy programme and slowly got to grips with looking up births and marriages, trying to note all the women whose names had changed after marriage. She'd asked Grandpa about people's birthdays and anniversaries when she went round Uncle James's for dinner. Grandpa had been happy to oblige, mostly because he wanted a cigarette and couldn't step outside until Ariel stopped talking about the importance of knowing one's family history.

'What has the library got to do with us?' Chloe asked.

'Ah... nothing. I had a book to return. Yeah, let's do something Sunday. Shall I bring Rocket?'

'Definitely,' Madge said. 'We could go up to the Crescent with hot chocolate? I think the weather will be good enough.'

'That would be nice,' Ariel said. What she was thinking was, *The fresh air might help me sleep. Is there a correlation between fresh air and sleep? Should I start leaving the window open at night? Burglars, though. I'll leave it on the latch. What was Madge saying? We're going to... to the Royal Crescent. It will be pleasant.*

So. She was busy.

She was not worrying about the necklace's curse.

She was making the most of the time she had, and sleeping where she could.

She almost believed all of those things.

After a weekend revision session in which Ariel grew so frustrated with biology terminology that she threw a pencil out of her bedroom window, she texted Grace. *How are things? Revision makes me want to move to the moon.*

Grace did not respond.

Ariel wondered if they would have a proper conversation again before they finished secondary school. They'd *sort of* spoken once or twice since the autumn. Mostly when a teacher made them work in the same group, or when Ariel was blocking a doorway Grace wanted to get through. But that wasn't really talking, was it? It was Grace saying 'excuse me, please,' and Ariel ducking out of the way, or Ariel saying 'what if we looked at the role of women in *Macbeth*?' and Grace saying 'yeah, that's original,' and Ariel shrivelling up.

Ariel wondered if she should just walk up to Grace and demand a conversation. A proper one, where they could talk about the fight they'd had. But—she didn't want to fight again. Not like last time, when Grace had been so angry she could barely speak. They'd known each other a decade, survived spats and petty disagreements, hung out with one another's families. But Grace's face on that last day made Ariel wonder if she'd ever really known Grace at all. Or, said a sneaky voice in Ariel's head, if Grace ever really knew *you*.

Head pounding, Ariel laced on her shoes, clipped Rocket to her lead and threw open the front door. Twenty minutes later found herself where she always went when she needed breathing space: the graveyard, via a flower shop. With her family's steady run of untimely demises, the McLeans had long ago invested in a substantial plot. It wasn't a vault—Seb would have liked a vault—just a long-ago designated bit of grass, big enough for several coffins. Here was Grandma's headstone, here was Aunt Katie's. Her father still had not gotten around to Nicole's. Ariel brought it up sometimes, but it always made her father rub his eyes as though he was trying not to look like he was tearing up.

Ariel tidied the graves, discarding old cut flowers and clearing a few stray weeds. The McLeans had at least half a dozen graves, attended to by various cousins. Not even Grandpa was old enough to remember everyone there, but he always came on Grandma and Aunt Katie's birthdays, and he always took Ariel and Seb on Mother's Day and Nicole's birthday. The whole family would come at Christmas, too. When she was satisfied with her tidying, Ariel separated the posey she had bought into three parts. A few stems to Aunt Katie, a few to Grandma, the biggest and prettiest to the patch of grass where her mother's ashes were buried.

Ariel wondered, for the thousandth time, why Mum had elected to be cremated rather than buried as the rest. Maybe she couldn't bear the thought of being embalmed and dressed up for a casket viewing. Ariel certainly couldn't. She thought she wanted one of those eco-funerals, where your coffin was buried in a woodland. Back to the earth and all that.

When she was younger, Ariel hadn't realised that most people did not think about how they wanted their final resting place. Or at least, they didn't when they were aged nine, or twelve, or fourteen. She glanced over the graves, checking Rocket wasn't trying to wee up any of them, then realised two things simultaneously.

One, at least one person in her family's distant past knew the curse needed to be taken seriously. Why else would they reserve so much space in one go? You had to pay for it.

Two, some of the headstones had names she didn't recognise from her family history research. She moved closer, annoyed that she hadn't thought to come here sooner. She *knew* these names, she had grown up reading them. The headstones weren't all commemorating women, but a lot were.

Marie-Elizabeth, died in 1961. Regina and Maria, both died 1957. Aurelia, 1970.

She jotted them down in the notes app on her phone, then took one last look, inhaling the clean, green-scented air.

She wondered if she would make it to this family plot before her newest distant cousin made it to hers.

Chapter Fifteen

That night, lavender bag clutched in one hand, Ariel dreamt of her mother.

She was not sure if it was one of those dreams that was actually a memory, or perhaps an amalgam of memories, or if it was just her imagination.

In the dream, Nicole Scarlet sat on the sofa in their house, reading a weighty book. This seemed accurate: like Ariel's father, she had been an academic. Something caught her attention and she looked up, seeing Ariel.

'Little miss,' she said. 'Come read with me.'

In the way of dreams, Ariel was immediately snuggled up next to her mother, peering through her arm at the book.

'What language is this?' Ariel asked. The words—they weren't words, they were hieroglyphs, or ciphers, or moving pictures. Ariel studied them, but couldn't decide. Some of the swirls and patterns made up the shape of a tree with leaves falling from its branches. She wanted to reach out and touch them.

'This book is in English,' Nicole replied. 'You and I are speaking it now.'

'But—'

Ariel looked back at the book. Now all the pages were blank. She reached for the book, determined to see closer—

Outside, a siren wailed.

Ariel sat up in bed.

She picked up the medical dictionary. She didn't want to, but made sure she could read a few lines before settling back on the pillow. It was four o'clock already. She could get up and start breakfast or put together a slow cooker for dinner, or do a yoga flow routine. While she waited for her body to muster up the energy to move, she tried not to scratch her not-quite-healed hands and thought back to the dream.

Was curling up on the sofa with Nicole a memory or wishful thinking? She didn't have enough memories of her mother to know for sure.

She hoped Sophey texted a confirmation about Alexandria's arrival soon. She wanted to know who Josephine was, and she wanted to know what the deal with the necklace was, and she wanted to be able to sleep through the night(ish) again.

As she swung out of bed and padded down the stairs, she decided that she would take one of the three.

Chapter Sixteen

As spring rolled through Southend, Ernest Bezzina organised his shop for the summer season, and resisted his assistant's attempts to organise him. Sophey, knee deep in schoolwork and stock deliveries, took three phone calls pertaining to a doctor's appointment Ernie kept changing. She wrote several sticky notes and rang him herself on the day of the appointment.

'You aren't my personal assistant,' he told her, torn between amusement and irritation when she called his home phone at eight o'clock in the morning. 'I gave you this number for emergencies only.'

'All doctor's appointments could become an emergency,' she said seriously. 'Anyway, your surgery keeps clogging the phone line.' Sophey had recently sold an early edition of *The Catcher in the Rye* via the phone to a buyer so pleased that he mailed a thank you card to the shop, so Ernie conceded she had a point.

With his appointments fulfilled, Ernest banished Sophey from shifts until her exams were finished. Although he wasn't traditionally bothered by legal technicalities, he did not think that being closed down for child labour law infractions would do his reputation any good. Besides, Sophey was one of those teens capable enough to run businesses or nations or planets one day: he wanted her to have the GCSEs to prove it. He was also, not unreasonably, terrified of Sophey's grandmother, from whom he had recently fielded two phone calls about how hard Sophey was working. They came to a mutual agreement that she could return to the shop when exam season was over.

With the summer solstice approaching, Ernie took delivery of a huge bough of flowers that never wilted and arranged it in the window around a set of handwrought metal garden furniture that did not warp or age in the weather. Sophey, sneaking in when she needed a break from revision, added some flourishes: a dress owned by one of the nicer Mitford sisters, a parasol that never broke, citronella candles that actually repelled gnats.

It was, Ernie thought as he stood outside one afternoon surveying the window, perfectly summery.

'Makes me want to have a barbeque,' said a voice. 'Even in this.' The sky was full of angry black clouds, blobs of rain hitting the pavement intermittently.

'All you need for a successful barbeque are the right clothes and the right attitude,' Ernie said lightly.

The man standing next to him was tall, with a slick of blonde hair and a well-cut suit. His tinted sunglasses were the sort that Ernie, purveyor of exclusive goods, appreciated as unaffordable to most.

'Spoken like a true Brit.' The man laughed.

'You're not from here?' Ernie was surprised; he had an ear for accents after a youth spent in the navy, and this gentleman's was solidly Home Counties English.

'Lived all over,' the man said. 'As I hear you have.'

'You hear correctly. What else have you heard?'

'That you've been running this place by yourself for decades. Ever think about retiring?'

'Sometimes,' Ernie confessed. 'But what would I do with myself?'

'Take a few trips,' the man suggested. 'Mediterranean, maybe.'

Ernie let the comment sit in a moment of silence, and then another moment of silence.

'Tristan Oldfield Matthews,' the man said when it became clear Ernie had an eternity of moments available. He took a heavy, embossed business card from his jacket pocket. 'I run museums. You might have heard of us? Oldfield Curiosities.'

Ernie rubbed the compass tattoo on his arm and said, 'aren't you a try-hard Ripley's Believe It Or Not?'

Tristan Oldfield Matthews laughed. '*They'd* like to be us. We only deal in the genuinely magical.'

Ernie waited. A breeze rustled off the Estuary, up through Southend high street and into the side roads. Ernie was glad he was wearing a cardigan.

'Artefacts and antiquities,' Matthews said eventually. 'We'd love to branch out into the smaller towns and cities, like Southend-on-Sea.' He pronounced it like one would an item on a foreign menu.

'We're not for sale,' Ernie said. 'Sorry to have wasted your trip.'

'You'll not even let me walk through the door?'

'Oh, of course. Where are my manners? What are you looking for today?'

Matthews pushed open the front door. Ernie followed, taking note of the man's shoes—hand-tooled, more expensive than the suit—and the way he walked, like he already owned the shop. Ernie did not miss that Matthews glanced up at the evil eye hung above the door, or that he brushed his fingers against a cloth baggie hanging from a nail on the inside doorframe. Ernie suspected that Matthews wanted him to notice the act of noticing.

Ernie took his place behind the counter, grateful for the excuse to lean for a moment, and watched Matthews take a turn around the shop, taking in the jewellery cabinet, the clothes rack, the bookshelf. A cabinet in the corner rattled slightly as Matthews passed it, but if he noticed *that*, it did not phase him.

'I'll take these,' Matthews said eventually. He was holding up a set of cushions. 'My wife's redoing the front room. These will be perfect.' He placed them on the counter and picked up one of the labels, moving it between his fingers. 'Encourages good feeling and perfect for social occasions, hm? She'll love them.'

'Eighty pounds, please, sir. Which currency will you be paying in today?'

'What are my options?'

Matthews' expression twitched towards a smile as Ernie said, 'We prefer British pounds, US dollars, euros, Maltese lira or Greek drachma. Other currencies are welcome.'

'Do you take AMEX?'

'Sorry. We're cash only.'

'Of course you are.' Matthews counted out four crisp twenty pound notes, and Ernie handed him a receipt before sliding the cushions into a large paper bag.

'I hope your wife loves them.'

'I'm sure she will. And if you change your mind... you know where to find me.'

Ernie watched Matthews walk out into the rain, then examined the business card. Selling his shop, of course, was out of the question. Researching Tristian Oldfield Matthews wasn't. Ernie picked up the phone and dialled his friend David. 'Hello you. How's tricks? Mm, here too. Listen, have you heard of a Tristan Oldfield Matthews? Yes, that's one person...'

<u>McLean Family Tree (In Progress)</u>

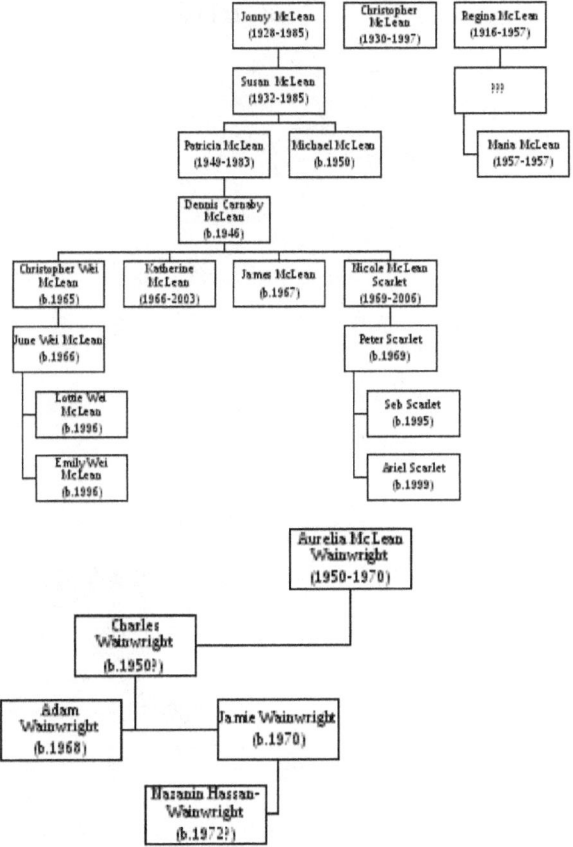

Summer

Chapter Seventeen

As the days grew longer, Bath swelled with tourists. The city was always a tourist trap, but in the summer months visitors seemed to multiply by the minute. Living away from the city centre, Ariel had easy access to local shops without risking life and limb to pop into a pharmacy or pick up groceries. She loved and loathed tourists in equal measure. They were sweet enough when they were taking photos of Bath Abbey or queuing for the Roman Baths or asking for directions to where Jane Austen used to live. But she had never known fury like a tourist late for their train home, or arguing over a bill, or shouting at whichever travelling companion had misread the map.

Her Saturday job at the sandwich shop, meanwhile, was losing some of its gleam. All its gleam. Ariel was not sure, on reflection, if it had ever gleamed and instead just shone a bit in the right light. Carol spent two thirds of the workday talking with customers about other customers and asking Ariel to hurry up mixing that tuna sweetcorn. Ariel had yet to see Carol mixing tuna sweetcorn. But the pay was okay, and Carol didn't mind if Ariel needed to come in earlier so she could leave earlier to walk Rocket while her dad was away at a work thing.

It was as a Saturday shift finished that Sophey finally texted Ariel with the date of Alexandria's arrival, arranged to coincide with half term. Ariel, walking home, texted Seb that she was coming to visit. Well, she texted him the dates of the trip, an emoji of a train, an emoji of a parasol on a beach and the emoji of something that looked a bit like a pie. She was grateful for Carol's wages if not for Carol—her father gave her a few pounds a month on the proviso that she helped out in the house, attended school and did not construct a meth lab in her bedroom—but the train fare was ridiculous.

Seb replied with a thumbs up emoji and a dancing lady emoji. Ariel packed an overnight bag, booked her train ticket and did a food shop to make sure there was enough in the freezer for when her dad while she was gone.

———————— ⧉ ————————

There were tourists in Essex, too, coming off the train from London. Instead of Bath's brash hen parties and happy couples, or its dozens of walking tours of international travellers, Southend's visitors seemed to be extended families and groups of teens, taking picnic baskets and boom boxes to the beach. A few couples got off the train at Leigh-on-Sea to visit cockle sheds or quaint pubs, but the majority of people visiting the centre of Southend were more casually dressed and carried fewer luxury branded items than those who made the trip into Bath. They were also darker skinned and more likely to be wearing a hair covering. Ariel wondered if that was down to geography, with Southend being so easy to get to from London. She knew Bath wasn't the most diverse city to live in, but now she wondered about its visitors. It was hard to tell how wealthy someone was when they wore trainers and a rain jacket for sightseeing, or high heels and a short dress for a night out. Everyone dressed like that. And you had tourists from all over, or whose parents were from all over, or whose parents had parents who were from all over. She'd have to look more closely at their shoes to figure out their monetary status, she decided. Not everyone who visited Bath was both white and well off, but she knew the city's Regency architecture and picturesque boutique shops harkened back to a time when one type of person lived upstairs, and another type lived downstairs. She'd never really thought about it until she saw Southend's tourists, though.

'Two visits in two months,' Seb said. He met her from the station with his flatmate, Karishma. Ariel remembered her from her last trip: petite and brown skinned, always wearing the same boxy band t-shirts Seb liked so much.

'I'm here because you're not coming home,' Ariel said haughtily. 'While I'm thinking about it, Grandpa told me to tell you that you should go to the Koko for gigs in London.' She handed Seb a bag with gifts from the family: his favourite coffee, a Sainsbury's voucher, a tin of biscuits from a local baker.

'Thanks, little miss. How does Grandpa know about the Koko?'

'I don't know, the internet? He also says, and I quote, "tell him not to pierce his tackle."'

Karishma snickered. Seb rolled his eyes. 'Lunch?'

'At the pie place? All right.'

Ariel waited in the queue to order while Seb and Karishma held down a table, the café bustling with lunchtime trade. She sidestepped a snotty child and walked backwards into—

'Ariel?'

A curtain of dark hair and a maroon dress, a cat tote bag full of textbooks, standing next to an older lady laden with shopping bags.

'Oh! Hi. Hi, Sophey.'

'You made it,' Sophey smiled, like she was genuinely pleased. 'Welcome back.'

'Thanks.' Ariel was acutely aware of Seb's presence in the vicinity. 'I'll... I was going to text you...'

She faltered. It had not occurred to Ariel to text Sophey when she arrived in Southend. The plan had been to message her tomorrow morning when Seb was asleep. They weren't going to meet until tomorrow afternoon, anyway, to go over the archival documents Ariel had requested, before Alexandria's appointment the following day.

'Nan, this is Ariel,' Sophey said, like she hadn't registered Ariel's lack of communication. 'She comes to the shop sometimes. Ariel, meet Irina.'

'Pleasure,' the older woman said. Although she was clearly old*er*, she didn't really look old enough to be Sophey's grandmother. Her hair was strawberry blonde, pinned back into a bun, and she wore a large crucifix around her neck. 'It's so nice to meet one of Sophey's friends. She never brings anyone round for tea anymore. Do you like reading those fantasy books too?'

Sophey was looking at her shoes now, fiddling with her plastic beaded bracelet. 'No she doesn't. Let's go to Marks and Spencer. See you later, Ariel.'

'Who was that?' Seb asked when Ariel returned to her seat. 'I didn't think you knew anyone here.'

'She works in that occult shop. Sophey.' Ariel had already decided that Seb needed a variation on the truth, because she couldn't keep finding excuses to slip away to Bezzina's Emporium. 'We got chatting when I got that vintage camera.' She had brought the camera back with her, to photograph the seafront while she was here.

'I love it there,' Karishma said. 'I want to get my mum some of their key chain charms. Do you know that girl well?'

'Not really.' Ariel moved in her seat. 'They have a lot of teas and little gift things as well.'

'I almost bought a wardrobe from there when I was in first year,' Karishma remembered. 'The guy was happy to sell it to me, what's his name—'

'Mr Bezzina,' Seb supplied.

'Yeah. He organised delivery and everything, and then we realised it wouldn't fit through the door of the bedroom in my halls of residence. I was devastated.'

'You're finishing your second year?' Ariel asked.

'Mm. Seb ended up living with us when someone dropped out.' She nudged Seb with her elbow. 'I think the other guy did us a favour, Seb's the cleanest person I've ever lived with.' She was looking at Seb as she said it, but Seb's eyes were on the door, clearly still thinking about Sophey.

'She's not like your usual crowd,' Seb remarked. Ariel supposed that Sophey did rather look more like one of Seb's friends than Ariel's, with her clompy boots and unkempt hair. Ariel wondered how many piercings Sophey had. Seb glanced at Ariel. 'I'm surprised you...'

'I what?'

'Bothered.'

'What is *that* supposed to mean?' Ariel knew she sounded like a child, and she didn't want to whinge in front of Karishma. But it was too late.

'She looks like she's less into Instagram than you and Madge and Chloe. She might have more braincells than Madge and Chloe put together. I think one of the badges on her bag was for that book I like. The horse one.'

'Please do not start talking books at me. And Madge and Chloe are smart! Chloe might apply to Oxford.'

'Didn't Chloe's entire family go to Oxbridge, and won't she be excommunicated if she doesn't? I'm just saying, if you want to invite that girl to hang out with us, it's cool with me.'

'Okay. Fine.' Ariel grasped wildly for a change of subject and spotted one poking out from beneath her brother's hair. 'Wait. Seb. Did you get another piercing?'

'It was my present to myself for finishing first year! And it's called an industrial.'

'Your ear looks like a cheese grater.'

Karishma burst out laughing and fist bumped Ariel across the table.

'So, tell me about Seb's love of body mod,' Karishma said once they were eating. 'When did it start?'

'When I learnt what good music is,' Seb said primly. He did indeed have a tattoo on his wrist of his favourite song lyric, signed by one of the band after a gig. He'd promptly gotten the signature tattooed too. He was saving up, Ariel knew, to follow them on tour around America someday.

'And the scales?' Karishma asked. Ariel suspected she was asking because Seb's other tattoo, taking up most of his left ribcage, was a child's drawing of an old-fashioned set of scales, signed with a wonky letter 'A.' Ariel took note of the fact that Karishma had seen Seb without at least part of a shirt on.

'That's my drawing,' Ariel confirmed. She looked to Seb to explain. It was his tattoo, after all.

He just shrugged. 'One of Ariel's drawings when she was little.'

'Are you an artist?' Karishma asked.

'Not really. I just like doodling. Remind me what you're studying?'

Chapter Eighteen

After an evening playing board games with Seb and Karishma, then a morning of helping Seb with his grocery shopping and pretending she wanted some time to herself for photography, Ariel waited while Sophey sold a woman a set of garden chairs. Ernest was out meeting Alexandria from her train. Ariel wondered if she should have bought something as a thank you for helping with the necklace. Maybe she'd wait to see how much help Alexandria could provide first. Trying to stay out of Sophey's way, she picked up a black pillbox hat with a veil, the sort you only saw on the heads of elegant goths or funeral attendees. Or both.

Ariel could not recall her mother's funeral. She had not long turned seven and wondered sometimes if her family had decided she was too young for the service. But Seb, then almost eleven, never spoke of it either. Ariel assumed that either he had been kept away too, or had buried the memory too deep to recall.

Ariel turned the hat over and over in her hands. In fact, she could not remember being told of her mother's death. That was the way of things, wasn't it? Maybe your brain stopped recording when it knew you were living through something traumatic. All she had were patchy images: staying at Grandpa's during the final days of their mother's illness, compiling the memorial box with Seb at the kitchen table with Uncle Chris and Aunt June, leaving flowers at the family plot.

She wondered whose funeral she would go to next. She wondered if she had even met them yet. Although, the way Grandpa smoked and drank, the next funeral would probably be his.

Sophey's forced cheeriness pulled Ariel out of her reverie.

'And we hope you love your furniture! We'd love to see a photo. Bye!' Sophey shut the door after the customer, flipped the sign to 'closed' and turned into the shop. She blew a strand of hair out of her face and rolled her shoulders. 'Let's get onto those documents.'

But first, of course, tea. Sophey and Ariel sat in armchairs, pouring over printouts of archival documents and comparing notes as a teapot of mint tea—fresh mint, with nothing but hot water—steamed gently on a side table. Ariel wondered what would happen if anyone ever tried buying these armchairs.

Ariel did not like to admit that she had missed the shop, the tea, and the company. She focussed on the documents instead, a pencil poised to make notes.

'Shit,' Ariel said after a few minutes. 'I think this is her. Josephine McLean. Born 1842, died 1868.'

'Cause of death?' Sophey asked.

'It says suicide.'

'Married?' Sophey asked.

Ariel scanned the page. 'Er... no. But she had a sister...Henrietta. I'm sure these are the right sisters, there's an Albert McLean listed as their brother. It says that Henrietta and her mother... they both died on the same day in 1867. So Josephine died a bit later.'

'In that case,' Sophey said, 'I think we can say we've found our necklace's starting point.'

'Okay...' Ariel flicked through her notebook, gathered the paperwork and made several amendments to her family tree and the list of victims' names. 'I think we have our list of curse victims.' Sophey peered over her shoulder to read.

'You've missed one,' Sophey said.

'Have I?'

'Cameron McLean, 1989, accidental overdose.'

Ariel examined a record from the 1980s. 'I assumed Cameron was a boy.'

'Could be,' Sophey said, but she sounded like she disagreed. Ariel added Cameron's name. They both surveyed the list.

Henrietta McLean (horse and carriage accident), 1867, aged 27. (Her mother, Charlotte, died with her, aged 52.)

Clemency McLean (fell off a wall), 1882, aged 8.

Jemima McLean (tuberculosis), 1900, aged 3.

Marie McLean (field nurse), 1916, aged 20.
Kathryn McLean (influenza), 1918, aged 19.
Ada McLean (choking), 1930, aged 10.
Laura Marie McLean, (house fire), 1936, aged 22.
Susannah and Sophia McLean (Blitz), 1943, aged 9.
Lily McLean (train crash), 1952, aged 29.
Regina McLean, (childbirth), 1957, aged 21.
Maria McLean (cause unknown), 1957, aged two days.
Marie-Elizabeth McLean (electrocution), 1961, aged 17.
Aurelia Wainwright, née McLean (car accident), 1970, aged 20.
Patricia McLean (cancer), 1983, aged 34.
Cameron McLean (accidental overdose), 1989, aged 23.
Jenna Torres McLean (hepatitis), 1995, aged 15.
Katherine 'Katie' McLean (accidental drowning), 2003, aged 37.
Finally:
Nicole Scarlet, née McLean (cancer) 2006, aged 37.

On another page, Ariel had started on a proper family tree. All the long-lived relatives were male, of course, but something twisted inside her every time she read that Freddie McLean had outlived his daughter Aurelia by thirty years, or that Gerald, Henry and Frederick McLean all lived to retirement age, while their older sister Clemency hadn't made it past the age of eight. She also wished people wouldn't keep naming their children after their loved ones. There were only so many variations of *Marie* and *Albert* that one could make without confusing cousins.

'Even if Alexandria can't confirm the curse's providence... I think we can say for sure that there is one.' Sophey's voice was a little husky, like there was a lump in her throat.

'Thanks for taking the archive papers,' Ariel said, for something to say. She was inherently uncomfortable with other people's tears and generally not completely sure about displays of emotion.

'That's all right,' Sophey said. Her voice was back to normal, thank God. 'Sorry if my nan was too much, yesterday.'

'She wasn't,' Ariel said immediately. 'She was fine.'

'Do you want to hang out later?' Sophey asked. 'I've got a free afternoon. Ernie and Alexandria are going to the pub. Ernie says it's important for

Alexandria to settle in before she looks at the necklace tomorrow, but I think he wants to catch up with Alexandria before the work starts.'

'I can't,' Ariel said truthfully. 'Seb and I are going to Hadleigh Castle. In a bit, actually.'

'Ooh,' Sophey said. 'I love it there. It's so atmospheric. You'll get a lot of photos.'

Ariel wasn't sure if she was relieved to have a ready-made excuse not to spend time with Sophey or if she felt guilty that she had automatically reached for an excuse. Would it really be so bad to hang out? But they had nothing in common except for this shop. What would they talk about?

Ariel tidied up the paperwork and made sure her notes were accurate. She looked back at the names. Josephine and Henrietta McLean.

'Alexandria will be able to fill in the gaps,' Sophey said, watching Ariel page through her notebook.

'What's she like?' Ariel asked. 'What are her... skills?'

'She's quite...' Sophey searched for the right words. 'Unusual. A bit like how Ernie's quite unusual. Practically, she specialises in objects. She can do other stuff too, but I think Ernie's thinking that she'll be able to get more from the necklace than he could.'

Ariel thought about what someone 'a bit like Ernie' might look like. She was willing to try anything.

'I'd better get going,' Ariel said. 'I'm meeting Seb at the bus station.'

'Alexandria will be here from ten o'clock tomorrow,' Sophey said.

'I'll be here at half past nine.'

'How was the photography?' Seb asked when Ariel found him outside a glass bus station so ugly she hoped the lads smoking outside would fail to stamp out their fag ends.

'Great,' Ariel said. 'Remind me where we're going again?'

'Hadleigh Castle. In Hadleigh. You passed it on the train coming in.'

'Did I?'

Seb thumbed through his phone and showed her a picture.

'Seb! That is not a castle. That is *a pile of stones.*'

'It *used* to be a castle. Now it's good for fresh air and nice views. That's our bus, let's go.'

'It had better not rain,' Ariel grumbled. 'You'll owe me.'

Chapter Nineteen

At nine twenty-nine the following morning, Ariel arrived at Bezzina's in good spirits. She had fallen asleep at two o'clock, which felt positively early. She was confident it was partly to do with the sheer amount of fresh air she had inhaled at the definitely-not-a-castle-but-quite-nice-landmark the previous afternoon, and partly because today was the day they got answers about Josephine and Henrietta McLean.

Hopefully.

Sophey flipped the sign to 'closed' as soon as Ariel was through the door (really, it was a good thing there wasn't a set list of opening times. No one could have trusted them) and Ariel arranged chairs so the four of them could sit down. She laid the necklace box onto the little coffee table. She wondered how long this would take. She'd arranged to meet Seb here so they could go for lunch, but now she thought about it she wasn't sure she wanted him walking in on some sort of ritual with their family's cursed necklace out on full display.

'How was Hadleigh Castle?' Sophey asked. Ariel suspected she just wanted to fill the silence.

'Pretty.' Ariel searched for ideas for small talk. 'I didn't know that John Constable did a painting of it—'

The door opened. Thank God. For a moment Ariel thought the woman crossing the threshold was Sophey's twin. Then she realised that this woman was much older, and although she was a similar height to Sophey, her hair was curled and bushy where Sophey's was straight and limp. Her skin was much darker than Sophey's olive pallor, too, and better taken care of. She was also extremely well dressed, wearing a jacket that Ariel had seen online for four figures, and her silk palazzo pants and blouse were as stylish as Sophey's tartan skirt and ankle boots were raggedy.

'Alexandria,' Ernest was saying, 'you remember Sophey, my assistant, and Ariel Scarlet, who owns the necklace.'

Alexandria shook Sophey's hand and said, 'Always a bright light, Sophey Cartwright. Don't burn out.' Her accent was from somewhere further south than Barcelona. Sophey frowned at Alexandria's words, but Alexandria was turning away. She smiled up at Ariel and held out her hand. Her grip was firm, and Ariel realised Alexandria was covered in tattoos, just like Ernest: an evil eye on this knuckle, a set of snakes on that wrist. Where Ernest wore a compass on his forearm, she wore a mirror, shaped out of vines. 'The girl with the cursed tree,' Alexandria said.

'Cursed necklace,' Ariel corrected. Alexandria made a *hm* sound. 'Thank you for coming to see me,' Ariel said, and hoped she sounded genuine. She really was grateful. Nervous, too, just a bit.

'I hear it's an interesting case. But first... tea.'

Ten minutes later, as the four of them nursed cups of smoked black tea, and Alexandria was alternately studying the necklace and Ariel's notes.

'Early to mid-Victorian?' she asked no one in particular.

'We think so,' Ariel replied. She did not like smoky teas—they tasted like drinking one of Grandpa's cardigans—but she did not want to jeopardise Alexandria's comfort.

'A gift?'

'That's what we thought.'

'Hm.' Alexandria set down her cup and picked up the necklace. She closed her eyes and ran her fingers over each stone, each link, every surface. She hummed a little, and it sounded like a song or a prayer.

'Definitely two sisters,' she murmured after a moment. 'A betrayal. False words. A...' she paused and Ariel wondered if she was thinking about the right English word, or reaching for a way to describe something magical. 'A marriage. No. *Not* a marriage. And then a curse.'

She opened her eyes and blinked several times. Her eyes were watering slightly. The necklace was smoking again, and Alexandria's fingers were already a bit pink. Ernest silently passed her the jar of poultice he'd given Ariel. Alexandria weighed it in her hand for a moment, then placed it next to the necklace.

'*Not* a marriage?' Ariel asked.

'A prevention. Do you have paper?' Again, she addressed no one in particular, and Ariel handed over her notepad and pen.

'This is one of Alexandria's more unusual gifts,' Ernest said with a hint of pride. 'Ally, are you sure you don't want more tea before you try this?'

Alexandria took one sip, like she was appeasing him, and laid one hand on the necklace and held the pen with the other. She closed her eyes and took several deep breaths. The room was silent for five seconds, ten seconds, a minute. The necklace continued smoking. Alexandria winced. Ariel looked at her watch, and then at Sophey—surely they should intervene? Sophey caught Ariel's glance and looked at Ernest. He was watching Alexandria carefully.

Two minutes. Three. Five. Ariel turned her teacup in her hands. Sophey rolled her bracelet up and down her wrist. Ernest sat perfectly still, eyes never leaving Alexandria's face. Ten minutes. Alexandria opened her eyes, which were watering. She put the pen down, applied poultice to both her hands and took a deep breath. Slowly, shakily, she began to write.

Chapter Twenty

Tuesday 1st May, 1866
　　Darling Henrietta,

I have so much to tell you about our stay in Paris! I am so sorry you are too unwell to come on our trip. Your French is so much better than mine, for a start, so you would love watching me humiliate myself on every outing. The city is everything we thought it would be! Father keeps saying, 'it's a shame about the French,' but you know what he's like. There are so many interesting people here, from all over. A family from Texas, they do something in oil, a couple from New York, and the most interesting gentleman from Marrakesh. Tomorrow we visit Notre-Dame. I will sketch it for you and enclose the paper.

Keep warm and take plenty of fresh air to rebuild your strength.

All my love,

Josephine

Saturday 26th May, 1866
　　Dearest Josephine,

I am absolutely boiling with jealousy here. I cannot believe a small cold kept me from our trip. I will be irritated about it forever! Your new friends sound very bohemian. I adored your interpretation of Notre-Dame and have put it up near my bureau.

Not much to report here, I'm afraid. My friend Maud has joined the suffrage movement. I'm not really sure why; her life is going brilliantly as-is, especially with lovely Mr Bartlett waiting to marry her. Sometimes I think she gets bored.

I am almost completely better and already scheming about when we can next travel to Europe...

All my love to Mother, Father and Bertie,
Henrietta

———————— ❧ ————————

M onday 13ᵗʰ August, 1866
          Darling Henrietta,
Greetings from Rome! It is the most wonderful city and we have again met the most fascinating people: a novelist from the Far East, a doctor from Johannesburg and a family from Bolivia. A wonderfully eccentric Scottish lady we met on the train has given me a book by Mary Wollstonecraft. She said she had read it back-to-back and that it was time to pass it on. It is quite enlightening—your friend Maud would like it! (No, really, I think she is right to join the suffrage movement. The more I see of the world, the more I realise how sheltered we have been at home in London.)
Enclosed is a sketch of the Colosseum.
Love,
Josephine
P.S. I may have good news when next I write!

———————— ❧ ————————

F riday 24ᵗʰ August, 1866
          Dearest Henrietta,
The news is only just confirmed but I wanted you to be the first person I tell—even if someone else will tell you before I am home, so to speak. I am engaged!
I know we assumed you'd be the first to marry, since you're older and so much more, well, refined, but I think I've met someone who matches me perfectly. He's intelligent, he asks me questions and actually waits to hear an answer. Professionally is a man of medicine, although he is also a most passionate writer of philosophy, specialising in ethics. I am sure he will be published soon. He has loaned me several books by notable figures, and I am already learning so much.
Although I am in no hurry to leave Rome, or the Continent in general, I cannot wait to see you again and for you to meet John.
All my love,

Josephine

M onday 24*th* September, 1866
     Dearest Josephine,

To say I'm shocked is an understatement. You were always the slower of the two of us to form attachments! But I suppose one knows when one has met one's soulmate. I am so pleased for you, little sister, and I cannot wait to meet this distinguished gentleman and find out from you both how you met. It was in Paris, wasn't it? I can see it now, you lurking in the corner at some party and a dashing gentleman sweeping you off your feet and following you across the continent.

I admit I am a little jealous, but mostly because I am missing this most special part of your life. I hope the rest of your destinations are boring and have terrible weather, so you hurry home to see me and I can hear about everything.

Love,

Henrietta

S unday 7*th* October, 1866
     Josephine,

Little sister, I am crying so much I can barely write. I am so very sorry for what transpired between us this morning. I was so looking forward to seeing you and hearing about your adventures, and I am still in shock at what you have done.

Josephine, you <u>cannot</u> marry this man. You know this. You knew it when you wrote me from Rome, you knew it in Paris and Berlin and Turin and the others, and you knew it when you brought him to the house this morning. Perhaps you took ill on your travels and forgot your common sense? It does not matter that he is a doctor. It does not matter that he wishes to become a great academic. No one in the family will permit you to make such a grave error. I implore you to see sense and break off the engagement before word gets around that you plan to travel to Greece and the Near East with this man. You know what the aunts and uncles will say. You know what God would say.

All my love,

Henrietta

---⊷◉⊶---

S*aturday 13th October, 1866*
    My dearest Henrietta,

I am so disappointed at how you behaved at our homecoming last week. I thought my sister, of all people, would put my happiness above such irrelevances as the opinions of strangers. For my part, I am sorry to have left things so badly with you and Mother and Father and Bertie. I hope my absence will soften them to my wishes.

I had hoped you, of all the family, would see what John and I mean to each other when you saw us together. But of course, you couldn't, because you refused to meet his eye. I suspected Father wouldn't want him in the house and warned John in advance (he is, for his part, far too well-mannered to be any less than complimentary about my family). I assumed you *would have the basic decency to shake his hand and wish him a good day. You do not deserve his grace.*

Did you know that John taught himself and his little sisters to read, and paid to send them both to school? Did you know that he graduated from the University of Edinburgh and knows some of the McLean family from Scotland? Did you know that he has written several papers on moral philosophy and a colleague has recommended he present them at the South Place Ethical Society? You did not, because you refuse to look past the superficial. If my circumstances were just a little different—and let me be clear, by that I mean if John shared our skin colour—you would be nothing but excited that I am engaged to a doctor.

Henrietta, I will marry him. I've found a vicar to do it. We both hope you will come. I've enclosed an invitation. It's the only one we're sending to my side of the family since the rest have cut me off so sharply. I trust you will not cause Mother, Father or Bertie greater distress by forewarning them of the date of the wedding. They already know to expect my marriage; I see no reason to drag out their dread. Better to tell them once it cannot be undone. I know you would all love John, if you got to know him a little. I am the product of all of you, after all.
    With love,
    Josephine

---⊷◉⊶---

M onday 5th November, 1866
     Dearest Josephine,

Please forgive my previous behaviour. I have been reflecting on my thoughts and actions and I will of course attend your wedding. I look forward to celebrating your union and I look forward to apologising to John for my previous behaviour, in person.

All my love,
Henrietta

S aturday 8th December, 1866
     Henrietta,

Now it is me crying so much I cannot see. I am sick to my stomach at your actions. I expected Father to engage in nefarious behaviour, but not you. My soul is crushed with grief and anger.

I have telegrammed John's sisters to inform them of his death. He has many friends here in London, of course, all of whom were present at the church while we waited eagerly for his arrival. They consoled me while we waited, they reassured me when I expressed my fears that John had changed his mind, and they informed and comforted me when they learnt what had happened. They have been my family today, and they will be my family from today onward.

I will not give details of John's funeral, nor his final resting place. I should like to join him there one day, and I suspect that telling you any details might cause another... accident.

I wonder if you understand the magnitude of the damage you have caused. I do not think you do; your mind has always focused on the superficial rather than the spiritual. I keep asking myself if you realised, when you shared your invitation with Mother and Father, the likely consequences of your actions. You are not a cruel person, I keep telling myself, just an ignorant one. For Mother and Father's part in this, I will never speak to them again. I wish the best to Bertie, who is too young to have had anything to do with it, and I pity Mother, who has neither the means nor the inclination to think for herself... but Father acted with a ruthlessness I can never forgive, and Mother of course will agree with him on all matters. I have no interest in corresponding with you any further. If your actions *were well intentioned, then may our estrangement be your punishment. If you had <u>any</u> inkling of what Father might do, then I trust you understand when I say that the Lord will punish you as He sees fit.*

Josephine

W*ednesday, 27th February, 1867*
        Dearest Josephine,
    Please let's meet. I miss you, and I am worried about you. I know you are staying at the awful boarding house to which I address this note—Maud told me about it, from when she saw you at that suffrage meeting. You'll catch your death there. Maud told me you looked sickly. I suspect you picked something up on your travels. Let us meet at St James's Park, at the bridge on the lake, on this Friday at four o'clock. The air will be good for you, and it is public enough that you won't dare to utter the foul thoughts you wrote in your previous letter. I will bring the carriage, so you can come home straight away if you'd like. Mother and Father would be so happy to see you again. Bertie too.

    Your loving sister,
    Henrietta

F*riday 1st March, 1867*
        Darling Josephine,
    I am so grateful you have decided to reconcile. I repeat what I told you earlier this evening: the match was unsuitable, and it had to be stopped. I regret the way Father went about it, of course, but I am pleased for your future nevertheless. I am glad you too have seen the light and I trust that our relationship will recover in the fullness of time. To celebrate your return to the household and assure our friends and neighbours that you are indeed back on the right path, Mother has invited a small number of our loved ones to tea next week. Father's friend Mr Cunningham will be there! Need I say more...

    Thank you so very much for my wonderful necklace. I am sorry that you brought it all the way across Europe as a birthday gift for me, and I only just got to open it. It is beautiful. Not what I would normally choose, but I have already tried it on. I will wear it tomorrow evening, in fact—Mother and I are going to the opera!

All my love,
Henrietta

———— ⟋⟍ ————

P ALL MALL GAZETTE, DECEMBER 10TH 1866
    BIRTHS, MARRIAGES, AND DEATHS
DEATHS

Ingram, John, aged 29, of Bethnal Green, 7th inst.

———— ⟋⟍ ————

P ALL MALL GAZETTE, MARCH 3RD 1867
    BIRTHS, MARRIAGES, AND DEATHS
DEATHS

McLean, Charlotte, aged 52, of Stamford Hill, 2nd inst.

McLean, Henrietta, aged 27, of Stamford Hill, 2nd inst.

———— ⟋⟍ ————

P ALL MALL GAZETTE, JANUARY 1ST 1869
    BIRTHS, MARRIAGES, AND DEATHS
DEATHS

McLean, Josephine, of Whitechapel, aged 26, 29th ult.

McLean Family Tree (Completed)

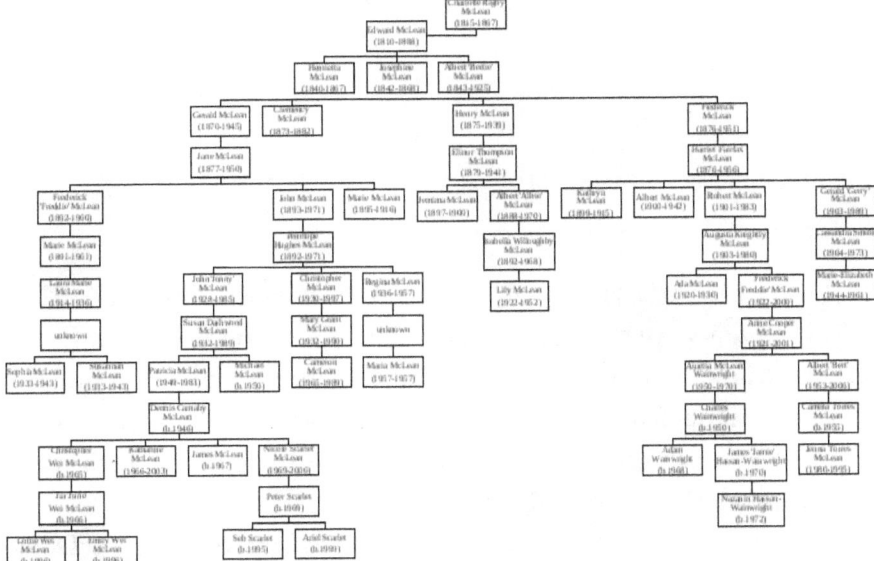

Chapter Twenty-One

After reading Alexandria's letters and newspaper snippets, Ariel helped Sophey wash the teacups, then took her notebook outside. Ernest and Alexandria were in quiet conversation, Alexandria applying poultice to her hands. As Ariel left, Ernest placed a blanket around Alexandria's shoulders and she lit a pipe. Ariel found a metal bench on Southend high street and read through the letters again.

A few yards away, a couple sat with their daughters, eating McDonald's.

'This is a one-time thing,' the mother was saying. Her long, blonde hair danced in the breeze, and she kept tucking it behind her ears to stop it from getting covered in ketchup. 'Because the oven is broken and our landlord is sh—'

'Lazy,' said the father quickly. 'He's going to take a while to fix the oven, so it's McDonald's for lunch and dinner at Gran's.'

'Do we have to go to Gran's?' one of the children asked.

'Gran's is too hot,' her sister agreed. 'She always leaves the radiator on.'

Ariel stifled a smile—Grandpa drove Uncle James up the wall for the same reason. She looked at the children again. The older girl was blonde like her mother, with her mother's straight, fine hair. The younger daughter was blonde too, but her hair was a curly afro; she was a paler version of their father. The girls wore identical butterfly clips, the sort Ariel herself had coveted at that age. The parents wore matching cord necklaces, the cheap type you bought from a market stall with half a heart each. All four of them were obviously related, she realised. They looked the same, but different.

Statistically, shame would not be the thing that killed Ariel Scarlet.

'Want to go for a walk?' Sophey asked. She was standing in front of Ariel, and Ariel hadn't even seen her approach.

'All right.' Ariel followed Sophey in the general direction of the seafront, climbing down a long flight of steps and crossing the road to reach the seafront. They walked along in silence. The tide was in, coming all the way up to the sea wall, and Ariel found she was grateful for the feel of the salty, biting air when she took deep breaths. After a while Sophey stopped and guided Ariel back across two lanes of traffic to an ice cream parlour.

'Is your oat milk thing a vegan thing or do you eat regular ice cream and chocolate?' Sophey asked.

'I could eat an ice cream.'

'Then it's time you had a Rossi's.' Sophey strode inside. 'I'd like two ninety-nine cones with a flake, please,' she said to the guy behind the counter. To Ariel she said, 'grab a seat.'

Five minutes later, Ariel was making her way through a creamy, gently melting ice cream and trying to figure out how to neatly eat the flake protruding from it.

'Want to talk about it?' Sophey asked, consuming her own ice cream with relish. She had read the letters over Ariel's shoulder in the shop but hadn't commented.

Ariel shrugged. 'We've solved the 'why'.'

Sophey nodded. 'Ernie and Alexandria are working on the 'how.' Alexandria's here all day. When I left she was talking about focussing on the necklace's origins. And stinking up the shop with her pipe.' Sophey wrinkled her nose. Ariel realised that she hadn't noticed that she'd left the necklace in the shop. She wasn't sure she wanted to look at it. She ate some more ice cream.

Sophey, for her part, seemed content to let Ariel find her words in her own time.

'I'm not sure how I should feel,' she said eventually. She wasn't sure why she was saying anything at all, but Sophey had bought her an ice cream, so it felt only fair to give her a few thoughts in return.

'So how do you actually feel?' Sophey asked. 'I'm not sure there's established social etiquette for what to do when you read the private letters of your long-dead feuding great aunts.'

Ariel licked her ice cream and thought for a moment. 'Ashamed,' she said eventually. 'Embarrassed.'

'Because...'

'Because it sounds like I'm related to horrible racists!'

'So are all white people,' Sophey said. She licked her own ice cream. A bit dripped onto her wrist and she mopped it up with a serviette.

'What do you mean?'

'Think about it. Everyone's got family history, haven't they? Odds are, if you're a white person and you look into your ancestry, you'll find someone who had sympathies with Hitler or someone who profited from enslavement. Like how everyone's got at least one rapist and at least one murderer in the family.'

'I think you're overestimating how many rapists and murderers there are.'

Sophey just said, 'also everyone's related if you go back far enough.'

'Great. Lovely.'

Sophey finished her ice cream and started on the cone. 'Our children would be fine,' she said around a mouthful.

Despite herself, Ariel laughed.

'Want a tea?' Sophey asked. She crunched her flake with gusto. 'Ice cream makes me thirsty.'

'Go on then.'

'It's not just that they were racist,' Ariel said when they both held cups of tea. Sophey made an infinitely better brew than this café, but Ariel was glad of the warmth of the mug. 'It's that the sister—Henrietta—ratted out Josephine's forbidden wedding to her family, and then the family... what did they do? Hire someone to shoot the fiancé and throw his body in the river? Hire a randomer off the street who wouldn't mind beating someone to death and dumping his body? That's just...'

'Middle class social climbers navigating the marriage market?' Sophey asked. Whatever she saw in Ariel's face made her say quickly, and more gently, 'I'm not sure we'll ever find out the details.' Ariel sipped tea, and Sophey continued, 'speaking of John...'

'What about him?'

'John Ingram is quite an anglicised name. He could have been... he could have been loads of things. African, lascar, Italian. Jewish.' She scratched her nose. 'Although the family lived in Stamford Hill, that's got quite a big Jewish population. They might not have minded Jewish as much as they'd have minded something else.'

Ariel did not know what to do with this commentary, so she said, 'What's *lascar*?'

'Lascars were what they called sailors or militiamen from places sort of vaguely in the east. India, Southeast Asia, northern Africa.' Ariel was not great at geography, but she was confident that Southeast Asia and northern Africa were not close to each other.

'Does it matter? Wait... Italian? Italians are just Italian.'

'A while ago someone came into the shop trying to sell an old sign saying "no blacks, no dogs, no Irish,"' Sophey said. 'The rules change.' She did not seem as perturbed by this as Ariel was, but then she had barely raised an eyebrow during their entire cursed necklace investigation, aside from when Ariel burnt her fingers. Ariel wondered if Sophey was one of those children who started reading the moment they were home from the maternity ward. It would not surprise her if Sophey already been accepted into a top university.

'So John Ingram could have been from pretty much anywhere and believed anything and it would have been a problem, even if he was a doctor.'

'The list of acceptable characteristics for Josephine and Henrietta's husbands would likely have been "white," "protestant," and "professional." We know he was a professional, so it must have been the other things.'

Ariel thought about that. 'I don't know Victorian history,' she said finally. 'I don't know what Henrietta would have considered so inappropriate she needed to put a stop to it.'

'I've just listed half of the planet,' Sophey said thoughtfully. 'Maybe the details don't matter. Curse is still the curse.'

They sipped tea. It really was not as good as the one Sophey made. Ariel looked over at the man behind the counter. He was more of a lad. Clearly he had no one at home to teach him how to make tea, and so he would not go far in life.

'I want to look into the details,' Ariel said after a minute. She squinted into the dregs of her mug as she tried to tie her thoughts together. 'Those letters were so vague. Maybe John could have been anyone, but he wasn't, he was a whole person. Then he was just a line in an obituary.'

'I'm sure there are ways to find out more,' Sophey said thoughtfully. 'They might not even involve me singeing your fingers.'

'It's good to have goals,' Ariel agreed, and they lapsed back into silence.

'Something else is niggling me,' Sophey mused after a while. 'We know from the dates that Henrietta died the day after she got the necklace, right? Killed in a carriage accident with their mother. So she didn't have any direct descendants. Nor did Josephine. *You're* descended from the brother, Bertie. Who had to sit around and watch his sister and mother die horribly, then his remaining sister took her life, and then—' she checked her notebook, where she had scrawled an approximation of the family tree. '—his daughter and three of his granddaughters died young during his lifetime. He would have suffered a lot.'

'Do you think that was what Josephine wanted?' Ariel asked. She thought of the toddling boy, in the scene with the tree in the garden, and wondered what he made of his sisters' feud. 'Do you think she wanted her family to have to live without their loved ones the way she had to live without John? Or do you think she was more interested in people knowing that her dad had him bumped off?'

'Maybe a bit of both,' Sophey said. 'You're thinking about how we can break the curse, aren't you?'

Ariel nodded. 'Do you think Alexandria or Ernest will know how?'

'I think they'll both know quite a lot but prefer for us to figure it out by ourselves.' Sophey pulled a face at her tea. 'Shall we go back and start trying to figure it out?'

'All right. Thanks for the ice cream.'

B ack at the shop, which smelt strongly of smoke from the pipe now sticking out of Alexandria's jacket pocket, Ernest and Alexandria were pulling tarot cards over the necklace.

'The Tower,' Ernest said, flipping over an old, worn card with an expert *flick*.

'Three of Swords,' Alexandria's *flick* was no less impressive, her own deck of cards far newer and brighter than Ernest's.

'Ten of Swords.'

'Five of Cups.'

'We get it,' Sophey said. 'The necklace is bad.'

Ernest chuckled. 'It never hurts to try the basics.'

Ariel, who had no idea how tarot worked, just said, 'Do either of you have any thoughts on how the curse was laid onto the necklace?'

Alexandria picked the necklace up, running her fingers over it and turning it so the gems caught the light. It wasn't smoking any more, and Ariel hoped it didn't start again. Alexandria's fingers looked sore. 'I'm almost certain Josephine cursed it herself. It was made in London, so the line that she bought it in Europe was a ruse to get Henrietta to take the gift. I think she had help with the curse unless she was already gifted in the arts. The magic involved is powerful. It would have taken a lot of energy.'

'Does how the necklace was made have anything to do with it?' Sophey asked. 'It's still bugging me that we don't have a maker's mark. Aren't gemstones powerful in their own right? What if the stones were magical before Josephine even thought about having a necklace made? We should know everything we're dealing with to have the best chance of breaking the curse.'

'You're right,' said Alexandria. 'Crystals, gemstones... anything of the earth can hold great power. Providence is important for items,' she continued, and Ariel thought she would have been an excellent teacher, 'because they have a long memory. Knowing the location the gems were mined would be helpful. Knowing which goldsmith worked the metal would be useful.'

'But we're never going to know for sure, are we?' Ariel said.

'I don't think so,' said Ernest. 'Some things are lost to time.' Alexandria shook her head in agreement.

'So let's focus on Josephine and John for now,' said Ariel. 'Josephine laid the curse, she wanted it. We know it's something to do with remembrance.' The granddaughter clock chimed and Ariel jumped. 'Shit, it's one o'clock. My brother will be here—'

In one fluid movement, Ernest swept the necklace into his pocket, stuck the case behind a cushion and stood up to flick the door sign to 'open.'

'Back to normal,' he said. 'Alexandria, be a customer.'

She pulled a face at him. 'Sell me something worth buying.'

They bickered back and forth like an old married couple as Ariel shoved her notebook into her bag and glanced at the time and—

'Hey, Ariel.' There was Seb, walking through the door like this was a normal day. 'Ready for lunch? Oh, hello... Sophey.'

Sophey smiled at him and looked away.

'Ready to go?' Ariel asked, suddenly very ready to be somewhere else. She wasn't sure she had an appetite for savoury food after her ice cream, but her stomach rumbled. Maybe discovering family secrets was like having a cold, and you needed to keep your strength up.

'Sure. Would Sophey like to join us?' Seb didn't look like he was just being polite, and Ariel had a sudden rush of gratitude for having a brother who liked who she chose to spend her time with.

Sophey looked at Ernie, and then at Ariel. Ernie said, 'You're probably over hours already this week. Go and have a nice time.'

Ariel said, 'Sure.'

Chapter Twenty-Two

Ariel, Seb and Sophey went, of course, to the pie shop. Sophey seemed content to eat while Seb and Ariel argued over whether or not it should be legal to sell bottled water when you could get it safely from a tap.

'What brought you to Southend?' Sophey asked Seb when the siblings went quiet. Ariel tensed, wondering if this was where their father came up in conversation, where the siblings danced the how-much-do-we-tell-a-not-family-member-about-the-family dance. She didn't think she'd mind Sophey knowing about all the fights Seb had with their father, though. She had already seen one branch of the McLean family tear itself into pieces.

'I liked the degree programme,' Seb replied. 'And I wanted to live by the sea. I've always liked water.'

'He was swimming before he was walking,' Ariel said proudly. She could not remember this herself, of course, but there was a framed photograph in the Scarlet house of Seb and Nicole, Seb barely a year old, wearing enormous armbands and splashing around in somebody's swimming pool, supported by a beaming, sunburned Nicole.

'Why not a nicer town?' Sophey asked. She shifted in her seat. 'Everyone I know who goes to university gets out of here and stays gone.'

'Where'd they go?' Seb asked.

'Edinburgh, Nottingham, Bristol. Oxbridge.' Sophey sounded wistful, like she wasn't worthy of mentioning such institutions.

'What would you do if you went to uni?' Seb asked.

Sophey's eyes shone. 'History or classics or archaeology. Archaeology is really expensive to get into, but it's so interesting. But...' she looked down at the table. 'I don't know. We'll see.'

'For what it's worth, *I* like Southend,' Seb said. He stabbed a forkful of omelette happily. 'Ariel's starting to like it too.'

'It's growing on me,' was all Ariel would say.

Chapter Twenty-Three

That evening, Seb found Ariel sat on the floor in the house's tiny living room, tinkering with her new-old camera on the coffee table. His flat-mates were all out at work or doing whatever students did in Southend, so Ariel took the opportunity to use the coffee table to set down the camera and examine all its components. It was a small miracle that it seemed to be in full working order, and Ariel wanted to make sure it was in the best shape possible. Plus, it was easier to let the events of the day wash over her when her hands were busy.

'Looks cool,' Seb commented, and sat cross-legged on the sofa across from her.

'I think I've already got some decent shots from it,' Ariel said. 'And if they turn out badly, I'll get some really cool shots *of* it. I like Bezzina's Emporium,' she added carefully after a moment.

'It's brilliant,' Seb agreed immediately, eyes glinting. 'Last time I was in there I was tempted by a set of writing pens,' Ariel made a mental note of that for his next birthday. 'Have you seen the clothes?'

'I have,' Ariel said. She wasn't sure if she was ready to admit she'd sold customers items, so she just said, 'the whole shop is quite something.'

Seb watched her tinker for a few more minutes, flicking occasionally through a grubby Agatha Christie paperback. They often sat like this back home, Ariel working on some arts and crafts project and Seb sitting nearby with a book. Ariel missed it. What she hadn't missed was the bite to the silence she knew accompanied Seb having something to say and working himself up to say it.

Should she say something first—

'So why'd you bring the necklace up here?'

Ariel's heart thumped, even though she had known, deep down, what this was about when Seb sat down. 'What do you mean?'

'Ariel, please. I have eyeballs. The case was behind a cushion on that chair when I walked into Bezzina's Emporium, and you've been cagey every time you've been near that shop. I'd rather you were honest with me.'

'I don't like your new ear piercing.'

Seb didn't even bother rolling his eyes. 'Do I need to phone Dad?'

'*No.*' Genuine fights between the Scarlet siblings were rare. Ariel could count on one hand the times she and Seb had really, truly, fallen out. She did not want to add to the list today. She pushed away the camera and moved from the carpet to a chair, so they were facing each other properly. 'Promise you won't interrupt 'til I'm done?' This, too, was a time-honoured Scarlet sibling tradition. If they had something to get off their chest, the other person couldn't interrupt until they'd finished speaking. Seb nodded.

Ariel took a deep breath. 'Right. So. I wanted to know for sure about the curse, and I thought Bezzina's might help...'

True to form, Seb said nothing until Ariel finished explaining her meetings with Sophey and their research, and Alexandria's input, and finally Josephine and Henrietta's letters. She got up to find a glass of water and when she came back, Seb was absently playing with one of his bracelets.

'Why didn't you talk to me about how much this was worrying you?'

'Didn't want to worry you.'

Now Seb did roll his eyes. 'And the curse is real? *Really* real?'

'Definitely. I'll show you the letters. They're insane, Seb.'

Seb continued fiddling with his bracelets. Ariel wondered if he was going to argue with her, like their dad would have done. But he just sighed heavily and said, 'what do you want to do about the curse?'

'Break it. Obviously.'

'Okay.' Seb twiddled his bracelet a few more times. 'Do you want to meet up with Sophey and Ernest Bezzina tomorrow? We could ask them what they think. Properly this time. No sneaking around.'

Ariel appreciated how quickly Seb grasped that Sophey and Ernest were the experts. 'Yeah, I do. I'll text Sophey and get the notebook with the letters.'

Ariel was gratified that Sophey replied to her message in the time it took for her to fetch her notebook from her bag and hand it to Seb. When she looked up from her phone at Seb reading, he wore the same expression he had when they were in Spain on a family holiday, back when their mother was alive. A local child held a small octopus and was methodically smacking it against the concrete of the harbour wall. Little Seb stared at the child for so long they noticed his presence but did not stop bashing the already-fairly-squishy mollusc until it was definitively *not alive*. Their parents hustled Seb away just in time for him to vomit into the harbour.

'You're not going to puke, are you?'

'Not this time.'

'It's bad, isn't it?' Ariel said in a small voice. She sat on the sofa next to her brother and read over his shoulder. *You know what God would say.* She swallowed and turned it over. 'I didn't think it would be something like that,' she said. She was surprised her voice cracked a little bit. 'I thought it would be, I don't know, an estranged husband having it off with the butler. Something...'

'Understandable?'

'No. Well yes, but that's not the word I'm looking for. I don't know.'

'You know this doesn't reflect badly on us or our part of the family, right?' Seb said quietly. 'We aren't Henrietta or her parents.'

'No. But we're—we're guilty by association.'

'Ariel, it was a hundred and fifty years ago. No one can be held personally responsible for something their ancestors did. That would be like punishing all modern Germans because of Hitler.'

'Grandpa has a good go at that,' Ariel said in a small voice, but she knew what he meant. She returned to her camera.

'Ariel. What's bothering you?' Only Seb would have known that she still wasn't satisfied. Ariel was glad he was part of this now too. She hadn't realised that hiding her necklace project from him had been so exhausting.

'I don't... I don't think it's enough to say it's nothing to do with us. Josephine made it about us when she cursed our family. Sophey said what you said, that we shouldn't be held responsible for Henrietta and what she did, but saying that it wasn't us and that Josephine shouldn't have cursed the necklace doesn't feel like... enough.'

'What does it feel like?' Seb asked gently. 'Use your pictures if your words aren't working.' This was something else they started when they were small. Ariel had never liked school even in the early years, never wanted to sit in a lesson when she could be using her hands to draw or go outside and look at things. Seb, by then old enough to read her story books and help her with her letters, used to encourage her to draw things when she struggled to articulate them. That was why his first tattoo was that wobbly drawing of old-fashioned weighing scales, created when five-year-old Ariel left him a note explaining that she wanted to make their parents a cake for their wedding anniversary. Despite their carefully-hatched plan to wake up at five o'clock in the morning and bake a Victoria sandwich, it had gone badly wrong—Seb was barely tall enough to reach the oven, and Ariel certainly not grown up enough to operate an electric mixer. Their parents were woken by smoke. The memory of Peter and Nicole, in pyjamas, waving a fire extinguisher around, still made both siblings smile, and for some reason Seb had kept hold of that drawing of scales. He got it inked over his ribs for his eighteenth birthday.

Ariel sat upright.

'What's that face?' Seb asked. 'What did I say?'

'The curse. I might know how to break it. Are you sure about coming to Bezzina's tomorrow? You don't have work?'

'Uni's done and I'm not applying for proper jobs until I hear about my internship. You've got your scheming face on, little miss.'

'It's just an idea. Sophey and Ernest will know what to do next.'

'Don't underestimate yourself, Ariel. You've got a good idea, I can tell. Your eyebrow twitches when you're pleased with yourself.'

'It's *just* an idea,' Ariel insisted, but she was touched by his faith in her.

———— ⟡ ————

Just before she went to bed, Ariel texted Grace.

Miss you. How's your summer?

She texted Sophey.

Had an idea. She added an emoji of a set of scales. Sophey texted back the quizzical face emoji.

She put her phone on silent, then plugged in her headphones and queued up a podcast about the environmental impact of the fast fashion industry.

She was surprised that she could feel herself drifting off before it was finished. She was unsurprised that her dreams were a whirlwind of handwritten letters, floating onto an inky black river.

Chapter Twenty-Four

Of course, Ariel had no reply from Grace the following morning—but she was too busy thinking about Josephine and Henrietta and her maybe-good-idea to mind. Seb wanted to go for a run with some friends, so Ariel said she'd meet him at Bezzina's Emporium and walked to Southend library. Ariel hoped Seb's run made him feel better. She'd heard him talking to Karishma as she went upstairs the previous evening, telling her that Ariel had found some interesting stuff about their family history. 'It's disappointing,' he'd said.

'But not surprising,' Karishma finished.

'Yeah.'

Ariel had closed the bathroom door, suddenly aware of what a lack of talking might mean. She hadn't seen Karishma since.

Now, in the library, she found herself wandering the social history and politics shelves. She'd never been one for nonfiction, any more than she had been one for fiction. She was dreading A Levels or university, where you had to read whole academic articles and textbook chapters just to have something to talk about in class. Besides, right now, she didn't know where to start. With a fat polemic or a little paperback? History or current events? She wandered the aisles, wondering when current events were considered officially 'in the past.' How long did you have to wait? Was 9/11 history? Ariel didn't remember it, but Seb did.

'There you are,' said a voice. Sophey, today wearing... oh God, green trousers. Lichen green. With her boots and a huge grey jumper, she looked like an actual witch.

Ariel hid a smile. 'Hi. How did you know I'd be in here?'

'Just had a feeling,' Sophey said. Then she grinned. 'Kidding, your brother just arrived at the shop. He's bombarding Ernie and Alexandria with questions about the occult so I thought I'd return a few books and fetch you.'

'What are you reading?' Ariel asked.

Sophey held up a pretty paperback with a blue-green cover and an illustration of a truck. Ariel squinted: it was a lovely design, but the title was too swirly to read easily. *Aristotle and Something Discover... Something.* 'Just a bit of YA. Young adult.' Sophey dug around in her tote bag as Ariel thought, *I know what YA is.* Out came another paperback, with a gold and red design. This one's typography was mercifully easier: *The Song of Achilles.* 'Some Greek myth.' Finally Sophey dug out a small orange book with black and white circles. 'And some nonfiction.' *We Should All Be Feminists.*

'How do you read that?' Ariel asked as Sophey loaded the books onto a kiosk and set about logging them into the system.

'The nonfiction?' Sophey asked.

'Yeah. I can't get my brain to focus.'

'This one is really short. But I suppose I just like reading.' She glanced at Ariel's face. 'You don't?'

'It's not that I don't like it. Seb used to read to me all the time, and I do read what we're set in school. I just can't... get it. I don't get why people are happy to sit for so long.'

'Do you like films or TV?' Sophey asked. She didn't sound like she was being snobby.

'Not really,' Ariel admitted. 'I'd rather be doing something.'

'Maybe that just means that one day you'll be making your own films or TV.'

As Sophey and Ariel walked through town to reach Bezzina's Emporium, Ariel looked forward to talking properly about her idea with Sophey and Ernest and Seb. It might be a shit idea once it was out of her head. It might not come to anything. But she felt hopeful, for the first time since she brought the necklace to Southend, that the curse might truly be breakable.

'Hi Ariel.'

It took Ariel a moment to realise it wasn't Sophey who was talking to her. It took her another moment to realise that she *knew* the person who was talking to her.

'Grace! What are you doing here?'

'Visiting my sister.' Of course. Grace's older sister went to Seb's uni. That's how Seb had become interested in coming up here, because Carrie had come the year before and liked it.

After so many months of only seeing Grace in class (well, of seeing the back of Grace's head, or the side of her shoulder), Ariel almost found it hard to look her friend properly in her face. She'd spent so long on the receiving end of Grace's cold shoulder that she'd almost forgotten what it was like to have a real conversation with her. She hadn't changed, except maybe getting a little taller. She wore the same beautifully styled cornrows, the same immaculate nails, same 'G' necklace that she never took off except for PE and then she made the teachers lock it in a desk.

'How are you?' Ariel asked.

'Okay,' Grace said. Her gaze flicked to Sophey.

'This is Sophey,' Ariel said quickly.

'Pleased to meet you,' Sophey said, and held out a hand. Grace shook it once, bemused, and Sophey continued, 'Is that scarf a Liberty print?'

Grace glanced down at her handbag. The bag was fake leather, as all her bags had been since she discovered veganism, and a silk scarf was tied to one strap. Silk was okay, she had told Ariel, as long as it was vintage, 'because those moths would have died years ago anyway.'

'Yeah, it is actually. Good eye.'

'Thanks,' Sophey said. She looked at Ariel. 'I'm not completely terrible at fashion. We sell Liberty prints in the shop.' Ariel made a mental note to look.

'It was nice to meet you,' Grace said, clearly ready to leave the conversation. She hovered, for a moment, then said to Sophey, 'Be careful with her.'

'Excuse me?' Sophey said politely.

'Be careful with Ariel. She's only friends with people who look right in her photographs. People who agree with her. People who... fit in.'

Then she was gone, into a shop.

Sophey turned to Ariel, frowning. 'What was she on about? Is she—'

'It's nothing,' Ariel said. 'Ignore her.'

She strode ahead and shoved all the feelings she had about Grace deep into the pit of her stomach. This was *her* day about *her* curse. She had been feeling optimistic not ten minutes ago. Grace wasn't going to ruin that.

'So, breaking this curse,' Ernest said. It was an hour later and, again, the shop was closed and the chairs arranged. Ariel appreciated Ernest's frank manner. It was just the three teens and Ernest, Alexandria off on a walk along the beach. Ariel suspected that Seb had talked her ear off about her psychic abilities and she needed time to grow it back. 'Alexandria and I have some thoughts, but it's your necklace.'

'I want to try anything to break it,' said Seb. 'But it's not my curse, really, it's Ariel's. She's the last girl in our immediate part of the family.'

'What about Em and Lottie?' Ariel asked. 'They're only nineteen.' Their mother's youngest brother, Chris, named his twin girls after he and Aunt June's favourite old timey authors. Nerdery was strong in Ariel and Seb's family.

'They're adopted,' Seb reminded her.

'Are they?'

'Yeah, course. Didn't you know? Uncle Chris and Aunt June decided not to have their own children just in case. The twins were adopted from China when they were babies.'

Shit. Ariel knew that already. Didn't she? She searched her memory for a single time she had heard Uncle Chris or Aunt June talk about the twins' birth or June's pregnancy. She realised she couldn't, despite whole summers spent together.

Ariel buried her face in her hands. 'I've told them how much they look like their mum, haven't I?'

'Yep,' said Seb. He didn't say it in a mocking way, or a judgemental one, just like he'd thought about Ariel's misunderstanding before. The handful of years between them felt like decades.

'I wouldn't worry about it,' Ernest said. 'I was out with my husband once and someone thought we were brothers. People see what they're expecting to see.'

Ariel did not feel better. 'So, the curse. I had an idea...'

'Go on,' Ernest said. Last night's inspiration withered and Ariel's stomach twisted. She felt like she was back in class, called on to answer a question she didn't fully understand. She blamed Grace for putting her off her game, with that catty comment to Sophey which wasn't even—

Ariel took a deep breath. She wasn't going to let her fight with Grace ruin an opportunity to break the curse.

She looked at Ernest, trying to form words to say while her brain did more thinking.

But he wasn't looking at her like she needed to have an answer. He looked like he was interested in whatever she wanted to talk about. Sophey leaned in and said, 'It's a really good idea.'

Yes. It was.

'We know the curse has to be about remembrance,' she heard herself say. 'That's what the gemstones spell. I... I think Josephine wanted her story known, wanted people to talk about how badly she and John were treated by her family and everyone.' She looked at Ernest, who gave her a tiny nod, inviting her to continue. 'I think Josephine was telling us how the curse can be broken too. I think she wanted people to know what happened to John. No one was held accountable for what happened to him. We're not even completely sure exactly what *did* happen. He got shoved out of history. So much of what you sell here is about balancing someone's bad feeling with something that will bring good feeling,' Ariel said to Sophey. 'I think the curse is rooted in the imbalance in Josephine's life. The injustice.'

'We need to balance the scales,' Seb said, and Ariel knew he was thinking about her drawing.

'I think that's a very good starting point,' Ernest said.

'Any ideas on how we actually do it?' Ariel asked. Now she had thrown the idea out there and no one had said it was stupid, she was willing to admit she had no idea what to do next.

'What about an exhibition?' Sophey asked. 'Something to tell the world who Josephine and John were and what happened to them.'

Seb's phone buzzed with a phone call. He glanced at it, uninterested, but ducked outside to answer.

'An exhibition might work,' Ariel said, although she had no idea how to put one together. She wasn't sure of the last time she attended one. 'If we can find information about John in particular.'

Sophey said, 'Josephine's letters said he was a doctor. There must be some record of his qualifications somewhere.'

'Where do we hold an exhibition about two Victorians?' Ariel asked. 'A museum? A library?'

'Or a website,' Sophey suggested. 'You can reach more people online.'

The door tinged as Seb came back in, face brighter than Ariel had seen for a while. 'I've got the internship! I start on Monday.'

'That's great! Really.' Ariel tried to make her face look like she meant it, and ignore that her first instinct was sadness and irritation that he really wouldn't come home properly this summer.

Seb scrubbed a hand through his hair. 'God, I said I'd come back with you to Bath for the weekend. I've got to grab some proper office clothes. And a haircut. Today. Want to come?'

'You should go with Karishma.'

'You sure? You love telling me how to dress.'

'Consider it a congratulatory gift that I'm giving Karishma a chance to do it.' Ariel updated him briefly on Sophey's suggestion of an online exhibition.

'That's a great idea. You'll be brilliant at that.'

Ariel, who had never made it through an IT lesson at school without being told off for reading *Vogue* in a spare browser, doubted this. But she appreciated Seb's enthusiasm. 'Are you going to be out all day?' she asked. 'You should take Karishma for a pity drink after she's watched you try on twelve identical black blazers.'

Seb looked quite pleased at the prospect and began texting furiously.

'You can hang out here if you want,' Sophey offered Ariel. 'Get some shots with the camera. Do something that isn't thinking about the curse.'

'I think that's a good idea,' Ernest said. 'I think you're onto something about balancing the scales.' He glanced at Seb and away, like he could see Ariel's tattoo shining through his clothing. 'But overthinking it won't make the solutions come faster.'

Chapter Twenty-Five

Ariel enjoyed watching the shop navigate the working day. Ernest working through a stack of receipts, frowning alternately at the paperwork and at the shop door, which clanged as a teenager pushed it open then clanged as it swung immediately shut, a parent calling from the pavement, 'Don't you *dare* go into that shop, young lady, unless you want to be grounded for a month. Those items aren't *safe*.' Alexandria, returned from the beach, leaning over a collection of seashells with a magnifying glass, muttering to herself. Sophey standing gingerly on a stool to reach a high shelf for a customer. Sophey standing on the stool again, and again, as the customer changed their mind.

After a while, Sophey and Ernest and Alexandria stopped noticing Ariel, stopped keeping half an eye on the camera in her hand. That was just what Ariel had been waiting for.

Click: the front door, with sunlight illuminating the *open* sign.

Click: the clothing rack, filled with beautiful silks and sturdy coats, wicker basket beneath full of scarves and hats.

Click: a stack of old alchemy books, neatly arranged and labelled. Two thousand pounds for all of them. Ariel stood well back.

'You go home in a couple of days, don't you?' Sophey asked. Ernest and Alexandria had gone into Leigh-on-Sea for a long lunch, with Sophey in charge until they returned. The shop was quiet, so Sophey immediately took her tea break. She decided it was Ariel's break, too, even though Ariel hadn't done much except get in the way.

'On Friday. But school is over for the summer soon,' Ariel said, trying to focus on the positives. 'I'll probably come back to see Seb. And work on this exhibition thing.'

'Have you had any more thoughts on how it could work?' Sophey asked.

'Not really,' Ariel admitted. 'I've seen some cool gallery websites online, like where someone's basically done an art show but it's on a website. If you can do that for free, and if we have enough information we can share, then that might be good. But if we can't find out more about John... There's always asking to do a presentation in assembly,' she said after a moment. 'But I think I'd rather chew off one of my toes.'

'Me too,' Sophey agreed. 'I think a gallery site would be great. We only need a handful of items we can share. Like if there's a portrait of either of them. I'll look into John's work. If his philosophical writing ever made it to publication, someone *must* know details.' She frowned, like she was annoyed she hadn't already found a manuscript in the library or amongst the Bezzina's Emporium stock. 'But you're really good at pictures, aren't you? You could design a website easily. You could make a Facebook page or something too.'

'Okay,' Ariel said slowly. 'I'll start planning it when we're on the train. Do you have any book recommendations?'

'Books?' Sophey asked, and Ariel had to resist the urge to say, *I can actually read.*

'About the Victorians.' Ariel shifted from one foot to the other.

'Oh, for context,' Sophey said. 'I'll send you some titles that should be in Bath library.'

'Thanks.' Ariel watched some pedestrians walk by the shop and stop to admire the flowers in the window.

'Are you going to tell your dad the curse is real?' Sophey asked.

'I think we should,' Ariel said. 'He deserves to know for sure. And Grandpa and Uncle Chris and Uncle James. I think we're just going to have to show him the letters and tell him.' Ariel rubbed her forehead. 'I don't know how he'll take it. I think we should do it this weekend, while Seb's at home.'

The door opened as the pedestrians walked in. Sophey pushed off the counter and Ariel gathered their teacups. She had a sick feeling in her stomach when she thought about telling her family about Josephine and Henrietta. It was one thing to have watched your loved ones die around you, but knowing why... she wasn't sure she wanted to watch Grandpa learn that his wife and two daughters were dead because of a Victorian feud.

'You'll be fine,' Sophey said, eyes on the visitors. 'It's always better to know about these things... Hi! Are you looking for anything in particular?'

As Ariel washed cups in the kitchenette, she could hear Sophey talking to the customers. 'We'd like something to erase memories,' a woman was saying.

'We have salves to help sleep and ease trauma,' Sophey replied. Her Essex accent was clipped when she spoke to adults in the shop, Ariel noticed. She wondered if *she* had a southwest accent. Seb didn't.

'No,' replied the woman, 'we want to *erase* memories. Oh, you have a spell book. We'll take that.' When Ariel returned from the back rooms, Sophey was rubbing the skin beneath her plastic bracelet, obviously thinking about something.

'What's up?' Ariel asked. 'Did those customers cause trouble?'

'No,' Sophey said absently. 'I was just... I think we should do the spell again. The one where we first learnt Josephine's name.'

Ariel was not keen to risk injuring her fingers again. 'We already know the curse is real.'

'We know where the necklace and the curse starts. And we know who the necklace ends up with. We don't know about the bit in the middle.'

'When the rest of the family started taking the curse seriously,' Ariel said, thinking back to the McLean graveyard plot in Bath. Then she thought about how her father had always brushed off the curse when she mentioned it. 'Maybe at first they just put the necklace in a cupboard and hoped all the deaths were bad luck.'

'Do you remember who passed the story down to you and Seb?' Sophey asked.

Ariel thought back. 'Auntie Faye told me about it first—she's my dad's sister. Mum used to talk about it a bit. Grandpa still does after a few whiskies.' She wracked her brain. 'I think... I think my grandma must have been quite aware of it. My mum's mum. Patricia. I remember people talking about how organised she was when she got her cancer diagnosis. She planned her funeral, she'd had her will sorted out for years and she even cleared out her stuff so no one else would have to. So she probably knew, or believed.'

'So we know people took it seriously by the late twentieth century.'

'We need to look further back.' Ariel rubbed her hands together. She was not looking forward to singeing her fingers, but if Alexandria could do it... Besides, the necklace clearly resisted magic in general. Sophey was as competent a practitioner as Ariel could hope to cast a spell and plumb the ether for answers to their questions. 'Can we do it now?'

Chapter Twenty-Six

F ront door, locked. Open sign, flipped to closed. Teen girls sitting cross-legged on the floor of the stock room with the necklace between them, check, check and check. This time Sophey did the spell, Ariel felt like she was standing on solid ground, like all she'd done to get into this new scene was step from one room into another. She wondered if that was because Sophey was getting better at magic or because they knew more about the necklace going in. This time, Ariel felt like she was really *inside* the vision.

A very old man sat in a very high-backed armchair, holding a teacup and saucer. He stooped so much his head barely touched the antimacassar. Ariel looked around the room. It could have been Victorian, she supposed, or... what came after the Victorians? The... Edwardians? This room contained a lot of wooden furniture, an open fire and some oil paintings. It felt... not modern. Ariel wished she was better at history, that she wasn't limited to thinking 'this place feels old.'

Movement caught her eye and brought her back to the scene. The elderly gentleman sat opposite two others: one middle aged, with heavy eyebrows and a gold pocket watch he kept passing between his hands, and one young with fair hair, gripping his teacup with an air of general anxiety.

'You two are the only ones who believe me,' said the old man. His voice was hoarse and his eyes watery, but he gazed at the other two seriously. 'I know your brothers humour me, Gerald, but they don't really believe in the curse like you do. Or you, Albie.'

'Of course we take you seriously, Grandpa,' said the younger man. 'We know what happened between your sisters.' Ariel's stomach lurched. This old guy was Henrietta and Josephine's little brother? It was one thing to know that the McLean sisters had another sibling, the toddler Bertie in the scene with the tree, but it was another to see him in old age. Albie was still talking.

'I know that necklace killed Jemima.' He looked with dislike at the table between them and Ariel saw, nestled amongst the tea set, a very familiar necklace.

'Father,' said the older man, Gerald, 'of course I believe the necklace is to blame for our... misfortunes.' Ariel racked her brain to put this Gerald into context. All the men in her family had blurred together.

'That's why I called you here,' Bertie was saying. 'I've cut everyone out of the will except for you two.' His voice was calm, but the other two's eyes widened. This was obviously not what they had been expecting to hear when they arrived for tea. 'On the condition,' Bertie continued, 'that you publish these.'

Bertie produced from the depths of the armchair a small stack of letters, tied neatly with a ribbon.

'These were exchanged between my sister and I before she died. My *other* sister. Josephine.' Gerald coughed with surprise; he'd taken a sip of tea at precisely the wrong moment.

'Uncle Gerald?' Albie handed him a handkerchief. 'Keep breathing, old chap.' Ariel wasn't worried. This dude almost definitely had decades ahead of him.

Gerald still looked uncomfortable as he surveyed the letters. 'You kept in touch with Josephine? After the humiliation she was willing to put our family through?'

'I didn't know much about it.' Bertie ran his thumb over the letters, then placed them carefully on the arm rest next to him. 'My mother and sister died suddenly, my other sister was estranged, I was sent away to school and our father shut himself up in his study.' Sounds familiar, Ariel thought. 'So when Josephine wrote to me, I wrote back. We even met a few times before she... she died too.'

It must have been half a century since the events he was describing, but Bertie's voice wobbled badly. Gerald reached over and patted him, somewhat reluctantly, on the shoulder.

Bertie took a slow sip of tea and said, 'Josephine told me she cursed Henrietta's necklace.' He took another sip of tea, and missed the glance his companions exchanged.

'Did she regret it?' Albie asked.

'I don't know. She was consumptive by then and half insane with grief. Maybe I am too. I'm so sure...' he gazed into his teacup. 'I'm sure I threw the necklace into the Thames once. I watched it sink. I could describe how cold it was that day, tell you about the breeze and the smell of the city. But a day later the necklace was back in the drawer my father kept it in.' The two men exchanged another look. Ariel, recipient of burnt fingers, was prepared to believe the necklace was welded magically to the McLean family. She understood the other two's hesitance to believe in the curse, though. They only had a handful of deaths to go by, in a time when reaching middle age wasn't a given. Bertie cleared his throat. 'I want you both to carry my sisters' story with you. I don't know if the curse can ever be broken—Josephine never said—but I want your children to know about it. The girls deserve to know that they should use their time wisely.'

'If that's what you want, Grandpa,' said Albie, still nervous looking but with an edge of steel to his voice that reminded Ariel of Seb, 'we'll do it.'

The scene dissolved around Ariel like water vapour. Ariel felt the heat of the fireplace dissipate, replaced by cool, fresh air. She was standing in a cemetery, surrounded by grass and trees. It smelt wonderful: a spring day, one of those where you can feel the earth waking up and stretching.

She was a few yards from a funeral, she realised, or the tail end of one. Mourners gathered in intervals near a graveside, some talking quietly, others walking along a path, presumably towards an exit and a wake. There were Gerald and Albie, their heads close.

'I'm ready to publish when you are,' Albie said. 'I've got a school friend who works at one of the publishing houses. He said he's willing.'

'Why would we ever do that?' Gerald asked. His pocket watch glinted in the sun as he checked the time.

'What?' Albie blinked. 'Because Grandpa asked and we promised.' He pulled from his coat the stack of letters from before. 'I've kept these safe, just like he requested.'

'My father dragged this family's name through the mud with his talk of Josephine and her escapades,' Gerald said grimly. 'It was bad enough that his poor mother and sister died in that carriage accident, but to say it was because Josephine had cursed them... and over that ridiculous marriage proposal no less.' Gerald blinked into the sun. 'We should leave the past where it is.'

'But the curse—'

'*Is* there a curse? My father said it himself, Josephine was half mad. She probably thought she did something to that necklace. She can't have really.'

'We *promised*—'

'Oh do grow up. We aren't publishing anything. And I'm contesting Father's will. We all deserve a portion of his worth.' To illustrate his point, Gerald produced a silver lighter from his pocket and in one fluid motion touched it to the letters in Albie's hand. Within a second the letters were ablaze and Albie let them go with a yelp.

He stared with dismay as ash floated gently to the pavement. 'You don't deserve your part of the inheritance,' he said.

'No one gets what they deserve,' Gerald said. He didn't say it with anger, or sadness. Just like you might say 'it looks like it might rain later' or 'I think we've run out of bread.'

Gerald set off to join the other mourners. Albie stared down at the ashes of Bertie and Josephine's letters.

The scene changed again. Ariel was in someone's bedroom, but it wasn't a welcoming, homely sort of bedroom. It smelt like damp, and a bare bulb illuminated an unmade single bed and glass bottles littering the floorboards. Someone had scrawled in blank paint over the wallpaper: *DESTROY THE NECKLACE*. A young woman was standing in a corner, her demeanour as grey as the room. She held a rubbish bag, and a bucket of soapy water stood at her feet.

'Right, then, Uncle Albie,' she muttered. 'All you've achieved there is that you're spending the rest of your days somewhere they won't let you hold a pencil. I hope it was worth it, for Lily. And Jemima.' She sighed heavily and began picking up bottles. Ariel remembered Lily's name from the list: she'd died in some sort of train accident. Ariel wondered who this woman was, clearing out her uncle's detritus. She was twenty-something, and her clothing seemed... nineteen sixties? Thereabouts. She was wearing a longish skirt and her hair looked like it had been styled with those rollers you left in while you slept.

Ariel wondered if she wanted to know the woman's name.

If she was a McLean, then Ariel already had it written down in her notebook.

———— ⟨∿⟩ ————

Ariel's fingers were not burnt, but she thought she tasted ashes.
'Bertie knew about the necklace,' she said quietly, 'and his grandson. Albie. Albie must have passed the story on. Even if he couldn't publish those letters, he made sure people knew enough to pass the legend down.' Ariel thought back to when Auntie Faye mentioned Nicole talking about the necklace, dramatically, over a few drinks. It would be easy to turn it into an anecdote, if you knew how to tell a story. Ariel wondered with a shiver if Nicole had ever thought about *her* death when she spoke about the necklace. She must have done.

Sophey stretched and surveyed the necklace. Ariel was grateful she wasn't nursing blistered fingers again. Maybe the necklace was tired from attempting to burn Alexandria's hand to a crisp. Ariel, certainly, was beginning to tire of stepping back in time and learning that another one of the men in her family had the integrity of a burst pimple.

'I'm not sure I'd risk pissing off Bertie's ghost,' Sophey said thoughtfully. 'Your family clearly isn't the sort to let a grudge go.' Ariel wasn't bothered by the idea that Gerald had incurred the wrath of another vengeful McLean. He deserved it. She helped Sophey tidy up the book and necklace.

'No wonder no one's tried breaking the curse before,' Sophey said when they were back in the front of the shop. 'You've got to really take it seriously first. Should we ask Alexandria to try to pick up on the contents of Bertie and Josephine's letters?'

Ariel considered. 'Maybe. If we think we really need them to find information for the exhibition. But...' Ariel looked at her shoulder bag, where the necklace was sitting snug next to a packet of tissues and some chewing gum, unsure how to put her feelings into words. 'They were private. I know why Bertie wanted them in the public domain, but it feels a bit...'

'Gratuitous?'

Ariel hoped she had a correct grasp on what 'gratuitous' meant. 'Mhm. I'm not sure we should publish Henrietta and Josephine's letters either. They weren't intended for publication. And it's been so long. Is it really necessary?'

'We want to share the essence of the story, not turn it into a soap opera,' Sophey reasoned. 'So probably not.'

Ariel was relieved they were in agreement.

Sophey looked at her watch and gathered the necklace and spell book. 'We'd better reopen. Are you sure you're happy to hang out here until closing time?'

'Definitely,' Ariel said. 'I can help out until Seb and I go back to Bath, if Ernest's okay with it.'

'I think he will be,' Sophey said. 'Any excuse to slope off with Alexandria.'

On the shop floor, Sophey flipped the open sign and Ariel rearranged some candles on the counter. 'Is Ernest...' She wasn't sure how to say what she was thinking. 'Isn't he old enough to retire?'

'He's old enough to have retired years ago. He's older than half the stuff in this shop. He won't, though.' Sophey twirled her plastic bracelet absently. 'He likes the people too much. But he is working too many hours. And he can't lift things anymore. That's why I'm happy to be here so often.'

'In that case,' Ariel said, 'let me know if you need anything moving that would take two people, and I'll help before I go back.'

'Are you sure?' Sophey looked pleasantly surprised.

'Of course.' Ariel had built up quite a lot of muscle from her years of self-defence classes. 'Consider it payment for all the tea.'

'You won't be saying that when you see some of what he's got in that storeroom.'

Chapter Twenty-Seven

The journey between Southend and Bath, crossing the south of England in almost a straight line, took around four hours on a good day. An hour on the train from Southend to London, on whichever overground line was working best (both Seb and Sophey had gone into great detail about different train lines and their respective pros and cons, and Ariel zoned promptly out of both conversations). Then half an hour on the Underground to get to Paddington Station; half an hour in which Ariel and Seb clamped on their headphones to block the noise of the Circle line, wondering how Londoners put up with the racket on their commute every day. From Paddington, it was just a couple of hours or so sat a train destined for Bristol or Weston-super-Mare, getting off at Bath Spa. The longest part of the journey, the one that would tip you into four-to-five-hour territory, was waiting for the bus to go to the right part of Bath once you were in the city.

Except for the hellish stint on the Underground and the twenty minutes they had spare at Paddington to buy an overpriced sandwich, Ariel spent the journey working on her website idea to share Josephine and John's story.

It didn't need to be complicated, she reasoned, in order to share the essence of the story. Just a page with information about Josephine and John's lives and their quest to get married, and some sort of clickable gallery with pictures that she could write a description for. She didn't want to include the necklace or the curse, she decided. Partly because it felt too personal, too close to so many of her family members. Partly because advertising that you owned a high value antique necklace was a good way to get burgled. But she wanted to mention John's death and his legacy, if he had one. Ariel scrolled through some Wikipedia entries about British life in the nineteenth century; she thought perhaps the site could include links to websites people could click on to learn more about the Victorian era.

Once they boarded at Paddington, Ariel googled Dr John Ingram. It took a while to find the right John Ingram, but Ariel was surprised to find he appeared on a couple of obscure lists of influential men of his time. Josephine's pride in his philosophical chops was not misplaced, by the looks of things, although Ariel wasn't familiar with his contemporaries, who were mostly scholars or civil rights activists. Reading about civil rights sent Ariel back in time, to articles about people involved the abolition movement. As the train rolled through Didcot Parkway, Ariel realised she didn't really know what abolitionists did, practically-speaking. She looked it up. She turned to a fresh page in her notebook and made notes, then more notes. She looked up terms on Wikipedia, clicking through link after link, and felt another stab of resentment towards school. She would have been more interested to study this than the Tudors, which only got exciting when Henry VIII got twitchy about having a son.

Maybe, said a small voice in the back of her head, if this came up in school, children would ask questions about it.

In the next row, someone's music blared terribly.

'Are you all right?' Ariel asked Seb when she realised he had folded himself over the tray table and buried his head in his arms. 'Is it the music?' her brother had gotten continuously quieter throughout the journey, but Ariel just assumed that was just what the Tube did to you.

'Not really,' he said. 'I'm just... are you sure you want to talk to Dad and Grandpa about the curse? You'll get in trouble for sneaking the necklace out of the house so often.'

'Twice. I'm sort of hoping that providing concrete proof the curse is real will nullify any bad feeling,' Ariel said. She had just learnt the word 'nullify' from her internet surfing and was pleased to use it so quickly. 'Also we've got a plan to break the curse. So they can relax! No more need to worry about all the women in the family. Uncle Chris and Uncle James will be pleased, won't they. And Grandpa. Because of Mum and Aunt Katie and Grandma.' Ariel knew she was rambling, but didn't know quite why. She wasn't sure she liked how unenthusiastic Seb was about sharing their news. 'And Dad... now we can *prove* that the curse is real.'

'Just... be ready for them not to take it as you hope they do.'

'Why?' Ariel asked. She had a sudden thought. 'Do you think they've known it was real all along? Why would Dad brush it off if he did?'

Seb put his headphones on, clearly ready to think about something else. 'I don't... I just... don't be surprised if they don't react like you hope.'

Fine, Ariel thought, I'll break the curse *and* be grounded until the rest of time for taking the necklace on a few trips. She went back to reading about Sophia Duleep Singh, and made notes on the suffrage movement.

When the person blaring music got off at Chippenham, Ariel stuck her tongue out at them.

Chapter Twenty-Eight

As the sun set that evening, Ariel and Seb sat down to fish and chips with their near-ish family. Dad, Grandpa, Uncle James. The takeaway was to celebrate Seb's internship, and to make Ariel feel better that half term was at an end. Uncle James brought wine and homemade lemon sorbet; Grandpa brought tobacco to smoke angrily on the patio. This sort of dinner was standard in the Scarlet-McLean clan, and Ariel was glad that she and Seb had Grandpa and Uncle James there too. She wasn't sure she wanted to have too many varieties of the curse conversation.

After the chip wrappers were discarded and Irish coffee poured, they retired to the sofas on the far side of the kitchen. Ariel sneaked a gulp of coffee for courage, then went upstairs to fetch the necklace. No point in pretending it still spent most of its time in the family safe. She presented it to their father in its box. His prematurely lined face aged a few more years when he saw what she was holding.

'Ariel, I've told you about this. Please don't keep—'

'Dad, please listen. For ten minutes. Please.'

Ariel, despite her finer tastes, rarely asked her father for anything important. She wasn't sure the last time she had asked for his time, for example, although she always took it when offered. Uncle James knew that, and so did Grandpa: with a glance at them, her father nodded and sat back on the sofa.

'The curse. It's real. I went to Bezzina's Emporium, a shop up by Seb, and they looked into it and the necklace is properly cursed. Because our great-great-something aunts fell out. Over, um, here's why—' she brandished her notebook. 'You can read it in your own time, the letters are really intense. And so that's why Mum died. And Grandma and Aunt Katie and everyone. But it's okay,' she continued. 'I maybe know how to break it. My friend Sophey, from Southend, she's going to help me.' Ariel plopped down on the sofa and beckoned Rocket for a belly scratch, just to give her something to do while she let everyone process what she'd said.

After a minute, Ariel looked at her grandfather and her uncle. Grandpa was rolling a cigarette, hands moving furiously. Uncle James was doing what he always did when his mother or sisters came up in conversation: digging through his wallet to uncover an old photograph of Dennis and Patricia McLean with their four children on holiday in Cromer in the nineteen seventies. There was a larger version in every McLean residence, but Uncle James always preferred this tiny one.

Seb and Ariel's father did not move at all.

'I'm going to try to fix it,' Ariel continued hurriedly. She wasn't sure she had made that clear. 'The curse will end with Mum. I won't let it hurt any more people.'

Grandpa stood up and shuffled to the French door, cigarette in one hand and lighter in the other. 'Now you know why you should have told them, Peter.'

'Told us what?' Ariel looked at Seb. Seb looked away.

Ariel looked at Uncle James. He looked away.

Ariel looked at Rocket. Rocket yawned and scratched beneath her collar.

'Dad? What should you have told us?' Ariel tried to ignore the churning in her stomach. She'd felt queasy with nerves all evening, but it was so bad now that she thought if she moved too fast, she really would puke. The coffee had been a bad idea.

'Did you know the curse was real all this time?' She had a sudden vision of her father in a shop like Bezzina's, handing over the necklace and asking for help.

'No,' her father said. He seemed to be choosing his words carefully, measuring them out bit by bit. 'I never thought too much about the curse.' Uncle James stood up, too, and strode out to the patio. Grandpa was onto his second smoke, but Ariel could tell by his posture that he was listening through the open door. Uncle James shut it firmly behind him.

Ariel waited. Seb abruptly scooted over on the sofa so they were shoulder to shoulder, and took her hand. Ariel looked at him, surprised. They were a hugging family, but not a cuddling one. Her brother's palms were sweating.

'Dad,' Seb said. His voice was low and he was hunched over, but he looked up at their father. 'I think I already know.'

Seb was shaking, and that scared Ariel more than anyone else's behaviour. 'Dad. It can't be that bad—'

'Your mother's alive.'

Everyone in the room stopped breathing.

'Pardon?' Ariel heard her voice but wasn't aware she had made the decision to speak. There was a rushing in her ears, and she could barely hear above it when her father said—

'Your mother. She's alive. She lives in Manchester.'

Ariel stood up from the sofa, walked into the kitchen area and vomited into the sink.

After a minute, or thirty seconds, or an hour, her father was there, smoothing back her hair like he had when it was long, when she was little and she had a stomach bug, handing her a damp cloth to wipe her mouth, saying 'Don't worry about the dishes.'

Ariel hadn't even noticed that there were dishes in the sink. It was hard to see, because her eyes stung.

'Don't touch me!' She was surprised at the volume of her voice, even though she still couldn't hear properly.

Seb was standing next to her now, too, or maybe he had been the whole time. 'Manchester?' He was shaking so badly Ariel could see it through her tears. Grandpa and Uncle James were back from the garden, watching as the Scarlet children clawed at their seams. 'I knew you were lying about something but I didn't really think—I thought—' he was crying too.

Their father reached out a hand, but Seb pulled away. He leaned on Ariel, who was leaning on the sink. *I should run the tap*, Ariel thought dimly. She could smell puke. She ran both taps and threw washing up liquid haphazardly onto everything she could see until the sink smelt like bubbles again. When she turned back, her father had sunk into a kitchen chair. Seb was still shaking badly, staring at their father. She was vaguely aware that Rocket, tail between her legs, had inserted herself between Ariel's calves and the counter. This struck Ariel as a sensible reaction.

Grandpa handed Ariel a glass of water. Uncle James guided Seb to a kitchen chair, the furthest from their father. She hadn't seen either of them move. She remembered thinking about how your brain stopped recording after a shock.

A shock.

She sat down next to Seb, who was looking at their father his fists clenched. 'Talk. Now.'

'Your mother is alive,' he repeated. 'She lives in Manchester.'

'Repeating that won't make it make sense,' Seb growled.

'Mum was ill,' Ariel whispered. 'For years.'

'She was,' their father agreed. 'But it wasn't cancer. She's an alcoholic.'

Ariel looked at the wine bottle on the table.

'It started after your Aunt Katie drowned,' their grandfather said. 'She always liked a drink, but after Katie it became...' he looked at Uncle James.

'Terrible,' James finished. 'Your father would ring me at three o'clock in the morning because she was passed out in the kitchen and the oven was on. She forgot to pick you up from school. She lost her job.'

'Then she crashed her car.' Their father was looking into the middle distance. 'You two were in the back.'

The car accident. Ariel remembered it as well as she remembered anything from the age of five. She hadn't been scared by all the noise and the shouting until she saw Seb crying, and then she cried too.

'It was a miracle no one was hurt,' their father continued. 'I mean, it was the middle of the *day*.'

'What happened?' Ariel asked.

'She went to court. She did community service. She enrolled in programmes to help with her drinking. And absolutely none of it made any difference.' Their father's voice wobbled for the first time all evening.

'So I left her. I took you two to Grandpa's and told her I couldn't watch anymore.'

Ariel remembered that, too. A week of Grandpa taking them to school and Uncle James or Uncle Chris or Aunt June cooking dinner. Evenings doing homework with Em and Lottie, comparing their different school uniforms. Their mother was very ill, each adult explained, and she needed special help. Daddy was there with her.

Eventually their father had picked them up and taken them home, to this house, and told them—

'You said Mum was gone.' Ariel looked at their father properly for the first time. 'You took us home and when we asked where Mum was, you said she had *gone*. And you let us think...'

'You smarmy bastard,' Seb was saying. Time was slipping still: Ariel had not seen him stand up. 'I always assumed you were too much of a coward to tell us to our faces that she died, so you just didn't mention it and hoped we figured it out. I thought you were happy to let Ariel drive herself *insane* about that necklace because you were too devastated to be a competent parent.' He scrubbed a hand through his hair. 'Then when you wouldn't get a headstone, I wondered if something... Oh God. *That's* why there was no funeral. We weren't too young to see the cremation. You just got rid of her and let us think she died of fucking cancer. And now you've got no excuse about why you weren't around more. I let you persuade me *for years* that you were too grief-stricken to notice that Ariel and I basically raised ourselves but actually you just weren't interested—'

'It's not just your dad's fault,' Uncle James spoke up.

'I know it fucking isn't, I'm not even *started* with you—'

'Your mother was sick,' Grandpa interrupted. 'The sort of sick you only get better from when you want to. The sort your loved ones shouldn't have to watch. Your father made the right—'

'Do not. Justify. Anything. To me.' Seb whirled out of the kitchen and Ariel heard the front door slam.

Her father looked at her. 'I'm sorry,' he said.

Ariel just shook her head. She gathered up the necklace—how silly, to think the evening would be about that—but left her notebook. She found her way upstairs and cleaned her teeth, then picked up her mobile phone.

'Hello?' Sophey sounded blurry, like she had been sleeping when the phone rang.

'Sorry it's late. The curse isn't real. What are you doing this weekend?'

Chapter Twenty-Nine

Sophey found Ariel and Rocket in Alexandra Park. Ariel texted her the location, and Sophey came straight from Bath Spa train station. She was red in the face by the time she climbed up the path, dozens of stairs long. As a child, Ariel looked out over the view and thought this was the top of the world. You could see so much of Bath from here: the Abbey, the Royal Crescent, the roof of the Roman Baths. How easy life had been when this was her whole existence.

All Ariel told Sophey on the phone the previous evening was that the necklace conversation had gone very, very wrong.

Seb had not returned home, but texted Ariel that he had taken the late train to Southend. After a night in which Ariel slept for five minutes and turned her duvet upside down from tossing and turning, Sophey had texted at around six o'clock in the morning. *I'll be there by half past ten.*

As Ariel and Rocket arrived in town, Ariel's cousin Lottie messaged the McLean cousin group chat: *Hey Seb and Ariel. Your dad texted our dad who called us. We're so sorry about everything. I'm in Nottingham and Em's in Plymouth until the semester ends but we're here if you need an ear.* Emily added her own message, a GIF of a cat offering someone a hug. Ariel knew she should be grateful that the twins, away at university, were willing to reach out. But she mostly felt hot, sharp stabs of anger and resentment that other people were already discussing her mother, that the Scarlets were the hot topic of conversation for the day. And, probably, the decade.

She was trying to figure out if she wanted to say this in the group chat when she saw Sophey striding towards her, backpack on one shoulder.

Instead of saying hello, Sophey sat down on the bench and said to Ariel, 'you look terrible.' She took in Rocket. 'Hello, creature.'

'Sophey, this is Rocket. Rocket, this is Sophey.'

'Pleased to meet you.' Sophey held the back of her hand out to Rocket, and the corners of her eyes crinkled briefly as Rocket snuffled her fingers. She looked back to Ariel. 'What happened?'

'The curse isn't real,' Ariel said dully. 'Mum's alive, and she's in her forties.'

Sophey looked like she wanted to say something, but didn't.

'Sorry about making you do the stairs,' Ariel said. 'I forget how hard it is until I'm walking it.'

'I need the exercise.' Sophey shrugged, although she was still quite pink. 'Are you sure I'm okay to stay at yours?'

Ariel nodded. She hadn't asked her father's permission to have a friend stay. At sunrise, when she gave up on sleep and found him in the kitchen searching for caffeine same as her, she told him Sophey would arrive later and left the room. Then she messaged Carol at the sandwich shop, asking to work the early morning shift and could Rocket please stay tied up outside while she did so. Although Ariel had not told Carol about her home life, Carol gave Ariel a free sandwich for breakfast and let her finish half an hour early. The sandwich tasted like cardboard, but she appreciated it.

'I don't know what to do,' Ariel said. 'Once I knew the curse was real, I thought "now I have to figure out how to break it." But this isn't like that.' She looked down at the city. 'I was the girl whose mum died. I don't know how to be the girl whose mother left and everyone lied about it. I mean, what do I even tell people? Hi, weird news, turns out Mum's been in Manchester this whole time and no one mentioned it. And it turns out the curse can't be real. It can't, or Mum would be dead by now. I'm sorry I wasted your time. And Ernest's. And Alexandria's.'

This was why Ariel phoned Sophey and not Madge or Chloe. Sophey already knew about the necklace, about the curse. Ariel's other friends knew of the legend, of course, but she had no idea how she would explain Bezzina's Emporium or Ernest or Alexandria to them. She certainly didn't know how she would tell them about her mother. Madge gave her a funny cartoony card, every Mother's Day, because she knew Ariel hated the occasion. Chloe always remembered Nicole's birthday and sent Ariel a message. Grace, back when they were talking, used to ask Ariel questions about her mother, and would invite Ariel round to her house on the days when Ariel felt too blue to go home.

Ariel did not know how to tell them it had always been a lie.

Sophey did not offer any words of wisdom. She just said, 'Is that the Abbey down there?'

'Yeah,' Ariel said. 'Want to see Bath properly?' she asked. 'If your bag isn't heavy, we could go into the city now and do tourist stuff.' She picked up Sophey's rucksack. It was light, although she could feel the outline of a couple of books tucked into the top.

'Are there any more hills?' Sophey asked.

'Not until we catch the bus to mine.'

'Then yes, please. I'd like to go inside the Abbey. And see the Roman Baths. And the weir.'

'You researched Bath on your way here, didn't you?'

'Yes. Can we do the open top bus tour?'

'Absolutely not.'

They did, though. Ariel had to admit, her mood improved just watching Sophey take in the city's sights. Sophey went all the way to the top deck on the tour bus and ooh-d and ahh-d at every opportunity. She even took notes as she listened though disposable earphones to the little voice narrating each stop. Ariel sat Rocket on her lap and breathed the clean air, leaning into Rocket's fur every now and then. Rocket's grubby dog smell made Ariel feel better, too. Eventually Ariel persuaded Sophey to a café for lunch, the sort of place she normally avoided because it was full of tourists and university students. Today it felt nice to see her city through an outsider's eyes.

Sophey was more animated and chattier than Ariel had seen her. Ariel didn't know if this was because Sophey was a history nerd or because she wanted to distract Ariel, but it was quite entertaining. And it worked. 'Did you know that Mary Shelley wrote *Frankenstein* here? And that Jane Austen didn't like living here? And that—'

'Ariel?'

Ariel looked up from her panini. *Please,* she thought, *let this not be someone who wants to stop and chat.*

It was Madge, with Chloe just behind her. Madge's normally brown hair was dyed pastel pink and her olive skin more bronzed than usual. She had probably been to the family's villa in... Tuscany. No, Naples. That was it. They had all been planning to go there when GCSEs finished. Ariel stood up from the table awkwardly and gave Madge a one-armed hug. She went towards Chloe too, but Chloe ducked out of the way. For her part, Chloe looked the same as ever: long blonde waves, clothing purchased entirely from the sort of shop that gave you free prosecco as you browsed, and cheekbones people paid a lot of money for. The first time they had met, Ariel had been reminded of a very young Princess Diana.

'Sophey, this is Madge and Chloe. Madge and Chloe, meet Sophey.'

'Is this your girlfriend?' Chloe asked, surveying Sophey.

'What? No. She works near Seb, we met when I was visiting.'

'Hello,' Sophey said. She was taking in Madge and Chloe as Madge and Chloe were taking in her. Chloe's gaze snagged on Sophey's oversized military-style jacket with hand-sewn patches. Sophey's gaze snagged on Chloe's bracelet, a four-figure gift from her parents on her sweet sixteenth. 'Ariel's told me all about you,' Sophey continued. 'Madge is doing languages, right?' Ariel had mentioned to Sophey once that Madge was taking two language GCSEs, when she spotted an old-timey map of the world in the shop.

'Yeah I am,' Madge said, relieved to be on stable ground. 'I want to do linguistics or be a translator. Travel a lot.'

'My mum used to work for the UN,' Sophey said. 'If you're interested, I could ask if she knows any good places to apply for internships? Maybe not *with* the UN,' she added hastily, like she didn't want to overpromise. 'But that sort of thing.'

'Really? That would be so kind.' Ariel had known Madge long enough to know she really meant it, and that when she had first approached their table she hadn't known what sort of person she would find in Sophey.

Sophey smiled. 'No problem. I wish I had a head for languages.'

'What do *you* do?' Chloe demanded.

'My GCSEs are History, Religious Studies and Geography,' Sophey said. 'My school makes us do a language and all the sciences anyway, so they're the ones I got to choose.' She thought for a moment. 'Oh, did you mean for work? I'm an assistant in an antiques shop.'

'Of course you are,' Chloe said.

'We have to go,' Madge said after the silence stretched on for just a bit too long. Ariel could not look at Chloe. 'We're getting coffee.' Madge glanced at Ariel awkwardly.

'You invited me,' Ariel remembered. Their group chat had been active around the same time Ariel was puking into the kitchen sink. She had completely forgotten to respond. 'Sorry I ignored you. There's been... home stuff.'

Madge, to Ariel's eternal gratitude, just nodded and gave Ariel a one-armed hug of her own. 'Call me if you need to,' she said into Ariel's ear, and Ariel hugged her back, hard. Chloe just walked away, clearly ready to be somewhere else.

'We'll get hot chocolate soon. Promise.'

Madge gave Rocket a quick pat on the head and half-smiled at Sophey. 'See you Monday, A.'

Chapter Thirty

After dinner in the city, Sophey borrowed Seb's old room and left it cleaner than she found it. Peter did not leave his study to greet her, and by the sounds of the radio floating out of his office on Sunday morning, he spent the night at his desk. Ariel took Sophey out to breakfast, and after walking Rocket they visited the Roman Baths. Ariel had been a few times with school or with family, but never with someone so unselfconsciously excited by chunks of old stone that she stopped to take notes.

'Is it... significant?' Ariel asked as Sophey paused in their walk for the thirtieth time to scribble something in her notebook. She felt like an idiot as soon as she said it: of course the Roman Baths were important. Ariel knew from primary school that when the Romans invaded what would become Britain, they found hot springs, worshipped by locals because every culture appreciates a warm water source. The Romans immediately built a temple, baths and various leisure facilities. Ariel wasn't sure how many cultures would put a holy building and a sauna in the same complex, and she appreciated the Romans for it.

'Quite significant,' Sophey said, as though she hadn't registered that Ariel was being obtuse. 'It's quite rare to have such a complete ancient site and relatively large swathes of information about what it was for. I suppose it's not a coincidence that Bath Abbey ended up built on the same site,' she added. 'This area's been sacred to people for millennia.'

'And now it's an altar to capitalism,' Ariel said, having read the entrance prices. She trailed after Sophey and spent five minutes looking at a collection of Roman hair combs. They looked so similar to her own collection at home that she wondered what would happen if she used one of these old ones. Assuming it didn't break as soon as she pressed it into her hair, it would probably do a solid job taming her flyaways. She turned back to Sophey, who was gazing into a cabinet with a skeleton.

'This guy was from Syria,' Ariel said when she'd read the information. She must have known this before, from previous visits, but she felt she should have remembered it sooner, given her research into John Ingram. She wondered if the McLean family, back in the 1860s, had any idea that Romans were not just Italian.

'They should rebury him,' Sophey said quietly. Her eyes were still on the skeleton, arranged carefully in a glass cabinet. 'People should be left where they've been laid to rest.' She chewed her lip, but then brightened and turned to Ariel. 'Did you say there are curse tablets here somewhere? We had a guy try to sell some to Ernie a while ago, he ended up reporting them as stolen artefacts... before I could have a look.' She sounded as disappointed to have missed ancient tablets as she was to see an unburied body.

'They're further along, I think,' Ariel said, and Sophey tramped onwards, notebook clutched in her hands. Ariel hung back, looking at the Syrian man in his cabinet.

After they'd had their fill of Roman Baths—meaning, after Sophey had run out of space in her notebook—Ariel took Sophey to the Holburne Museum. A mansion-like building at the end of a sweeping Regency street, the Holburne was home to a wide collection of paintings, some excellent ceramics and the personal collection of a hoarder, William Holburne. Wealthy and landed, Holburne's treasure trove consisted of items picked up on his travels: textiles, jewellery, miniature portraits. A substantial collection of gilded spoons. Visiting the Holburne as a child made Ariel simultaneously claustrophobic and desirous of material wealth. Sophey, of course, loved it all and took several photos to show Ernest ('we could display our cutlery like this!').

'I did some reading,' Sophey said later as they stood in one of the upstairs art galleries, gazing at an enormous portrait of an aristocrat and his wife and child. It was so big it could only ever have been commissioned by a posho with more space than sense. You had to stand several feet away just to see it properly. The man in the painting waved his hat towards some trees, his wife following his gaze as the child stood at her skirts.

'Go on,' Ariel said.

'Coming—huh. I've just noticed, he's at the dead centre of the painting,' Sophey remarked. 'What a poser.'

'Originally it just showed him and his wife,' Ariel remembered from a long-ago school trip. 'They painted in the child later on. And changed the wife's dress colour. Sorry, what were you saying?'

'Coming to Bath got me thinking about the McLeans and how they ended up down here from London. Bristol was a trading port. They could have been traders overseas.' Ariel let the unsaid part of that sentence hang in the air as Sophey walked to the information plate next to the huge painting. Ariel followed, barely taking her gaze from the portrait. She really couldn't imagine having the space for it. Sophey was leaning toward the information, so Ariel did too.

'George Byam and his wife Louisa,' Sophey read. 'Third generation plantation owner.' She rocked back on her heels and looked at Ariel.

'Bristol was a key port in the eighteenth and nineteenth centuries. Spices, medicines...'

'People.'

'If he was British, I think John is too young to have been enslaved,' Sophey said. 'The dates on the letters are too recent.'

Ariel, whose comprehension of historical dates was limited to 'Jesus in year zero' and 'World War II finished in 1945,' was unsure what to make of this. She shuffled her feet and looked at the information plate as she absorbed Sophey's words. 'So that's... good. For him.' She thought back to the contents of Henrietta's letters and searched for the words to articulate what she was thinking. Not finding them, she began to wander around the gallery, Sophey at her shoulder. Eventually she said, 'it's like you said before. We might never know details. I still want to know, but specifics don't change that the McLeans didn't think John was an actual person.'

Now they both faced a picture called *The Auriol and Dashwood Families*. Also enormous, it depicted nineteenth century Bengal, according to the information. Well dressed women in silk, well dressed men in breeches, tea poured by a retinue of Indians.

'Do you think we'd find the McLean name attached to a picture like this, if we looked hard enough?' Ariel asked.

'Maybe.' Sophey eyed the painting. 'Are you still... do you want to continue working on your project?'

'I don't know. Is there any point if the curse isn't real after all?'

Sophey twisted her beaded bracelet. 'Your family, your necklace, your decision. About the curse—'

'I don't want to talk about it.'

'But Nicole—'

'Made it past forty. No curse, or not anymore. Maybe someone else broke it. Maye we're just good at self-fulfilling prophecy.'

Sophey looked like she itched to say more, but to Ariel's relief she just fiddled with her bracelet. 'I've got my train soon. Are you okay to walk me to the station? There's no way I'll remember the route.'

— ❧ —

At the train station while Sophey dug out her ticket, Ariel felt a little forlorn. She did not know if it was because she hadn't realised how interesting her local history was until she saw Sophey being interested in it, or because she wasn't ready for Sophey to disappear back to Essex. Probably it was the realisation that when Sophey boarded her train, Ariel was out of reasons to avoid her life.

'Come back to Southend soon,' Sophey said. 'We might need more hands in the shop over the summer.'

'I will,' Ariel said. 'School ends for good in a few weeks. I'll text you.'

They weren't really on hugging terms, so Sophey just nodded at her and walked towards the ticket barriers.

Ariel wandered aimlessly towards the centre of town. She didn't feel like going home, but she didn't feel like doing much of anything else, either. Maybe she would give Rocket a bath. The girls had left her napping in the kitchen. Rocket disliked bath time and always tried to escape to the muddiest part of the garden, so it would be a good distraction from Ariel's father working in his office. He hadn't told Ariel he would be working, but he never needed to. Every disagreement in the household was followed by the tap of fingers on a keyboard as he worked on a book or paper, or marked assignments.

Ariel wasn't sure she had the heart to watch Rocket's betrayed face when she got out the dog shampoo, though.

'Ariel!' She turned and there were Madge and Chloe again.

'Oh, hey.' She tried to make her face look friendly. 'We have to stop meeting like this.'

'Want to hang out?' Madge asked. 'I need to buy a present for my Australia cousins. They're arriving *tomorrow* which is a week before we thought they were, and Mum's panicking and says we need to give them gifts. I'm already giving the little ones my bedroom and I think that should be enough, but then Mum got a bit stressed about duvet covers and I thought, I will volunteer to find them gifts if it means I can stay out the house. I invited Chloe since you were—busy. But if your friend's gone, do you want to come watch me find tourist crap?'

'Go on then.' Ariel followed them into the gift shop for the Roman Baths, avoiding Madge's glances by dodging around clusters of tourists. She and Sophey had browsed, briefly, but neither of them were interested in novelty soap or plushie toys, so they went straight on to the Holburne Museum. Now, Ariel wondered if she should have encouraged Sophey to buy a souvenir for herself. Bath was a pretty cool city, if you were a history nut.

'So, who was that girl really?' Chloe asked as they browsed. She hadn't bothered with inquisitive glances; she preferred to start with a blunt force question and work backwards.

'No one,' Ariel insisted. She picked up a plastic figurine of an owl. She suspected the only thing it had in common with the Roman Baths was that it, too, would last several thousand years.

'*A*,' Chloe said. 'She dresses like a bog witch and she studies religion. You normally have such high standards.'

'I know,' Ariel admitted. 'She...' Ariel searched for the words. 'She works in this occult shop in Southend and she was kind of... useful.'

'Useful?' Madge asked. Her eyebrows, dark under her pastel fringe, moved sceptically as she surveyed a set of novelty tea towels. 'Bread knives are useful. Sanitary products are useful. You aren't friends with them.'

'I'm not friends with her, either.'

'You looked friendly,' Chloe said as Madge selected a handful of tea towels and headed to the till. Chloe and Ariel mooched after her, dodging tourists. 'She came all this way to see you.'

Ariel weighed up the pros and cons of explaining the curse here, in the gift shop of the Roman Baths, while a group of Americans cooed over overpriced beauty products. 'I was just being polite. I don't think she has any friends. Do you guys want to go for hot chocolate when we're done? I'm sorry I missed our coffee thing yesterday.'

Chloe and Madge did want to go for hot chocolate.

Ariel kept the topic focussed on Chloe's father's upcoming retirement party.

She continued ignoring Madge's sideways looks.

Chapter Thirty-One

When she finally nodded off on Sunday night, Ariel dreamt of Bezzina's Emporium. It was darker and dustier in the dream than in real life, with blinds pulled down and the window empty. She was sure she could smell it, even asleep: the musty smell of a room closed up for years. Suddenly Sophey was there, scrubbing a display case with a bucket of soapy water. The only thing inside the case was a miniature, decaying tree. Ariel didn't know why Sophey didn't take the tree out of the case before cleaning it. Except it didn't really matter because the dust was thick enough to eat, and she was only using a tiny cloth, so all the dirt was swirling around and into the air—

Ariel woke up coughing and did not fall back to sleep.

The next morning, she felt like her head had been stamped on. Until she remembered it was Monday, she had planned to go back to bed after she'd taken Rocket for her walk.

She and her father still had not spoken, aside from the basics of confirming who would be indoors that week and when to let Rocket out into the garden. When Ariel put a load of washing on, she left her father's clothes in the laundry basket. She mixed one of those electrolyte drinks, the sort you take to rehydrate after a stomach bug, and hoped the salts would make her feel better.

They did not.

As she was grabbing her school supplies, she noticed some plans for Josephine's website on a bit of scrap paper. She balled it up and chucked it into the bin, hoping the thud of paper would make her feel better.

It did not.

On her way out of the house, she noticed that someone had bumped into her dad's car, badly enough to leave damage requiring phone calls to the insurance company.

That made her feel a little better.

Lessons were harder than usual. Ariel struggled to pay attention, which was normal, but today she couldn't summon up the energy to pull her focus back to class every time her mind wandered. She was told off for daydreaming twice, and wondered if she ought to alert the school to the fact there had been a Family Situation. When Nicole died, the grief councillor had sat with her for hours.

The thought made Ariel want to puke again.

At lunch, Ariel huddled with Madge and Chloe, none of them saying much. Ariel played with her new-old camera as Madge scratched away at some homework and Chloe scrolled through her phone.

Across the courtyard, Ariel could see friendship groups of varying sizes and with varying levels of comradery. She wondered which type of group Sophey would sit in. Would she fit with Carys and the two Hannahs, all three obsessed with the latest boy bands and Japanese manga? Would she gel with Jodie and Kat, the two only openly gay girls in the school? Most likely she would sit with Amanda and Emmy, two bookish girls with enough awkward facial hair between them to elicit the nickname the Chuckle Brothers.

'So what's actually up?' Chloe asked. She put her phone on the table with a *smack*. 'You've been weird all weekend and all morning. Is it your mum again?'

'Yeah,' Ariel said immediately, glad she could answer a question honestly. Madge reached over and squeezed her hand. 'When did you dye your hair?' Ariel asked her, desperate to think of something else.

'Start of half term,' Chloe replied before Madge could speak. 'If you were better at checking the chat, you'd know that. Just like you'd know she went to Naples.'

'Chloe,' Madge said, a sting in her voice. 'I don't think now's the time. And I don't care that you didn't notice. It's just hair. And they told me I have to dye it brown again even though the summer holidays are quite soon.'

'I like it,' Ariel said. 'It suits you.' She wasn't sure why she hadn't said it sooner.

'Thanks, I—'

'So, Sophey.' Chloe's voice was broken glass.

God. 'What about her?'

'Are you sure you're not...'

'What? Yes. God. Yes. She helped me out with some family stuff. She's actually all right.'

'She seemed it,' Madge said, with a glance at Chloe.

Chloe shrugged. 'You can do better.'

'I told you, we aren't really friends—'

'I mean, even *I* would be better than—'

'Seriously, we aren't—wait. Is that—are you—'

Oh no. Months ago, *months*, Chloe had swiped some sparkling wine at a family party on a skiing trip in the Alps. Then she rang Ariel in the middle of the night to talk about, amongst other things, whether or not they would make a cute couple. Ariel had never mentioned it and fervently hoped she would never have to.

'*No.*' Chloe flushed. 'But seriously, that girl is going to bring you down. She's worse than Grace.'

Ariel stood up, flipped Chloe off and spent the rest of the lunchbreak in the toilets, sitting on a dry-ish corner of the sinks. Her finger hovered over Grace's name in her phone contacts. Should she reach out again? Was it finally time to call her friendship with Grace a past tense situation? Maybe she should ask Seb, but she didn't want to give him more to think about. She stuffed her phone back into her bag and was counting backwards from one hundred when Madge came to check on her.

'You didn't need to come find me,' Ariel said. 'You're Chloe's best friend. You can't get in her shit books too.' Madge scrubbed her hand through her hair but nodded.

'What's up, A?' she asked. 'You don't have to tell me, but at least tell me if it's something really bad.'

Ariel took a deep breath. 'You remember the curse?'

'Of course.'

'It's not real. Or not anymore. Mum's been living in Manchester.'

Madge gaped at Ariel for long enough that she wondered if she'd said the words out loud or just imagined them, so she elaborated enough to give Madge the general idea.

'Shit,' Madge said eventually. 'God, no wonder you don't care about my hair.'

'Your hair is *great*,' Ariel insisted. 'It's fine. Honestly.'

'No, it's not,' Madge said gently. 'Are you staying at your dad's?'

'Unfortunately. Rest of the family's in the shit books too.'

'They knew?'

'Uncle James and Grandpa definitely did.'

'Fucking Uncle James,' Madge said. 'Never trust a bachelor.' She hugged Ariel, but held her delicately, like she was an expensive piece of china. 'It will be fine,' she said, 'Eventually.'

'Eventually,' Ariel agreed. 'Go and hang out with Chloe.'

'Are you sure?'

'Yeah. I'll be fine. We don't both need to deal with her stink eye. And I think I could do with some quiet time.'

Chapter Thirty-Two

Ariel wished she wanted to go to school. She really did. She *tried* to make the most of it, to tuck away her resentment and appreciate state-mandated education in a nation willing and able to educate girls and young women. She'd heard too many stories about child marriage and civil war to refuse to engage at all. But the day was too long, too rigid, requiring too many hours of concentration she did not have, especially after months and years surviving on a handful of hours of sleep. Homework took away from precious time with Rocket or her photography; exams were a test of Ariel's memory, not of what she had learnt, and it rarely felt as though those were the same thing.

But the worst bit was finishing the school year when she had fallen out with most of her friends.

Friendship did not come naturally to either Scarlet sibling. Once they found someone on their wavelength, that person tended to stay in their life for the long term. There were ebbs and flows in their relationships of course, like the time Grace was on a road trip across America and she and Ariel exchanged handwritten letters, or when Seb's primary school best friend, Jake, moved to Malaga with his parents. But generally speaking, the Scarlets preferred quality over quantity. Madge and Ariel did text occasionally, but it wasn't the same as a conversation, which was near-impossible with Chloe glued to Madge's side. Most messages consisted of funny GIFs Madge thought might cheer Ariel up (they did not) or suggestions as to things they could do as a pair over the summer. Ariel did not want to think of the summer, all those weeks stretching on, but she did her best to appear moderately enthusiastic. And at least the summer holidays meant no school.

Although she really was grateful to have time alone with her thoughts and desperately needed the brain space to make her slow way through exam revision, there were times when Ariel wished she was better at chatting. She wished it in Maths, when Chloe ignored her except for when they did pair work on a tricky bit of algebra that Chloe understood and Ariel didn't. She wished it in PE, when Madge and Chloe joined one group and Ariel was left in a group with Grace, who did not look at her except for when they had to pass the ball back and forth. She wished it on the walk home from school, when dozens of her peers chatted happily to one another and Ariel strode as fast as possible towards her house for an evening of dog walks and home-work and yoga and meditation apps that did nothing to stop her dreaming about a dusty old shop and falling leaves. Sometimes she dreamt of Nicole, too, standing under a creaking, decaying tree. She looked just like she did in photos from when Ariel and Seb were little, just like Ariel remembered her: cheerful and vibrant.

Ariel did not know if she wanted to know what Nicole looked like now.

She didn't quite know why she was bothering, but she retrieved the crumpled paper from the bin and continued working on Josephine and John's website. It was more fun than reading the medical dictionary, she sup-posed. She had a few paragraphs typed out, and she'd found a blurry portrait of John online. She wasn't sure if it was legal to use it on her own site—she had a list of things to ask Sophey and Ernest about. She hadn't managed to find out much more about John's background, either: from the grainy por-trait, he was very dark skinned with short, curly hair, but that was about as useful as a chocolate teapot when it came to tracing his lineage. She won-dered what her History teacher would say if she explained she was working on this project more than she worked on her actual homework.

That being said, she was at the point where even homework was okay if it meant a bit of time she couldn't be thinking about Nicole or her father, to whom she still refused to speak. She leapt at the chance, in English, to do a summer reading project on the topic of 'award winning novels' in a pair the teacher had chosen. She even, thanks to Sophey's library habits, had an idea for the book they could study when the students gathered into their pairs on a grey afternoon. 'Hi,' Ariel said to her new partner, Amanda. Amanda did not look impressed that the teacher had placed her with Ariel. 'You're in Pho-tography, right?'

'You don't have to do that,' Amanda said.

'What do you mean?'

'You don't have to pretend you give a shit about who I am.'

Ariel was going to say something until she could have sworn she saw Grace, on the other side of the classroom, smirk. Instead she said, 'what do you want to do for the project? I know we've got the suggested list, but my friend really liked *Aristotle and Dante Discover the Secrets of the Universe*. It had a giant sticker for some award on the cover.'

Amanda blinked. 'My sister's been telling me to read that. Are you sure?'

'It fits the criteria and both of us know people who liked it. Might as well.' Ariel took a breath. 'What's your phone number?'

Chapter Thirty-Three

That Friday afternoon, as Ariel got in from a run with Rocket, a message pinged on the group chat she shared with Chloe and Madge, silent since Chloe and Ariel's falling out.

Chloe: *Ariel are you still up for my dad's retirement thing tomorrow*

Chloe: *Madge is coming*

Chloe: *Free booze*

Shit, the party. Dr Montgomery was retiring his post as an eminent gastroenterologist in order to spend more time fishing and visiting his holiday home in Saint Lucia. It was to be quite the event, months in the planning. Ariel had assumed her invitation rescinded.

Her phone buzzed with a text from Madge: *Please come to this thing or Chloe and I will be the only teenagers!*

Ariel messaged the group chat: *I'll be there!*

She eased her best clothes from the wardrobe and laid them out to decide what to wear, washed her hair and was choosing nail polish when her phone rang: Sophey.

'Hello?'

'Sorry for bothering you,' Sophey said, strangely formal in the way people can be over the phone when they don't know each other too well. 'But Ernie's had to go to Oxford and David won't answer his phone and the shop is rammed and I wondered if you'd be able to come up this weekend to help? You're the only person I can think of.'

Ariel did not know what she had been expecting Sophey to say.

'Erm...'

'Could you? Ernie will pay you.'

'Sorry,' Ariel said. She really did feel bad—and it would have been nice to see Seb, to whom she'd only spoken on the phone a few times since... that weekend. 'But I've got this thing tomorrow. Chloe's dad's retiring. Chloe's the blonde one,' she added after a moment.

'I remember,' Sophey said. 'It's okay. Say hi to Madge. And Chloe.' She ended the call.

Chapter Thirty-Four

A riel had visited the Montgomery home several times since meeting Chloe in year seven. The Montgomerys were good at parties: Christmas, birthdays, new year... Mrs Montgomery either had a lot of time on her hands or employed a highly skilled events planner, because each party was the sort to get featured in society magazines and talked about years down the line. 'Do you remember the winter wonderland they had in the garden?' 'Do you remember those mixologists they hired?' 'Do you remember when that MP was there and really rather good company?' Their home was the fanciest Ariel had ever been in, and that included the time her family visited Buckingham Palace. It wasn't that it oozed luxury... it was more than once you noticed that the painting in the front room was an original Jack Vettriano, you couldn't stop thinking about how much the rest of the house cost.

So Ariel wore her most expensive dress, and took a cab to make sure she didn't crease it.

The front door was answered by an East Asian woman Ariel had never seen before, wearing a starched black uniform and balancing a tray of canapes on one arm. She took Ariel's jacket—also the most expensive one she owned, although she wished she hadn't bothered as soon as it was whisked from her hands—and led her out into the vast garden, via a stop at a temporary bar in the chrome-and-tile kitchen. Ariel thought she recognised one of the bartenders from the last time she was here.

Ariel found herself under a marquee decorated with fairy lights, listening to a real-life string quartet, clutching a glass of lemonade. Madge was right: this party was full of Dr Montgomery's colleagues, Mrs Montgomery's friends and Chloe's much older siblings and their spouses. Ariel knew Chloe's family by sight, but she'd always been a little intimidated to approach them. If she had thought Chloe icily straightforward, she got a shock when she first met the rest of the clan. Besides, most of them were lawyers or surgeons or managing directors. Her father's position as a respected university academic lost its shine around these most sparkling of professionals. Ernest and Alexandria, Ariel suspected, would be made to take their boots off at the back door.

So she hovered, watching the string quartet. Sophey would have liked it, she thought suddenly. Her hand was halfway to her phone to text her—

'Ariel!' Chloe elbowed her way through the crowd, Madge hot on her heels. 'You came!'

'You invited me,' Ariel said awkwardly, but she accepted Chloe's hug nonetheless. She smelt like prosecco, which wasn't a great sign. 'Love your outfit, Madge.'

'And what about *my* outfit?' Chloe demanded, before Madge could say anything.

'Cute,' Ariel said. It wasn't cute: it was strapless, sequinned and at least one size too small in the bust, which Ariel suspected was why Chloe had purchased it.

'You're just in time for the speeches,' Chloe said, still hanging on to Ariel's hand.

Indeed, Dr Montgomery was standing on the little stage, string quartet silenced.

'...Thank my wonderful wife,' he was saying. The crowd *oohed* and clapped as Mrs Montgomery smiled, herself a vision in peach lace. 'My wonderful children,' Dr Montgomery continued, listing each of his progeny by name as well as the various historically respected institutions they now worked in or lunched at or walked past on their commute. 'And Chloe, our dear youngest, soon to follow us!' More applause. 'Of course, her grades haven't been *quite* what we're hoping for, but we live in hope she won't turn out like her mother!' The crowd laughed politely. Chloe's grip tightened on Ariel's hand.

'Want to sneak off?' she asked, then pulled Ariel and Madge through the crowd and into the vast cream living room, where she dug around behind a boat-like sofa and emerged holding a bottle. 'Champagne?'

'No,' Madge said firmly. Ariel shook her head.

'Don't be a square,' Chloe sniffed. 'This is the good stuff,' she added. 'Not prosecco. *Champagne.*'

'We're fifteen,' Madge pointed out.

'You're allowed at home,' Chloe argued.

'You've had four glasses,' Madge said. She didn't say it like she was judging Chloe, just like she needed it to be said. Chloe ignored her and poured a fifth. Clearly ready to talk about something else, Madge turned to Ariel. 'What have you been up to?'

'Just a bit of reading,' Ariel said honestly. 'I'm working on a website about my great-great-something aunt. She's the one who started the curse business.' She gave Madge and Chloe an abbreviated version of Josephine and John's story, leaving out the more awful parts of the letters. She didn't think she was up to sharing those quite yet.

'I didn't think you were into history,' Madge said when Ariel paused to sip her lemonade. Chloe, bored, was onto glass number six.

'I didn't either,' Ariel said. 'I don't think they teach us the right stuff.' She looked out at the window, to where Dr and Mrs Montgomery were now slow dancing to the string quartet. She let the silence sit for a minute, then said, 'you guys, I think we should speak to Grace and apologise.'

'What for?' Chloe asked.

'You know what for.'

Chloe hiccupped and fidgeted with her bracelet. 'No I don't. She was a bitch.'

'I think she was right,' Ariel said. She said it quietly but firmly, and she knew Chloe heard her by the set of her shoulders.

'This is your other friend talking, isn't it?' Chloe said.

Ariel was deciding how to respond when Madge said, 'I think Ariel's right about apologising and I think Grace was right about what she did.'

'Take that back,' Chloe snapped. Her face did not change especially, but the glass she was holding cracked.

'No,' Madge said. She said it gently but firmly, just as she had said no to Champagne.

'Then get out of my house.'

Madge and Ariel had both stood up when the waitress from earlier arrived. 'Miss Montgomery? Your parents would like to know—'

'Fuck off!' Chloe snapped to the waitress. 'Don't come back inside this room unless it's with a loaded tray.' The waitress blinked, once, but nodded and headed back into the depths of the house. It occurred to Ariel that she wasn't so much older than they were.

She and Madge looked at each other, and at Chloe, who was now drinking straight from the bottle and taking a selfie of the process.

'We need to have a proper conversation about Grace,' Madge told Chloe. 'But not when you're like this. Text me when you're in bed so I know you're not choking to death on your own puke.'

Chloe clicked another photo.

'*I* don't have anything to say to you,' Ariel realised. 'Except that Grace was absolutely right. Also you're a spoilt brat and I'm sorry that your parents are horrible.'

She did not wait around to see Chloe's reaction, although she thought she heard the sound of a glass hitting a wall.

Ariel and Madge trekked around the ground floor until they found the room containing their jackets. Inside, texting furiously, was the waitress from earlier. She looked up guiltily when the door opened, but Madge said, 'we won't tell.'

'I'm sorry,' Ariel said to the waitress. She knew it wouldn't make any difference whatsoever, but she wanted to say it anyway.

The waitress shrugged, like she knew Ariel was thinking both of those things.

The girls called a cab from the Montgomery driveway.

'Do we need to tell a teacher?' Madge asked as they waited. 'Is she... having a breakdown?'

'I'd have a breakdown in that house,' Ariel said. 'Who talks about their kid like that?'

Madge fidgeted with her phone, then said, 'you're right about Grace. We should apologise properly.'

Ariel thought about the unanswered texts. 'I don't think she wants to hear us out.'

'I might write to her,' Madge said thoughtfully. 'I've always been better when I write stuff down.'

'You're good at words,' Ariel agreed. 'Put a good one in there for me, will you? Not that I deserve it.'

'I don't think you don't deserve it as much as you think you don't deserve it,' Madge said.

Ariel snorted. 'I take it back, that sentence made no sense.' But when the cab arrived and dropped Madge at her house first, Ariel leant across the seat and hugged her friend. 'Thanks for being there.'

It occurred to Ariel, alone in the car as it made its way to the Scarlet house for an evening curled up with Rocket, that aside from that last conversation with Madge, she could have gone up to Southend this weekend after all.

Chapter Thirty-Five

Finally, finally, school ended. Ariel's father was on a trip to Patras and Athens for conferences and it was agreed that Ariel could stay in the house alone as long as she phoned Grandpa and Uncle James once a day and went there for dinner once a week.

Ariel immediately booked more shifts in the sandwich shop, took Rocket for longer walks and spent more time on Josephine's website. She'd found a free website builder and slowly begun creating pages, but she still wanted to speak to Ernest and Sophey about those small details before she made it public. There was too much she still didn't know about John Ingram—Josephine's letters said he was educated in Edinburgh, but had he grown up in the UK?—but other than Sophey and Ernest, she didn't know who to ask. Most of her teachers had told her off for daydreaming once too often for Ariel to consider them anything other than irritants.

Seb, on the handful of times she could get hold of him, told her to stay busy and that they would arrange for her to visit soon. His internship sounded horrendously stressful, but he was very cheerful when he told her about all the hours and terrible bosses and bitchy colleagues he put up with. 'It's better than being at home, I know that much.'

She couldn't really disagree.

With her website project in limbo until she could arrange to go and visit Southend, Ariel set about developing the photos she'd been taking with the vintage camera. The student exhibition had got back to her: they wanted a few shots for the café wall. Ariel's dark room was a converted airing cupboard, too small to do anything other than stand, lean and work. Seb and Uncle James had put it together when Ariel was twelve. *Bougie,* Grace joked when Ariel showed her it. *Dad said it saves him bothering with laundry,* Ariel replied.

Now, Ariel wondered if Grace had been joking.

She shook her head, as though the motion might get her thoughts in order, like shaking a snow globe and watching the glitter settle. This teeny space was hers, and she was going to create something in it, and she was going to go to that café and drink its overpriced beverages and look at her work on the walls.

It took her quite a while to realise what was wrong with the photographs. So long, in fact, that over a week of the holidays passed. Ariel and Amanda met up to talk about their book project; Ariel endured a frosty dinner with Grandpa and Uncle James; Ariel's father returned from Greece with loukoumi Ariel refused to eat; Ariel sent an eighth consecutive text to Grace with no reply. When she next sat down with the photos properly it was early in the morning and she'd not long awoken from a nightmare so unnerving that she got dressed, clipped Rocket to her lead and went straight out for fresh air before it got too warm.

She thought, as she and Rocket walked, that the nightmare had been about Bezzina's Emporium. She was fairly sure Sophey had been there, and Ernest. And... Chloe and Madge? No, not just Chloe and Madge. Nicole featured too. All Ariel knew for sure was that she had woken up angry and frustrated, and then sad, and then she looped back round to the sort of angry that makes you slam things just to hear something louder than your feelings. She slammed every door she went through on her way out the house.

The walk with Rocket helped. She could get by with almost no sleep and consecutively terrible dreams, she decided, as long as she could get up and look after Rocket. The park was close to their house, and she was permitted to go there alone as long as she always took her phone with the GPS turned on, and left her father a note. The fresh air and quiet morning sounds always calmed her mind.

Statistically, a stranger in the park would not be the thing that killed Ariel.

It did feel more like a probability than a possibility, though,

She tightened her grip on Rocket's lead as they walked home, repeating what she had told herself time and time again: Rocket was small but ferocious, the park nearly always contained other dog walkers, most of whom

Ariel or her father knew by sight; if anything happened, there were road traffic cameras nearby.

Statistically, statistically.

When they got in, Ariel made a coffee and picked the photos back up, sorting them into an order for her scrapbook.

They weren't bad. Ariel had half a mind to make a sort of portfolio out of them. There were some of Sophey and Ernest and Alexandria which might look nice in the shop, but the rest could go in the huge, decadent scrapbook Ariel had been keeping for a special project. She thought she might write a sentence or two next to each one, explaining her motivations or the styles she experimented with. That was an adult thing to do, wasn't it, to show off one's work and make it sound like instinctive decisions had been thought through.

She stopped sorting when she realised what was wrong with almost every picture.

She had a shower, packed a bag, clipped on Rocket's lead back on and took the next train heading into London.

Chapter Thirty-Six

If Ariel had been hoping to make a smooth, if slightly dramatic, entrance to Southend, she was sorely mistaken. This was Rocket's fault. The dog was small enough to sit on Ariel's lap on the train (just about) and well behaved enough to be trusted on a train (just about) but she made life a lot harder when it got to navigating stations and climbing down to the Underground. Rocket, like her owner, was unconvinced that a metal tube in the ground was an acceptable way to travel, and flatly refused to go near an escalator. This culminated in Rocket climbing out of Ariel's arms and up to her shoulder and refusing to move, like an extremely hairy parrot. In the end, Ariel took Rocket for a walk outside Paddington Station for a while and poured her some water from a flask, then scooped her up into an extremely large shopping bag and carried her down to the Underground using the lifts.

Neither of them enjoyed the remainder of the journey, but neither of them bit the other, so Ariel counted it as a success. When they stepped into Southend high street at lunchtime, both dog and human were happy to inhale the salty air and wander down to the seafront. Both were devastated to find that the beach was off limits to dogs between May and October, and both resolved to sneak down at dawn tomorrow.

She had *not* missed Southend, Ariel assured herself as she let out Rocket's retractable lead and walked along the path by the sea wall. It was just the smell of the sea, the warm summer light on the Estuary, the miles of sand stretching out at low tide, that appealed to her. Seb was right, about living by the sea. It was good for you.

Speaking of Seb, he did not know she was coming. To lessen the surprise, she texted him as she walked back up to Bezzina's Emporium and then bought a large box of his favourite chocolates from a shop. She didn't know why she hadn't thought to put Rocket in a shopping bag before now, actually; disguising one's dog as groceries to pop to the shops felt like quite the skill. In the queue to pay—she wasn't using one of those self-service check outs, thank you very much, they were a scheme by corporations to justify firing their shop floor staff—Ariel skimmed the shop's notice board and noticed an advert for Bezzina's Emporium. It was handwritten, because of course it was, and advertised jewellery valuation, bulk purchase of vintage clothing and 'genuine occult items.' Most of the poster was covered by a glossy print out advertising mum-and-baby yoga.

It was only when she walked into Bezzina's, Rocket back on the ground, that Ariel realised she had forgotten to text Sophey. The shop was busy; a handful of people queued at the desk clutching their finds.

'Ariel? What are you doing here? Why did you bring Rocket?' To say Sophey looked surprised was an understatement, but she recovered her composure. Her hair was tied up with a scrunchie and her cardigans had given way to a sleeveless blouse, burgundy check skirt and black tights. She must have been baking wearing her tights, but as she stood on a stool to reach a high shelf, Ariel understood why she had chosen to cover up. The guy waiting for his item was arse height, and he knew it.

Ariel was about to explain, when she noticed that Sophey was teetering on her stool. 'Do you need—'

'Yes, absolutely.'

With that, Ariel had tied Rocket's lead to a hook behind the counter, handed her her favourite stuffed toy and began serving customers, starting by calling Sophey's creep customer over to the counter.

The day became a blur of people, with conversation snatched between tasks and clamouring customers. Most conversations went like this:

Customer: 'Excuse me, do you work here?'

Ariel: 'Yes, ma'am.'

Customer: 'I'd like this vase, please.'

Ariel: 'Certainly. It'll be thirty-five pounds.'

Customer: 'Oh, that's far too much. I can get it for ten down the road.'

Ariel: 'The flowers in this one will never wilt.'

Customer: 'Oh, well that's different! I'll give you twenty.'

Ariel: 'Thirty is our best offer I'm afraid.'

Customer: 'I'll go down the road then.'

Ariel thought it might never end.

'Why is Ernest not here? Is he still in Oxford?' she hissed to Sophey as she rummaged behind the counter for a suitable carrier bag before—

'Miss, how much is the dress in the window?'

'Let me check for you... Fifty.'

'Can I have it professionally altered?'

'Of course, ma'am, but not by us. We have the number of a tailor if you're interested. I think it's... Sophey, is it this number? Here you go, ma'am.' The girls couldn't speak again until Sophey ducked behind the counter to give Rocket a dish of water.

'When I rang you he'd gone to Oxford for a weekend trip to a museum. Today he's—he's in the hospital. A dog bit him. Could you grab the key charms from the stock room please? We're nearly out.' Sophey turned her attention to the latest customer and Ariel could hear their conversation as she dashed into the back rooms.

'Excuse me, I'd like to buy this mannequin.'

'I'm sorry, sir, that's not for sale.'

'Why not?'

'Because we need it to display clothes.'

'Is it magic?'

'No.'

'Oh, in that case, who cares then.'

Ariel returned with key chains. 'Is Ernie going to be okay?'

But Sophey was already serving someone. 'So that's three key chain charms and a set of teacups. Would you like a bag, sir?'

'Only if she's a blonde!' Ariel looked at the customer (white, tobacco-stained, owned about eight teeth) and at Sophey (curling her lip in the same way Rocket did when a dog got too friendly in the park). Then Sophey blinked once and wrote the man's receipt.

'Here are your items.'

The man looked down at the pile of goods on the counter. 'Where's the bag?'

'Oh I'm sorry,' Sophey said through gritted teeth. 'Was that you asking for a bag?' She turned her back to him and spoke directly to Ariel. 'I think Ernie will be all right. They're keeping him in for tests. Be careful with the snow globes. If they break, they unleash a bout of illness on the nearest people. I don't know why Ernie bought them, he thought they'd be popular Christmas presents.' She stomped off to get herself a glass of water as Ariel tidied up the counter and checked the ledger was up to date.

'Excuse me,' said a voice. 'Where is your mop?'

'Our mop?'

'My son just knocked over a snow globe.'

'A snow globe? Could you show me the label please? Sophey. Sophey! This child's about to need medical attention. Yeah, it was the snow globe.'

It wasn't until gone five o'clock that the shop emptied and Sophey locked up. 'What did you want talk to me about?' she asked. She still sounded a little formal, but Ariel thought maybe she was tired: the whites of her eyes were tinged red and she had dark circles. She pulled the scrunchie from her hair and raked her hands through her roots with a satisfied sigh. Ariel glanced at her phone. She knew Seb's internship demanded twelve-hour days, and she wasn't sure he had his phone on him. Sure enough, no response.

'Ariel,' Sophey prompted. She'd retrieved her tote bag from the back room and was repacking Tupperware, a water bottle and another paperback. 'Why did you come here?'

Well all right then. Ariel pulled the photographs out of her pocket. 'Look at these.'

Like Ariel, Sophey took a minute to realise what she was looking at. Ariel knew the moment she noticed what was wrong, because she exhaled sharply.

'Is this on every one?' But she was already leafing through the stack. She settled on a photograph of herself in the shop, absorbed in a task.

If you just glanced at it, the picture was only Sophey, in the shop, absorbed in a task. But if you looked closer, then closer still... Standing just behind Sophey was a woman holding a book.

She had definitely not been there when Ariel took the photo.

Sophey flicked to another photograph. This one was of Ernest, leaning over the ledger. Stooped next to him, looking up, was a tiny, extremely old, man. His skin was shrivelled, his eyes rheumy and his bones sticking out.

Next to the old man stood a woman, smiling happily, although her skin was covered in pustules and rashes, and it looked a lot like some of her skin and a good chunk of her bones had rotted away.

Now a photograph of Chloe. Behind her, a man glared out at Ariel with furious indignation. His expression, Ariel realised with a jolt, was a little like the one Chloe wore sometimes.

'Are they ghosts?' Ariel asked. She felt a little silly asking, but if she hadn't grown up with a cursed necklace, she wouldn't have believed in curses.

'I don't know. They seem very... specific.' Sophey rubbed her nose. 'They remind me of something. I can't remember what.' She shrugged. 'Figure it out tomorrow, I guess.'

Ariel waited for her to say something, then realised Sophey was waiting for her to speak.

'Oh. Yeah. I guess.'

'Right, so I have to put money into the safe. See you tomorrow?' Ariel had been thinking of asking Sophey if she wanted to grab dinner, but Sophey was clearly very ready to be somewhere else.

'Okay.' She gathered Rocket and made for the door. 'Have a nice evening.'

'You too.' Sophey's eyes were already on her phone.

Chapter Thirty-Seven

As predicted, Seb was unimpressed to find his little sister on his doorstep. He was even less impressed that she had forgotten to tell their father where she was until she was boarding the train out of London to Southend.

She had half forgotten.

She did not feel bad.

'Ariel, seriously, you can't act out like this. What if you got kidnapped and raped and your body was dumped and no one even knew where to look.' Seb was happy to see Rocket, of course, and was busy scratching her behind the ears as he said so, so the venom in his voice was neutralised.

'Dad's a scumbag. He deserved a bit of time stewing.'

'Whether or not he's a scumbag has nothing to do with the fact that you are fifteen and can't just fuck off halfway across the country by yourself.'

'I took Rocket.' Ariel handed him the chocolates. 'Peace offering?'

'You little shit. You're not having any of these.' Seb swiped them and put them in a high cupboard, like that would deter her. 'Why did you actually come, Ariel? Was it just to annoy Dad?'

'It actually wasn't. Something's up with that camera, and I wanted to get it checked out. And see my favourite brother.'

'God, don't say that. It'll turn out there's another one of us hiding somewhere.' Seb rubbed his eyes. He looked at Ariel. 'I've been thinking about everything. It's all pretty fucked, isn't it?'

She reached across the table to take his hand. 'Yeah, I think it is. Can I stay here for a bit? I'll be out at Bezzina's Emporium most of the time.'

'Course you can. We might have to deep clean the place when you're gone, though. Pets are against the lease.'

Chapter Thirty-Eight

The following morning, after an illicit sunrise excursion to the beach, Ariel arrived at Bezzina's clutching Rocket, a cushion for Rocket to sit on, plus some carrots for her to gnaw throughout the day, and a tin of loose-leaf tea and a packet of fancy coffee. She should have brought Sophey something yesterday, she thought. It was kind of rude, just turning up at the shop with a dog in tow. If Ariel had known Ernest was in hospital, she would have volunteered to come and help out straight away, instead of spending the week faffing about with her photos. She wondered why Sophey hadn't told her. Anyway, she left the house bright and early, and sure enough Sophey arrived to find her standing on the doorstep with Rocket.

'Morning!' Ariel said brightly. 'Do you need help with anything before we open properly?'

'You can polish the display cabinets,' Sophey said. 'There's a cloth behind the counter. Then sweep the stock room, and dust the window displays.'

Okaydokey. Ariel got on with it, glad for the manual work, as Sophey organised change in the till and tidied a few shelves.

'What happened to Ernest?' Ariel asked after she wrestled the vacuum back into its cupboard in the stockroom. 'You said... dog bite?'

'Remember the protesters outside the last time you were here?' Sophey asked. She put down some books and retied her hair into its bun. 'They're part of a group. Campaigners for Tradition.'

'Should I have heard of them?' Since she'd begun drinking less caffeine, Ariel had also tried limiting her exposure to the news. A desire to know when a war had broken out or when bad weather descended (or being caught not knowing who the prime minister was) warred constantly with her desire to sleep peacefully.

'Not really. They're a bit fringe. They think that Ernie's a Satan worshipper, they think the shop is corrupting the youth, they think we should be closed down for public health purposes. Common and garden faux-religious extremists. They've been coming to the shop a lot and last week they brought a dog with them. Huge thing, some sort of Mastiff-cross. Poor animal was terrified because they've *clearly* trained it to be scared of them and they've got it on one of those shock collars that ought to be *banned...*' she seemed to realise she was going off on a tangent. 'Anyway, Ernie went outside to offer them a bowl of water for the dog and something happened and it got scared and bit him. It was quite bad so we closed for the day and went to the pharmacy and they told us it was bad enough for the hospital so we went there and he was in A&E for *ages* with just some gauze to mop up the blood and he's still there because he's old and they want to check he's not got rabies or something.'

Ariel digested this. 'What happened to the dog?'

'I don't know. I reported the organisation to the RSPCA and the police but I don't think anything will happen. Next time we'll hear about it is when it bites a child and the news will be full of crap about how big dogs are dangerous and then the dog will get put down and it will have had an absolutely shit life.'

She sounded so dejected that Ariel wanted to pat her on the hand. She did not think they were at that point in their relationship, so she just said, 'at least Ernest's okay. He can bite, too.'

Sophey cheered a little at this and went to flip the *open* sign.

The day was immediately as busy as the last. A husband searched for an anniversary gift for his wife and left the shop clutching a leather handbag. A mother searched for a gift for her daughter's birthday and left with a key chain shaped like an orange Chevrolet Camaro. A teacher searched for a leaving gift for a colleague and left with a pen that always leaked.

'This is perfect,' the teacher said grimly to Sophey, counting out notes. 'That bastard's been nicking my stationery for ten years.'

During a lull, Ariel took Rocket to the street for a wee and some exercise. When she returned, Sophey had hefted a cardboard box onto the counter and was rummaging through. 'Someone donated these,' she said. 'I'm not convinced they're quite our thing.'

'Donated?' Ariel asked. 'Does that happen a lot?'

'Sometimes. Some old lady left Ernie the whole contents of her house once. Her family went ballistic, they thought they were going to inherit and sell it all... Sometimes people just leave boxes on the doorstep.' She pulled the first items from the box: fist-sized carved elephants.

Ariel leaned closer. 'Are they... ivory?'

'I think so. Ernie won't deal it unless he can prove it's from the nineteenth century or earlier, but even then he's not keen.' She dug through and made a little stack of items that could be worth pricing up: a woollen scarf, some war medals, a silver pendant. Then she wrinkled her nose. 'I can't see these selling.' She showed it to Ariel: a set of postcards, decorated with illustrations. 'I think they're William Blake.'

'The writer?' Ariel knew him from English class.

'He was an artist too, and an abolitionist. These might have been part of the abolition effort. I could check, but even if they are...'

They surveyed the postcards. Some were of fruit, or trees, or European military men. Some were of enslaved people being lynched.

'Leave them for Ernest to decide?' Ariel suggested.

Sophey was about to respond when the door opened and several primary school-age children piled through, demanding to know if they sold live insects.

(They did not.)

Eventually, eventually: closing time. Once the door was locked and money in the safe, Ariel made them both tea and dug out her photographs. Sophey stared down at the image of Chloe and the angry woman. 'I think I know what it is they remind me of,' she said eventually. 'Spirits.'

'Like whisky?'

'No. Like in Greek myth.' Ariel waited. 'In Ancient Greece, people believed in personifications of attributes. Like Eros and Nemesis and Nike.'

'Love... revenge... victory?'

'Exactly.'

Ariel examined the photographs again. Seb, laughing with Karishma. The woman in their photograph was young, their age, and held a cup. 'Could this be youth?'

Sophey had a look. 'Yeah.' She kept shuffling photos until she settled back on the one of Chloe. 'Zelos.'

'Who?' Ariel asked.

'Envy.'

'That would fit,' Ariel said. Now she thought about it, she wondered why she hadn't realised before. She glanced at her watch. 'Shit, I have to get home. I'm helping Seb clean the house. *I'm* cleaning the house.'

'Okay,' Sophey said absently. 'I think Ernie will be back in a few days. I'll phone him in a bit to check in. Do you still want to speak to him about your website?'

'Yeah. And you too, actually, if you have a moment.'

'I'll see,' Sophey said. 'See you tomorrow.'

Chapter Thirty-Nine

Seb, Ariel was relieved to find, recovered fully from the inconvenience of her visit when she cleaned the house while he was at boxing. She didn't do his housemates' rooms (Karishma was still here for the summer working at a local shop; the other two whose names she couldn't remember—okay, wasn't interested in—were back wherever they came from) but she wanted to scrub the common areas and Seb's room. Rocket's hairs hadn't covered the house yet, but she knew that they would and also wanted to show Seb she felt bad for worrying him.

'It hasn't been this nice since we moved in,' he said drily later that evening.

Ariel loaded dirty cleaning rags into the washing machine, alongside a stack of Seb's 'basically clean' towels and bed linen, then set the temperature to high. 'I could tell.'

'How's Ernest?' Seb asked. 'Didn't he get hurt in a protest?'

'How did you know about that?'

'Not all students sleep in and go clubbing. Some of us talk to local people at the boxing gym. Are you sure that shop is safe to hang out in?'

'I'm safer there than wandering around the shops,' Ariel reasoned.

'Speaking of safety... Dad told me you've been making vegetable pasta. Pasta out of vegetables.'

'Yeah. What about it?'

'Vegetables aren't meant to replace pasta. You're meant to eat them alongside pasta.'

Ariel looked at him. 'I don't understand what you're on about.'

'Just... just keep eating pasta. I told Dad...' he trailed off.

'To make me eat pasta.'

'Yeah.' Seb rubbed his hand through his hair and worried at one of his helix piercings. 'Basically.'

Ariel was mystified about why her cooking was the topic of conversation between her father and brother, especially when they were barely on speaking terms. She made *good* courgetti, back when she was still willing to cook for her father. He said he liked it. *He said a lot of things*, said a voice in her ear. She decided to change the subject. 'Want to watch telly?'

Seb grinned. '*Keeping Up Appearances?*' It was a Scarlet family favourite, and Seb kept up a TV licence just to watch old BBC comedies.

'Yes please.' Ariel dug a notebook and pencil out of her bag and settled into doodling absently as Seb lined up an episode.

Karishma joined them halfway through. 'I love this show,' she said, grabbing a blanket and plonking herself into an armchair. 'We had a neighbour just like Mrs Bucket. She complained when we invited her to our Diwali celebrations when we first moved in, so the next year we didn't invite her and then she complained about that.'

'We had someone similar,' Seb said. 'Our neighbour tried to get Ariel to get rid of Rocket in case she gave her children fleas.'

'What happened?'

'They moved to a posh bit of Bath and stopped bothering us,' Seb said happily.

'A posh bit of Bath?' Karishma asked. 'Isn't it *all* posh?'

'Not our bloody house,' Ariel said, and Karishma laughed.

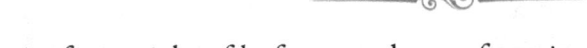

After a night of leaf-strewn dreams featuring Nicole hugging Ariel and Seb on the sofa at home—Ariel woke up and told herself her eyes were watering because of allergies and nothing more—Ariel returned to Bezzina's Emporium to help open the shop. She liked her job in the sandwich shop, mostly because Carol was good about flexible hours and hadn't fired Ariel when she disappeared to Southend with no warning, but she had to admit that she preferred the variety that came with spending time at Bezzina's. You could spend the morning vacuuming behind cabinets, lunchtime selling a set of haunted encyclopaedias to an enthusiastic university lecturer, and the afternoon dealing with protesters. Like today, for instance.

'What's going on?' Sophey's voice, coming from over by the clothing rack, was brittle enough to snap. Ariel followed her gaze through the window.

A crowd, marching in a circle, holding signs. So far, so much like before. But now they brandished sparklers, or tambourines, or air horns. Some wore balaclavas or scarves tied around their faces. Most of their signs indicated they marched for Campaigners for Tradition.

A chill settled over Ariel's shoulders. 'They remind me of the Westboro Baptist Church.'

'I think of these guys as a second cousin.'

'What do they want?' But Ariel could already hear them, chanting:

'Save! Our! Children! Save our children!' A couple with a child walked past the shop front. Or they started to. As Ariel watched, they ambled along the road from the high street, laden with shopping bags. When they saw the protest, one of the adults grasped the child by the hand and they crossed the street, glancing back Bezzina's as though the window contained a lot worse than summer furnishings.

'I'm going to talk to them,' Ariel said.

'What? Ernie tried that and now he might have rabies.'

But Ariel was already outside.

She hadn't decided to confront the protestors until the words were out of her mouth, and now she was directly in front of them she had to admit that it might not be her smartest idea.

She did not want to antagonise anyone physically more intimidating than herself in case she ended up on the evening news. This limited her options somewhat. Wait, there—just left of the main group, a woman of about Ariel's height and build. She brandished a sign that read 'PROTECT CHILDREN FROM PEDOS, PAGANS AND POOFS.'

Ariel was confident that *pedos* was not the correct spelling.

She was also confident that two of those things were distinct from the third.

She strode to the woman. 'Excuse me, can I help you?'

'PROTECT OUR CHILDREN!' The woman did not meet Ariel's eyes, but glared straight ahead to the door of the shop. She did not blink. Her eyes were blue, not unlike Ariel's own, and watered a little from the effort of staring.

'Because you've been out here for a while and we're open, you can come in.'

'PROTECT OUR CHILDREN!'

'I can highly recommend Bezzina's Emporium as a shop. They'll help you find what you need, even if you're not sure what you're looking for. Although... you might just need a dictionary.'

'PROTECT OUR CHILDREN!'

There was, Ariel realised, a literal child accompanying the protestor. She hadn't noticed it at first, because it was strapped to the woman's back. Ariel preferred those back slings to the ones where you wore your baby on the front of your body. What if you tripped and squashed the child?

'We have some children's items too,' she said, and waggled her fingers at the child. It was a toddler at the most, basically still a baby, and surveyed her nonchalantly, then grabbed a fistful of its mother's hair. That may have influenced the strength of feeling in the woman's next chant:

'PROTECT OUR CHILDREN FROM SCUM LIKE YOU!'

Ariel decided she had tried hard enough. It was 2015, not the dark ages, and this woman was a grown up. Her ignorance must be a life choice. 'Have a nice day.' Ariel turned to go, then on impulse turned back. 'I hope this shop and ones like it are here for your child, when they need it.'

She had just gotten through across the threshold of the shop when she felt something wet hit the back of her neck. She wanted to touch it, to confirm that what she thought was spit was in fact spit, but she didn't want to give anyone the satisfaction. Instead, inside she went straight to the toilet to wash her neck and hands, then went back to the shop and began tidying up.

Sophey watched the exchange grimly but continued on with her day. Ariel appreciated her gutsiness. Rocket, when Ariel went over to have a cuddle, snuffled into her hand and permitted Ariel to bury her head in her fur. Ariel appreciated her patience.

Eventually the protesters dispersed, presumably to the sewers from which they had emerged.

'**P**eople,' Ariel reflected as they tidied up that evening, 'are disgusting. Why can't you just say something to someone's face? Why spit on them?'

'Just rude, I guess.'

Ariel dug out her phone and looked up Campaigners for Tradition. 'Oh, God, they have a website. And social media. People are commenting.' She squinted at profile pictures and comment threads. 'Some are agreeing with the group. There's that dude who yelled at you about the *Percy Jackson* book. And that woman with her poor mother-in-law! She called Ernest a washed-up pansy hippie. Why would she say that? Her mother-in-law was happy enough. And the kid.'

'I suppose a lot of people will say things behind someone's back.'

Sophey's tone caught Ariel's attention. There was something lurking, just beneath the surface of her words. Something... sharp.

Ariel looked up from the phone. 'Are you okay? Has someone said something about you on here too?'

She was about to turn back to the phone when Sophey said, 'No, actually.' Her voice sounded a little wobbly, now, but she stared straight at Ariel. 'No one said anything online. But there's not a lot they can say that I haven't heard. What with me being a bog witch.'

Bog...

Oh God.

'You... how did you...'

'When I got into the train station I realised I hadn't bought Nan a present so I dashed back out. I was in the gift shop at the Roman Baths the same time you and your friends were.' Sophey's eyes were extremely bright, and her hands made fists.

'Sophey—'

'Please don't pretend to apologise. You're right. I don't have many friends. Any. Well. I thought I maybe did.' She swallowed. 'You know, I think I can finish closing up myself. You don't have to come in tomorrow. David said he might come by. And Ernie should be back the day after.' Sophey handed Ariel Rocket's lead and crossed her arms, waiting.

Ariel stood on the pavement for a long time after the door closed in her face.

'What's up?' Seb asked when she met him off his train that evening. 'You look like you did when Dad told us... about Mum.'

Ariel recounted the day's events. When she was done, Seb loosened his tie and said, 'so she came all the way to Bath when you were having a crisis and you didn't know how to explain your decent new friend to your terrible old friends, so you let them talk shit about her?'

'I joined in talking shit about her.'

Seb wound the tie experimentally around his hand. 'That's brat behaviour, little miss.'

'I know.'

'I guess the question is... did you feel bad about it when you realised she overheard you, or did you feel bad about it straight away?'

Ariel thought of her dreams. 'Straight away.'

'Well then.' They were at a crossing: Seb leaned his elbow on the button. 'That's something. How are you going to apologise?'

'I don't know. Just say sorry again?'

'That would be a good start.' Seb exhaled noisily. 'Lot of apologies floating around at the moment. That's the thing, though...' he stared off at the sky for so long Ariel thought he was going to miss their crossing when the green man beeped. 'Apologies don't mean being forgiven.'

Ariel didn't need him to tell her twice.

Chapter Forty

Ariel did not sleep much that night, but when she did, she dreamt of creaking tree branches and a rising tide in the Thames Estuary, water lapping over her ankles as she stood in the surf. Although Sophey had told her to stay away, Ariel knew that if she had any chance of fixing her damage, she needed to speak to Sophey properly. So she arrived at the shop at opening time, with Rocket and two posh takeaway coffees.

Sophey just stared at her, unblinking.

'I'm sorry,' Ariel said. 'I'm sorry that I didn't shut down Chloe's nonsense and I'm sorry that I didn't want them to know we're friends. We are. Were. Please take this coffee.'

Sophey did take the coffee. 'Me drinking this does not mean anything.' She unlocked the door and let it swing shut in Ariel's face. Ariel chose to ignore this and pushed through after her.

'Can I help with anything?' Ariel asked. 'Now I'm here.'

'You can clean the toilet.'

Ariel did not know if Sophey was being sarcastic or not, so she tied Rocket to her place behind the counter and dug some cleaning materials out of the rickety cupboard beneath the sink in the tiny staff toilet.

Oh, God, now she thought about it, this little room was rank.

No, not rank. Neither Sophey nor Ernest were the sort to allow a bathroom to become anywhere near 'rank' on the scale of clean-to-dirty. In fact, the bathroom itself was quite nice, with white tiling and cream paint. Various bottles of surface cleaner and toilet gel had all been used. The tiles around the sink were unblemished and the sealant was not gunked up; the bin was barely a third full; the toilet itself was clearly scrubbed regularly.

But.

The smell.

Ariel had not noticed it the handful of times she had used the loo: the first time, she had been too busy attending to her burnt fingers, and this week she had been too busy helping Sophey with the shop to spend more than thirty seconds in here. The longest she'd spent was when she dashed in when she thought she got her period, which she hadn't, but she took the opportunity to do a wee then dashed back out because Sophey was in the middle of a heated discussion with a customer about the Bezzina's Emporium returns policy.

Now she was paying attention, she couldn't believe she hadn't noticed it before: the little room smelt awful. Really, truly, awful. Like the sanitary bins at school when they hadn't been emptied for ages and the heating was on. Like the homeless guy Ariel saw on the way into town sometimes, who smelt like damp laundry gone stale. Like when Rocket was ill and Ariel came downstairs to a pile of dog puke and turds.

Ariel sloshed some toilet gel into the loo basin experimentally. Then she sprayed some surface cleaner onto some surfaces. Then she opened the tiny window that looked out onto a bit of alleyway.

Absolutely nothing improved.

Ariel walked out of the toilet, shut the door and sprayed the surface cleaner into the air of the corridor, then sniffed.

She could smell surface cleaner.

She walked back into the toilet.

She could smell nothing but the terrible smell.

So it was magic, then.

She washed her hands and strode onto the shop floor. She did not look at Sophey, although she was fairly sure Sophey was looking at her.

She sipped some coffee to collect her thoughts, then went to the display of dried herbs on the counter. She picked up a gauze bag containing dried mint, and after a moment an evil eye charm. She took a handful of coins out of her purse and added the items to the ledger, then took both to the bathroom. She hung the evil eye on a nail protruding from the inside of the door. Then she attached the baggie to the window fastening, so the fresh air would waft the scent through.

The smell, she was almost sure, was getting weaker.

Or possibly her nose cells were dying.

What could be causing this? If it was a curse, Sophey could fuck off and ask Ernest. What else could it be?

Struck by an idea, Arial crouched down to the little cupboard, but it was empty save for cleaning products, bin bags and a packet of sanitary towels. She leant into the space between the toilet and the wall, where the pipe went. *Yes.* There. Ariel scrabbled around until she could reach, then closed her hand over something solid.

Straightening up, she surveyed the item. It was a tiny glass ramekin, like her dad kept for serving salsa. It was full of potpourri, that fragrant stuff that people in films were always eating because they thought it was muesli.

The potpourri smelled repugnant. Like dirty dishcloths abandoned in a sealed plastic bag, like bloodstains on clothes, like old meat left in the sun. It was every horrible scent in the universe rolled into one.

Why Ernest and Sophey allowed such an abomination to exist in their staff facilities was beyond Ariel. She got a bin bag, tipped the potpourri into it, tied the bag off and took it outside to the big commercial waste bins. Then she went to the little kitchenette and scrubbed the glass dish with water so hot it scalded and set it on the drainer.

She went back into the toilet and inhaled deeply. It smelt—

Absolutely terrible.

Wait.

Ariel crouched down to the toilet pipe.

The ramekin was sitting right where she had found it, full of potpourri.

She picked it up, sat it in the little sink, and surveyed it.

She was *not* going to ask Sophey for help. But she wasn't sure what she could do without knowing who had put the ramekin there, and why. What if it was an angry customer, getting their own back because a product had caused them grief? The shop had its ledger, but there was no way Ariel would find that specific wronged customer just from a list of sales. Ariel thought about her own magical item. It was to do with balance and imbalance, wasn't it, magic.

How could she counteract this God-awful little bowl of hell? The evil eye and the mint were helping, she was almost sure of it.

Think, Ariel. You can when you need to. Magic. Energy. Energy? Ariel prodded at the potpourri. What normally went into potpourri? Fragrant flowers and plants, she presumed. Cinnamon sticks. Rose petals. Lavender. What had gone into this? She inspected the plant matter, gagging. She wasn't particularly knowledgeable about plants when they were fresh and alive, so she wasn't sure what she was hoping to achieve here. Wasn't there a type of flower in the tropics that smelt like a rotting corpse? She was sure there was, because Seb had gone through a phase in his early teens of wanting to be a botanist. And there definitely existed trees that smelt absolutely terrible. There had been a few in her neighbourhood, but they were so gross in certain seasons that residents successfully campaigned to have them removed and replaced with something less pungent.

Going by the variety of colours and textures in this bowl, whoever concocted the mix had a good idea of which plants to use.

Ariel whirled back onto the shop floor. She took her time at the counter, going through the various herb bundles and smudging sticks. She selected eight items and a small incense burner, the type with a lid. According to the label it was brand new, fashioned by a ceramicist in the Black Country. Perfect. She didn't need anyone's second hand negativity for this. She purchased all the items and wrote them into the ledger—this was going to be the most law-abiding, positive plant-mixing attempt on the planet. Then she went into the kitchenette and gently, slowly, shook the herbs and plant matter into the incense burner. As she did so, she focussed on everything she liked about Bezzina's Emporium: the cosy armchairs, Ernest's calm acceptance of anything that came through his door, the strange variety of customers. She thought of the last few days, working with Sophey. She enjoyed it. Her feet ached a little after a shift, and she wasn't quite sure about using the till yet, and the thought of those protesters made her nervous.

But even with Sophey's anger radiating off the walls, Ariel loved it here.

When the burner was full, she fixed the lid on and carried it to the toilet. She didn't want to set it alight; she didn't think it would be safe to leave it. The little holes in the lid would have to do. She wasn't sure, but she thought that potpourri lasted for ages because it was treated specifically. These herbs and plants would eventually decay and smell bad themselves. She had loads left, so she adapted some gauze bags and bits of ribbon and twine until she had enough baggies to hang them from every surface in the tiny room, and on the door handle outside.

She stayed in the corridor for long enough that she was fairly sure she could only smell wood, dust and a few herb remnants.

She stepped back into the toilet.

It smelt fine. Not fragrant. She couldn't smell any of the herbs and flowers she'd hung: not the mint, not the chamomile, not the rose, nothing. The room smelt like a clean bathroom always smells: like toilet gel and surface cleaner and hand soap.

Ariel strode onto the shop floor. 'Toilet's clean.'

Sophey had unclipped Rocket from her lead and was sitting on the floor with her, stroking her head. 'I believe you,' she said. 'I've been meaning to try the herb thing.'

'Who left that ramekin there?'

'Some old dude who thought some spices and trinkets could cure his wife's motor neurone disease. They didn't, obviously. So he left us that.'

Ariel respected the level of detail he'd gone to. She sat on the floor opposite Sophey. Rocket thumped her tail but did not move; Sophey had her full attention.

'You really hurt my feelings,' Sophey said after a minute. 'I *don't* have any friends. I suppose that's why it hurt so much.'

'You must have friends,' Ariel said. Everyone had friends, didn't they? Even if it was just your family.

'I have people I'm friendly with,' Sophey corrected. 'I had two best friends in primary school and at the start of secondary.'

'And?'

Sophey blinked a couple of times. 'Theresa moved to New Zealand at the end of year seven and I lost her contact details and when I looked her up on Facebook, she blocked me. Cassie died last year.'

Oh. 'I'm sorry.' A very small part of Ariel was relieved she'd grown up knowing the etiquette for what to say when someone lost a loved one. 'Was she ill a long time?'

'She stepped in front of a train at Rayleigh station.'

Oh.

'I suppose she had been ill for a long time, if you think about it.' Sophey glanced over at the shop's dark shelves. 'All the magic in this room and I couldn't persuade her to hold on until she went to uni.'

Ariel wondered what she could say that would make Sophey feel better. She wondered what would make her feel better if it were Grace or Madge or Chloe.

'So, yeah, I don't have any friends,' Sophey said. 'Unless you count my nan, which I sort of do sometimes and sort of don't sometimes.'

'I'm really sorry about Madge and Chloe,' Ariel said. 'Well, not Madge. Madge *is* really nice, she just takes a while to warm up to new people. Chloe... isn't nice. She has stuff on at home,' she added, out of loyalty.

'So does everyone,' Sophey said. 'It's not an excuse to treat other people like dirt. She doesn't treat *you* like you're friends.'

After the last conversation she'd had with Chloe, Ariel had to agree.

'I'm sorry that I didn't stand up for you either,' she said. 'I should have. It was... it was because I was ashamed to admit I made a friend who's a bit different. And because you knew about all the curse stuff, but Chloe and Madge know about the real-life stuff. They knew me when I would mark the anniversary of my mum's death and go to her grave on Mother's Day. Her fake grave,' she added after a moment. 'You're separate from that. I'm not the girl whose mum died to you, and I'm not the girl whose mum died but then turned out to just be fucked off in Manchester. I'm just a customer.'

Sophey scratched behind Rocket's wonky ear and Rocket hummed happily. 'You were a rude customer.'

'Yeah. I'm sorry about that too.'

Sophey was quiet, the sort Ariel knew not to interrupt. Eventually she said, 'Thank you for apologising. You're *not* off the hook,' she added. 'But we're... better. Want to come in tomorrow? Ernie should be back mid-afternoon. He can look at those photographs.'

'Please.'

Sophey nodded. 'All right then. Let's open up.'

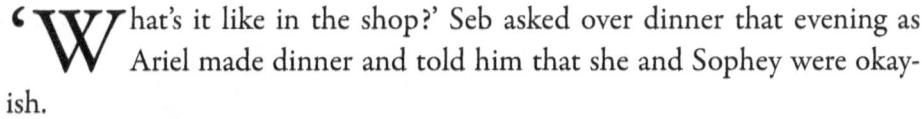

'What's it like in the shop?' Seb asked over dinner that evening as Ariel made dinner and told him that she and Sophey were okay-ish.

Ariel checked the oven. 'You've been in.'

'I mean what's it like to work in?'

'It's like the Holburne,' Ariel said. 'Well. It's like being in William Holburne's collection, but some of it's haunted and some of it might kill you. Do you want tarragon with this chicken or something else?'

Chapter Forty-One

The next morning, the girls couldn't open the shop. When Ariel arrived with Rocket, she found the door blocked by a small crowd of people. She recognised a few of them from the spitting incident: Campaigners for Tradition.

She hadn't slept well, obviously, and Rocket had gotten into a growling match with a Jack Russell on their walk *and* her favourite top, a pastel boat neck with embroidery on the sleeves, didn't really match her cardigan, which shouldn't have bothered her but did so she slung the cardigan into her tote bag in case of emergencies. The sky was grey and it was spitting, so if she were less vain she would have put the cardigan on before she left the house. But she was vain, and so she was chilly, and she really wanted a decent coffee. She would feel better about both top and vanity once caffeinated. Which couldn't happen until she could get through the door. Not that she had a key—where was Sophey?

'Morning!' said a voice, and Ariel found that Sophey was standing right next to her. How she materialised without making a sound, Ariel would never know. Sophey nodded at the crowd. 'How do you want to play this?'

'Without getting bitten?' Ariel eyed the protesters. Like before, they were mostly middle aged and holding signs. Some teens were there too, the sort Ariel suspected went to Bible reading group and judged those who didn't. 'Is that the dog?'

'Yep,' Sophey said grimly.

Well. Ariel could see what Sophey had been talking about. This animal was several times bigger and heavier than Rocket, straining at a chain lead. Some sort of Mastiff-Boxer-Ridgeback mix, bred for guarding and fighting and producing other dogs that did the same.

'Shall we just ask politely?' Ariel asked. 'Do unto others and whatnot.'

'That is what Ernie would recommend,' Sophey said. She looked worried, but she squared her shoulders and approached the crowd. 'Excuse me,' she said. 'I have a shift to start. Would you mind moving please?'

As expected, the crowd did not move at all. 'Go home,' one woman told Sophey. 'This isn't the right sort of place for you. I hope you see that one day.' She sounded genuinely worried, and Ariel would have appreciated that if she hadn't been holding a sign with a picture of Satan painted on it. She glanced at the other protestors. They seemed fairly harmless, but she didn't like how much attention the dog was paying to Rocket.

'Be that as it may,' Sophey was saying carefully, 'I do have a job to do. Please could you at least let us in?' Her hand was in her jacket pocket, and Sophey suspected she was texting David or Ernest for backup. Now Ariel thought about it, she should probably text Seb or Karishma. Seb, ensconced in an office somewhere along one of Southend's train lines, was too far away to help. But Karishma worked on the high street.

'No!' said one protestor. He was a teen, and Ariel wondered why he thought picketing an antiques shop was a good use of his summer holiday. 'You can't spread your evil if you can't open!'

You couldn't argue with that logic, but Ariel was tired of running on single-figure hours of sleep, and she wanted a coffee.

'Sir.' She stepped forward. 'Please just let us do—'

Ariel never got to finish asking the boy for anything, because at that precise moment, the protestor holding the dog on the chain let go.

Ariel, focussed on the teen, was unaware of this until she heard Sophey shout, '*Ariel!*' and, half a second later, Rocket screamed. Ariel felt the lead pull taught in her hand as Rocket tried to flee, but there was no space: they were surrounded by people and Ariel couldn't even move her legs to let Rocket through. Besides, it was too late: the Mastiff had bitten Rocket once and was lunging for her again. All Ariel could hear was snarls—all she could see was her tiny rescue pup baring her teeth, ears flat. Like her owner, she knew this wasn't going to go well. Ariel had half a second before the Mastiff sunk its teeth back into Rocket, so she did what she'd been taught not to do: she leant down and scooped Rocket up. You were meant to avoid picking up scared dogs, in case they bit you. You were meant to avoid getting in the middle of a dog fight, in case one of the dogs bit you.

The Mastiff bit Ariel.

Whatever he'd been trained to do, it wasn't a clean kill. He hung from her arm, shaking it with enough force she almost dropped Rocket. Ariel had seen dogs do the 'kill shake,' of course: Rocket had done it this morning with a stuffed toy. Ariel had never wondered what it might feel like.

Statistically, this dog might be the thing to kill Ariel.

He was *not* going to kill Rocket.

Ariel clung to her dog, and the other dog clung to her arm, and for the first time in years Ariel found herself praying. *Please let this be over soon please let this be over soon.*

Then, abruptly, it was.

Ariel wasn't sure of the order of events, but she thought Sophey shoved through the crowd, threw open the shop door and grabbed something from inside. The next thing she knew, the Mastiff yelped and let go of Ariel. He cowered in the gutter next to the shop, but Ariel couldn't focus on it because Sophey was pulling her through the door and locking it behind her. Only then did Ariel put Rocket down.

She couldn't tell what blood was hers and what was Rocket's. Rocket was shaking and whimpering, but the bleeding seemed to be slowing. Ariel would be taking her immediately to the nearest vet.

'Ariel, your arm.' Sophey, Ariel now realised, was on the phone to the 999 switchboard. She had been saying words like *assault* and *dangerous dog* and *my friend got bit.*

Oh yeah. Now she was safe, Ariel realised her arm hurt quite badly. She peered down and her skin was peppered with punctures, all bleeding with enthusiasm.

'We get Rocket to the vet first,' Ariel said. 'I'll be okay with some bandages.'

'Ernie said that,' Sophey said. She fished a first aid kit from behind the counter with one hand. 'Sit down. I'll clean you up and get you a tea and in a minute someone is going to come to get that dog before it kills someone. She's okay,' Sophey said into the phone. 'I don't think she's going to pass out. Okay, yeah, thanks.'

'Is the crowd still there?' Ariel sank into a chair and found she lacked the energy to look out of the window for herself. Sophey clicked off the phone and glared out of the window, then began efficiently applying disinfectant to Ariel's arm.

'No. They've fucked off and left that poor dog behind.'

'What did you hit it with?' Ariel asked.

'Rounders bat. I feel terrible but—Ariel. *Ariel.* Don't close your eyes. Phone your brother. Do it now, while I'm watching. For fuck's sake, not the vet. Rocket will be okay.'

A knock on the door. Both girls and Rocket jumped. Sophey applied a dressing to Ariel's arm before she got up to open it.

'David! If you'd been here half an hour ago...' Sophey's voice cracked.

'You're perfectly capable of handling things.' David said smoothly. 'Look at that dressing on your friend's arm.'

'Don't bullshit me,' Sophey snapped. Ariel thought vaguely that this was the first day she could remember Sophey swearing, but now she was swearing quite a lot. 'Go and make Ariel a tea. Black tea, lots of sugar. Phone Ernie while you're at it. He's getting discharged today. Go *now.*'

Ariel's arm attended to, Sophey turned her attention to Rocket. 'I'm not used to working with animals,' she said grimly. 'Sorry, creature, this is going to hurt.' Ariel watched as Sophey dabbed disinfectant along Rocket's side. Rocket squeaked, but she lay still. 'Ariel. I can't hear you talking to your brother.'

Fine. Ariel rang Seb's phone and left a message. Did she actually have Karishma's number? Wait, yes, because she'd sent her a photo of Seb as a preteen.

'Karishma? It's Ariel. Do you know the office number of the place Seb's working? It's not *really* an emergency. I'm fine, mostly.' Ariel became aware that she could see blue lights. She'd always hoped that she'd get the police called on her for doing something fun, like discovering a government scandal and chaining herself to railings to publicise it. 'Yeah, I'm at Bezzina's Emporium. Okay. Thanks.' Ariel clicked off the phone and surveyed Sophey and Rocket. Ariel felt a bit ill, now she wasn't doing anything in particular, but she was fairly sure she could stand up. 'Soon as we're done here, Rocket's going to the vet.'

'Of course,' Sophey said. She stood up to open the door. One hand was back on her mobile, speed dialling another number, but it rang out. She cursed too quietly for Ariel to hear and stuffed her phone back into her pocket. 'Now stay awake long enough to answer these people's questions. DAVID. BRING THE TEA.'

Chapter Forty-Two

That evening, sat in Seb's kitchen, Ariel tried to decide who was in more trouble with Seb. Was it Ernest, for selfishly going to hospital and leaving Sophey to run the shop alone? Was it Sophey, for allowing Ariel to hang out there and serve customers? Was it Ariel, stupid enough to put herself between two fighting dogs?

Really, Ariel thought, the problem was bigotry. If bigotry didn't exist, those protesters would never have brought that dog...

She felt bad about the dog. The *thunk* as Sophey hit it with a rounders bat might be worse in her memory, or might have been terrible in real life. And there was no way it wouldn't be humanely destroyed now.

What a shit life.

Seb brought her out of her philosophical reverie by slamming a container of Chinese food on the table. 'Eat,' he growled. 'Then call Dad.'

Ariel picked up a fork in her left hand. At the hospital, where the police insisted they visit, a doctor told Ariel that she was lucky to have full use of her arm and that the bruising would go down in time. Antibiotics should take care of any infection but in the meantime, don't be an idiot again.

At the vet, where Ariel insisted they visit, the vet said much the same thing about Rocket, except for the idiot bit. Like Ariel, Rocket received stitches. Unlike Ariel, she also got a plastic cone, to discourage her from licking her wounds.

Ariel was not looking forward to the conversation with their father, so she ate slowly.

'Thanks for leaving work to get me,' she said. Karishma, sitting next to her, raised and lowered one shoulder. 'Any time.'

Seb, across from them, scowled. 'You're not going back to Bezzina's.'

'I bloody am. I have to speak to Ernest about those protesters. He said that there's a case to ban them because they incite violence.' Ernest had been leaving the hospital as Ariel and Sophey arrived. He hadn't been surprised to see them, but maybe that was because David had called ahead.

'Fine. Do that. Then no more.'

'Seb, you're nineteen. How much power do you have over me?'

Seb gave her the finger. Ariel added this to the number of times they'd truly fallen out.

After she'd done the dishes (extremely hard with one arm in bandages), she went out to the house's tiny patio.

'Dad?'

'Ariel?'

'How's your conference?'

'Fine. It was nice to do one in Bath for a change. How are you and Seb?'

'Seb's fine. He loves his internship. I'm... Rocket and I had a small scrap with another dog.' Peter Scarlet heard through Ariel's forced serenity in a nanosecond.

'Ariel? Are you both okay?'

'We're fine now. I just have some bruising and a little bit of some stitches.'

'Stitches?'

'Just a few! Those ones that dissolve. Not proper ones.'

'Ariel. Explain everything.'

She did, and when she was done, she said, 'Don't bother telling me not to go back to Bezzina's. Seb already tried.'

'You shouldn't go back—'

'And you shouldn't lie to your children about their not-dead mother. Bye, Dad.'

Ariel hung up.

It felt a lot like something Chloe would do.

She did not care.

That night, she took some of the painkillers the hospital gave her and, for the first time in years slept for ten straight hours in a deep, dreamless, sleep.

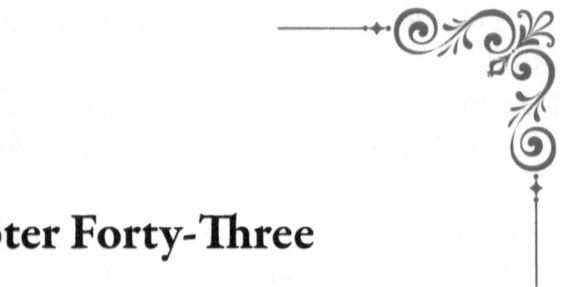

Chapter Forty-Three

In a change of tradition, Sophey texted Ariel to meet her and Ernest at a café in Southend for lunch.

When she arrived, they were already sitting at an outside table and had a dish of water for Rocket waiting. A walking stick learned on Ernest's chair.

The first thing Ernest said when Ariel sat down was, 'I will take care of your vet's bill.'

Ariel nodded slowly. She could afford the bill for Rocket's consultation, because she had taken out insurance for Rocket before they left the dog shelter. But she appreciated the gesture. 'Okay. Thank you.' She looked at Sophey. 'What happened yesterday?'

'After Karishma collected you from hospital, David and Ernie and I kept the shop open for the day. The police guy we spoke to came back and said that they're looking at maybe trying to make Campaigners for Tradition illegal and could we all please give testimony that they incite violence.'

Ariel lifted her arm. 'This do?'

Ernest lifted his cane in response. 'If you're happy to make a statement, it would help,' he said.

'Will it, though?' Ariel asked. 'Won't they just rebrand under a different name?' She was sure she remembered Grace talking about how that happened with hate groups.

'Probably,' Ernest said. 'But sometimes it's important to get these things on the record.'

Ariel thought about Henrietta's necklace. She wondered what would have happened between the sisters if it had been possible to get things on the record back in the day. 'Then I'll do it.'

'You should know,' Ariel said when their food arrived, 'that my family don't think I should come work for Bezzina's Emporium anymore.'

'Mine think the same,' Sophey said.

'What are you going to do?' Ariel asked.

'Carry on as before. What are you going to do?'

'Carry on as before.'

They both nodded. This seemed reasonable.

'You two,' Ernest said, when the bill arrived and he placed a handful of notes and change on the table. 'Go and spend a day off.'

'In Southend?' Sophey asked doubtfully. 'Ariel's seen the beach.'

'Try a park. Breathe in some green space. Don't come back to the shop this afternoon.'

'Do you feel guilty about the protestors or am I over hours or do you want me out of the way so you can do something magicky in the shop?' Sophey asked suspiciously.

'All of the above. Go away now.'

Chapter Forty-Four

In the end, the girls walked to Priory Park. It had green space aplenty, and Ariel was surprised at how well the sounds of the town floated away once they were amongst trees.

'Was your top salvageable?' Sophey asked as they walked.

'My top?'

'The one you were wearing yesterday. There was a lot of blood...'

'Oh.' Ariel hadn't thought about it. 'I think a nurse cut it off me. I wore my cardigan home.'

'Wasn't it quite expensive?' Sophey asked.

'Yeah, it was.'

'Will you... get another one?'

'Haven't thought about it,' Ariel said honestly. 'Probably not.'

They wandered for a while, finding a walled garden with manicured flower beds and a pond. Rocket lingered close to Ariel even when Ariel unclipped her lead. Ariel hadn't thought she'd miss Rocket's insatiable appetite for squirrels. She wondered if dog therapy was a thing. Probably for celebrity dogs. Or royal dogs. The Queen probably had therapists for her Corgis. Ariel wasn't sure what they'd need therapy for. Living in proximity to Prince Andrew, maybe.

'Want to do a tarot reading?' Sophey asked suddenly.

'Um. Okay.'

Sophey wandered to a bench under a tree and brushed off leaf litter. In Southend, Ariel had noticed, it didn't rain nearly as much as it did in Bath. This was an improvement as far as Ariel was concerned, but it did mean that outdoors objects felt a little dustier. She settled on the bench next to Sophey.

'I've never done a reading for someone else before,' Sophey admitted. 'But I want to learn tarot because Ernie finds it really helpful.' She pulled a pack of cards out of her bag. They didn't look very much like the ones Ariel had seen Ernest or Alexandria with. The back of the cards had the pretty blue-black hue of a night sky, and the images were all smudged blue and white lines.

'I'm honoured,' Ariel said lightly. 'Do I need to do anything?'

'Shuffle them,' Sophey said. 'And if you have a question, hold it in your mind while you do it.'

'If I have too many questions?'

'Just shuffle.'

Ariel did so, slowly. 'What now?'

'Flip over three cards. I, er, I haven't learnt the longer readings yet. This is for your past, your present and your future.'

Ariel turned over three cards at random. She wondered if she was meant to experience something in particular when she touched a card, like a flurry of emotion or a little shock of electricity, but she didn't feel anything other than the glossy cardstock.

'The Tower,' Sophey read. 'Death. And Six of Coins.'

A chill settled onto Ariel's spine. 'What do they mean?'

'Devastation and change,' Sophey said slowly. 'And generosity.'

Ariel looked down at the cards.

'Hm,' she said.

Then she burst into tears.

'Oh God,' Sophey said. 'I'm so sorry.' She scuffed the cards out of order hastily. She patted her pockets for a tissue and dug one out for Ariel, who blew her nose noisily.

'Sorry,' she said after a moment. 'I'm not normally a spontaneous crier. That's all my blubbing for the next five years.'

'It's okay,' Sophey said. 'Sometimes you need to let it out. And you had quite a traumatic day yesterday. Which, er, which card set you off?'

'None of them. All of them. The first two might be accurate, but the last one can't be. I'm not a generous person.'

'It's also about being generous with your time.'

'I'm not sure I'm good at that either.'

Sophey didn't say anything. She just looked out over the pond and flower beds and folded her hands into her lap. Ariel was grateful for the silence. She dabbed at her face and hoped she wasn't too snotty.

'You should carry on with your learning,' Ariel said eventually. She felt she owed Sophey an explanation for her waterworks. 'The first two cards *are* accurate. Not just about my mum or the necklace, although...' she glanced down at the Tower card. It showed a tower struck by a lightning storm, halfway destroyed. 'Although devastation is a good word for it. And I guess change is happening whether I want it or not.' She looked down at the Death card: a figure walking across a flurry of skulls and bones. She thought about her father's face as he sat in that chair at home and talked about Nicole's illness. She thought of Seb, happy and thriving up here at this concrete seaside. 'But I think things started falling apart a long time ago. Do you remember Grace?'

'You used to be friends,' Sophey said. 'You and Madge and... Chloe.'

'Yep, we were like the gruesome foursome of our school. I don't think you'd have liked me if you met me a couple of years ago. Or you'd like me less than you do now.'

Sophey did not dispute this.

'Last year... Grace was getting involved in Black Lives Matter. You know, the thing in America?' Sophey nodded. 'She was saying that it should be talked about just as much over here, too, and that Britain was just as bad in loads of ways, and Madge and Chloe and I said that at least our police don't carry guns and Grace said we were missing the point...' Ariel thought back to long discussions during lunch and at the school gates while they waited for various buses. Perhaps discussions wasn't the right word. 'I agreed with Grace. I didn't understand all the words she was using, but I understood what she meant. Or I thought I did.'

Ariel watched Rocket half-heartedly stalk a squirrel. The squirrel did not seem to care.

'But Chloe really didn't like it. She kept saying that Grace was making a fuss over nothing. Because Grace was asking teachers if she could talk in assembly and stuff, and they were happy for her to do it. Grace got other students involved too, and they were talking about setting up a club to talk about race and social issues and stuff. Anyway. Eventually, Chloe told Grace that she should know her place and keep quiet. And Grace was so angry, she threw Chloe's phone into the school fountain. She got suspended for a day and had to write an apology letter.'

'What has this got to do with you?' Sophey asked. She shuffled her tarot cards absentmindedly.

'Grace said we hadn't defended her to the teachers.' Ariel's voice sounded hollow to her own ears. 'She said she was justified in how she responded and that if she had really wanted to teach Chloe a lesson, she should have punched her hard enough to knock out her braces. I said that violence made her no better than racists. I know it was a *really* bad choice of words,' she said hastily. 'As soon as it was out of my mouth, I realised how it sounded. I was on Grace's side. But before I could explain, Grace walked away. She didn't speak to me, or look at me really, until we met that day in town.' Ariel did not like to think about how close this sounded to her conversation with Madge and Chloe about Sophey. 'So I'm not a generous person,' Ariel finished. 'Not when it matters. I didn't defend Grace. I didn't defend you. I'm just like Henrietta McLean.'

If Ariel's inability to stand up for her friends didn't kill her, her humiliation over it might.

Sophey was quiet for several minutes, shuffling some cards. Ariel pulled threads from her cardigan and took in the view. Then Sophey said, 'I think the curse is real.'

Ariel was caught off guard at this change of topic. 'Why?'

Sophey turned in her seat to look properly at Ariel. 'Does your mother know who you are? Is she well enough to know that your dad left her and took you and Seb?'

Ariel struggled to think properly. 'I think so? Dad said that he goes to see her sometimes. He mails her photographs of us, and school reports and things. He said that she wants to get better but she relapses a lot.'

'Do you believe him?'

Ariel shrugged. 'I don't know what better looks like for an alcoholic. I don't know what truth looks like on my dad, because I'm questioning every conversation we've ever had. What does this have to do with the curse? She's over forty and she's not dead. So the curse can't be real.'

'I think she's over forty *and* the curse is real.'

Ariel flapped her good hand: *go on*.

'For a while I thought the curse is doing its job but really slowly. Alcohol poisons you. So if she's been dependent all these years, she's been dying all along. Maybe especially if she's just mentally stable enough to know that your father told her children she died because he thought it was kinder than letting them watch her in her current state.'

'So even though every other woman in the family died well before their fortieth birthday, she's the exception because the curse is taking its time and making her suffer.'

'Yeah. But what if the curse is killing her slowly because it's not as strong as it used to be? Your grandmother, your aunt Katie, they both made it to their late thirties. You're almost sixteen, that's older than a lot of the women in your family. Maybe the curse is weakening because Josephine's wishes are coming to fruition.'

This, Ariel had to admit, was a good idea. Both good as in, it made sense and good as in, she wanted it to be true. Despite her best efforts, a tiny flame of hope flickered in her chest when she considered what Sophey was suggesting. She thought back to Josephine and Henrietta's letters. She thought about the sort of curse she would have created, if she were Josephine. She didn't want to stoke the hope, so she said, 'Josephine wanted people to remember what had happened to her and John Ingram. But they both vanished from history. Even after Bertie tried to keep the story alive, the necklace's curse is the only part that got passed down. My grandmother's generation didn't know who Josephine and John were. My aunt Katie didn't know.'

'They didn't know about Josephine and John specifically. But what if it's about your family learning to behave differently to how Henrietta and her parents behaved? A sort of... collective improvement.'

'I didn't stand up for Grace,' Ariel argued. 'I should have, but I didn't know how to. On the day you and I saw Grace in town, I told myself not to let my fight with her distract me from fixing the curse. But the joke was on me.' She rubbed her sore arm. 'I'm part of the reason the curse still exists. Just *wanting* to do the right thing might not be enough for Josephine. It wouldn't be enough for me.'

'You couldn't stand up for Grace months ago. What if you could now?'

Ariel looked out to where Rocket was sniffing around some flowers, squirrel abandoned. Sophey seemed to sense that Ariel had more to say and took in the view as Ariel tried to voice what she was thinking. 'Maybe. But what if the curse is so clever that even if I think I can do it, even if I think I am un—unlearning institutional racism, or whatever Grace called it, what if the curse knows that I'm only trying to improve so I'll live a long life and that doesn't count?'

'*Are* you trying to improve just to live a long life?'

Ariel picked up the three cards and examined them. The Six of Coins showed a smudgy figure handing six coins to another smudgy figure. She didn't know much about telling the future. If she hadn't had this reading, would it have occurred to her that generosity was a habit she might want to work on? She thought back to Grace's face when they last argued, the fury and disappointment emanating from her as Ariel wished, for the thousandth time, that she better knew how to articulate herself. She thought about all the work she'd been putting into Josephine and John's exhibition website, all the effort she'd made to find out if the curse was real in the first place.

'I wanted to break the curse for me,' she said quietly. 'I was so tired of checking both ways three times before I cross the street and reading the ingredients on food packets and worrying that an aneurysm would kill me while I slept. Then I was afraid that lack of sleep would kill me.' Ariel had to smile in spite of herself. 'You worry about worrying in the end, don't you? Some days I couldn't get out of bed, because I was so scared of what might be outside the front door. But then I would remember earthquakes and house fires and think, maybe outside is safer.'

'Life is what happens while you're worrying about being dead,' Sophey observed.

'I think it's "life is what happens while you're busy making plans."'

Sophey shrugged. 'Basically that's what I said.'

Rocket wandered over to where the girls sat. Ariel leant down to scratch beneath Rocket's cone and said, 'I came to the shop because I was tired of being afraid. I wanted to be a normal teenager. Did you know that other people our age are dating people? And thinking about where they might go to university or get a job?'

'I'm told that's the case.'

'That's all selfish, though, isn't it.'

'I don't think it's selfish to want to live past forty,' Sophey said. 'I think you can want that *and* want to be a better friend to Grace because it's the right thing to do. Would you have wished you'd stood up for Grace if you'd never known about John and Josephine?'

Ariel didn't even have to think before she nodded.

'There you go then.' Sophey folded her hands over her cards and gazed across the park.

Ariel looked back at the Six of Coins. 'There's a Latin proverb about living well while you're terrified, isn't there?'

'Probably. Or a song lyric by a naughties rock band.'

Ariel blew out her breath. Her bum was going numb. 'Thank you for the reading. Do you want to get ice cream?'

Chapter Forty-Five

The next day was bright and cheerful. Ariel woke with the dawn, of course. But she didn't mind waking up so early when the weather was this good—and not when she'd just had a dream as interesting as the one that woke her up. She sketched a couple of ideas down into her notebook then started her day. Or she attempted to sketch a couple of ideas into her notebook... her bite-free wrist was not her writing wrist. First proper job: taking her camera into Bezzina's Emporium and making Ernest a cup of tea while he was on his break. She texted Seb where she was going and, after a moment, Karishma.

'You learn fast,' Ernest said cheerfully—more cheerfully than he should have, in Ariel's opinion, given that he was consuming a large quantity of tablets with his tea. Ariel did not like to think about how wonky his tattoos would look with a bite scar shot through them. Maybe he didn't have any on his legs. She was struck suddenly by the image of Ernest in an old timey stripy swimming costume, reclining on a deck chair on the beach. She pulled herself back to the present before she could giggle.

'Do you know what's up with this camera?' she asked. She showed him the photos. Sophey, consuming tea herself, watched on. Rocket, on her cushion, crunched down a carrot.

'Ah,' Ernie said. 'Those are just personifications.'

'Like the Greeks believed in?' Sophey asked.

'Exactly. Nothing to be scared of. Not ghosts.'

Ariel did not think that *nothing to be scared of* was the same as *not ghosts*, but she was relieved nonetheless. She tucked the sheath of photographs back inside their wallet and slid the wallet into her bag. Maybe she could do something with them, for a project. Not all the photos had people in, after all. She decided to think about it while she helped Sophey clean the shop.

'Should you be moving your arm?' Sophey asked as Ariel helped her heft a wooden, lacquered cabinet, decorated with flowers.

'I'm using my good arm,' Ariel said, 'I can polish if you'd rather shove.'

Sophey dumped a duster in Ariel's hand and reached for the vacuum cleaner to clean behind the cabinet. 'This takes up so much room,' Sophey grumbled as she manoeuvred the vacuum to reach the wall. 'Can we move it somewhere less fiddly to clean behind? It could go in the window. We could do a wood theme.'

'Better not,' Ernest said briskly. 'That cabinet is an integral part of our security system.'

Sophey put down the hoover. 'Is that...' her eyes widened.

Ernest nodded. 'Best leave it there.'

Ariel looked between them. 'What is in that cabinet?'

'Nothing,' Ernest said. 'Nothing you need to worry about, anyway.'

Sophey looked like she disagreed, but she resumed vacuuming. Ernest continued drinking tea, so the cabinet couldn't be *that* strange. Or dangerous. Could it? Ariel decided to save asking about it for later. She had something more important on her mind that she wanted to ask Ernest about.

'Something else is bothering me,' Ariel said hesitantly when Sophey had put away the vacuum cleaner. To keep her hands busy, she picked up a blue dragon plushie from a shelf and turned it over in her hands.

'About the camera?' Ernest asked, although he looked as though he might already know the answer.

'About the curse. I wanted to know what you thought of Sophey's idea, that the curse is weakening because my family is learning. Could it really be as simple as that?'

'I think it's a good theory.' He looked at her. 'I also think that you have more thoughts.'

'It's just... it's not just my family, is it? It's the...' Ariel struggled towards the words and was grateful that Ernest showed no sign of rushing her. 'Josephine's family was of their time. But even though racism isn't acceptable anymore, it's still... in the... in the carpet.'

'How do you mean?' Ernest asked.

Ariel thought for a moment. 'It's like how there aren't any gay people on children's television.'

Ernest nodded. 'Once you notice it,' he observed, 'you can't stop noticing it.'

'No.'

They both sipped tea.

'What do you think this has to do with the curse?' Ernest asked her.

'It's just that if I were Josephine, I'd want the curse to hold until the carpet was... was clean.'

'It might never be,' Ernest said. He didn't say it like he was trying to warn Ariel, or express cynicism. Ariel thought back to the protesters outside the shop. She thought about Grace, and Sophey asking if she'd want to make amends even if she hadn't known about John and Josephine.

'We can't ask Josephine what she wanted,' Ariel said eventually. 'So let's hope she meant it to be about good intentions and just... leave the rest to the gods.'

'That's quite a heavy statement in a shop like this,' Ernest said thoughtfully. 'But I agree.'

'So do I,' Sophey said.

'Are you still happy to help me with the history bits of the website?' Ariel asked.

'Course.' Sophey frowned at Ariel's expression. 'Do you want to do something else?'

'I had another idea. A follow up. But it will need your help.' Ariel fished her notebook out of her bag and flipped to the relevant page, turning it round to show them. 'What do you think?'

Autumn

Chapter Forty-Six

Time flies when you're changing your life. It did for Ariel Scarlet, anyway. She was not sure what happened to August, but one moment she was up in Southend, working on her project with Ernest and Sophey, and the next she was in Bath, sorting through things in her bedroom and telling Rocket to stop sitting in boxes destined for the charity shop. She even sent some photographs into the student exhibition and enjoyed a mediocre coffee with her grandfather while he admired them on the wall.

'So these are all yours?'

'Yes, Grandpa.'

'Hm. I like the seascapes. And the ones with Rocket.'

'I like those best too.'

'Why didn't you include any of people?'

Ariel thought about how she didn't know how to take a photo on her vintage camera that didn't conjure up the subject's inner spirit. 'I thought I'd start with the nature stuff. Less likely to shout if I get the wrong angle.'

Her grandfather nodded his agreement. 'You've got quite the skill, little miss.'

'Thanks.'

Seated on too-low sofas next to a table made of an old door, Grandpa slurped an overpriced fruit smoothie. It sounded like a chemical toilet flushing. 'You should speak with your father. More than you have been.'

Ariel's grip on her cup tightened. 'I should also donate more money to charity.'

'He's sorry he lied.'

'I'm sorry I believed him. Grandpa, please,' Ariel added when she could see him start to speak. 'I'm old enough to make my own decisions about why I should be angry. So is Seb. I can't just stop being angry.'

'I know you can't. I just don't want you to end up like me.'

'Like you?' she asked, surprised. 'I'm not much like you, Grandpa.'

'All that fury,' Grandpa said, gazing up at the photographs. 'Turn it out or it might be the thing that kills you.'

Another thing keeping Ariel busy was that she needed to work as many hours as she legally could in the sandwich shop before the beginning of September. She had told Carol she wouldn't be staying on, and gave her enough time to find a replacement.

Carol did not seem bothered.

For once Ariel felt genuinely grateful that she didn't sleep. Those painkillers had helped her sleep for longer, but her wrist was almost back to normal and so too her sleeping pattern. She needed more hours in her day. Always, always, she was working on her project for Josephine and John. It was harder than Ariel had anticipated to hold all the moving parts in her head and build what she envisioned piece by piece. It required nonfiction books (or more accurately, audiobooks. She wasn't up to weighty tomes just yet), lots of phone calls to Sophey for advice and quite a bit of time utilising YouTube tutorials.

Although she still hadn't managed to uncover as much information about John's background as she'd have liked, she was hopeful that if she—they—could pull off her idea, it would be the sort of thing she would be talking about in years to come, the sort of thing teachers wanted you to put on your CV.

At Bezzina's Emporium, Ernest disregarded his walking stick and took receipt of an extremely large mirror.

'Through the looking glass?' Sophey asked drily as she polished it. She stopped. 'This *is* safe to stand in front of, right?'

'If it wasn't, you'd have noticed.'

'By the way, someone called the shop phone for you this morning. I wrote his name on a sticky note. Tristian... Matthew. Tristan Something Matthews.'

'What did he want?'

'He was asking if you'd changed your mind on his offer. Did he want to buy something?'

'Mm. He was in a while ago, looking at soft furnishings.'

'I took his number if you want to call him back.'

'I imagine I'll be hearing from him before long.'

Chapter Forty-Seven

September arrived, sunny and smelling of autumn. Ariel's birthday was approaching, her sweet sixteenth. Nicole always made a big deal of birthdays; Peter had to be reminded of them the day before, so Ariel had baked her own cake between the ages of nine and twelve, when Seb started to grow up and asked Aunt June to intervene. After that, Aunt June would cook dinner or Uncle James would construct a living room cinema screen out of bedsheets and set the smoke alarm off making everyone popcorn, and Ariel always got an iced sponge and cards with vouchers to her favourite shops. This year, Ariel gifted herself three things.

She was going to think of them as gifts, she decided as she walked a cone-free Rocket, because this was the first year that her impending birthday hadn't made her wake up in the night and rush to the toilet to vomit with increasing frequency as the day got closer. Although she wasn't honestly sure she was looking forward to turning the thoughts into action items, they would be sweet enough when she was done. 'Get it?' she asked Rocket as they walked. 'Sweet like cake. Oh, never mind.'

Gift number one: talking to Grace. Ariel invited Grace for coffee in the centre of Bath, only a week or so before the school term was due to start.

'I'm sorry.' Ariel said. It was her opening line, before hello, followed by a shortened version of the events of the last few months, followed by another apology. 'I know I've said it before, and I meant it then, but now I think I know why I should be sorry. I should have stood up for you with no caveats, because we were best friends. I should have done more to understand why you were so angry with Chloe, and why you were so passionate about Black Lives Matter. I don't expect you to forgive me, but please know I am really, *really* trying to be less awful.' Ariel stopped for breath. Was she babbling? She might be babbling. But what if Grace thought she was just saying what Grace wanted to hear?

Grace looked at Ariel over her cup and she must have believed Ariel, because her gaze softened. Ariel wondered if she was thinking of all the times, so many years ago, that Ariel would phone her in the early hours of the morning, crying over a nightmare about the curse. 'I believe you. And I'm sorry I froze you out. I talked to Carrie and... I shouldn't have given you the cold shoulder every time you tried to make amends. But... *you* understand why I can't go back to being friends straight away?'

'I do. I don't expect us to ping back to how we were before. I don't think we should—or can, even. But... fresh start?'

'I can do that,' Grace said. 'I missed you.'

'I missed you too,' Ariel said. They sipped their beverages in silence for a minute and Ariel thought, maybe, that she and Grace had a future.

Grace cradled her cup in her hands and frowned into it. 'I got a letter from Madge. We went for hot chocolate.'

'And?'

'We're okay. Better.'

'Did you speak to Chloe?' Now she'd asked the question, she wasn't sure she wanted an answer—but Grace just met Ariel's eyes and raised an eyebrow.

'No. Madge told me about that party. Have *you* spoken to her?'

'Not for months.'

Grace nodded, like she was satisfied. 'Carrie said you've been in Southend a lot.'

'Yeah. I'm working on a project for my great aunt Josephine and her fiancé. I have a prototype here, actually. Would you mind having a look?'

'Me?' Grace frowned. 'Why me?'

'I think it's up your alley. And you've always been honest with me whether I've wanted to hear it or not.'

Grace nodded amiably. 'All right then, I'll have a nose. Who was that girl you were with in Southend, by the way? Liberty Print Girl.'

'Her name is Sophey. She's also honest with me whether I want to hear it or not.'

'And you're...'

'Absolutely just friends.'

'Are you sure, A? You've traditionally not been that good with feelings that aren't crippling terror.'

This was more like the conversations she remembered having with Grace. 'Piss off. Yes. I am sure. Chloe suggested that too, for the record.' Ariel played with the little biscuit that came with her coffee. 'Sophey's just a mate who's a bit different to my other mates. You'd like her though.'

'I believe you. Speaking of Chloe...' Grace paused delicately. 'I can say this now you aren't in touch. Did you know that she had a crush on you?'

'Yeah. Weird way of showing it.'

'Oh God, so weird. Did you know she used to ask Madge and I why you would call us in the middle of the night instead of her? She was kind of obsessed with it.'

'What? Really? I used to call you and Madge because your parents didn't mind as long as I didn't keep you up for hours. The one time I tried phoning Chloe her dad swiped the phone off her and gave me a ten-minute lecture about wasting other people's time and how my problems were not his daughter's.' Ariel buried her head in her hands. 'Did Madge tell you everything that happened at that retirement party?'

'Yes... but I kind of also want to hear it from you.' Grace's eyes sparkled. 'Was it truly awful? Tell me all of it.'

'Okay, so...'

Chapter Forty-Eight

Gift number two was a conversation with Peter Scarlet. Seb and Ariel went for dinner with their father, the same day Ariel met up with Grace. It was early in the evening, the sun not thinking about setting yet. They met somewhere fancy enough that Ariel suspected that if she asked her father for a pony, he would buy one. Grandpa was there too, with Uncle James on one side and Uncle Chris and Aunt June on the other.

'I really am sorry,' their father said as soon as food had been ordered. Nice job, Ariel thought, making sure we're invested in sitting here until we've finished eating. But Grace had listened to Ariel's apology, so Ariel was going to listen to her father's. 'I made the best decision I could at the time,' he continued. 'Your aunt Faye and I grew up with a father who was so terrible that we often said, when we got older, that we would have done better without him there at all. That's not an excuse,' he added quickly. 'But it's a reason. You were both growing old enough and bright enough that you were going to start asking questions about Nicole's behaviour that I couldn't answer. I didn't want you to watch her fade like I was watching.'

'That wasn't your decision to make,' Seb said quietly.

'Maybe not,' their father said. He rubbed the bridge of his nose. 'I'm going to say what I always said I'd never say to my children.' Ariel and Seb waited. 'If you ever have children, you'll understand.'

'On the off chance that doesn't happen,' Ariel said, 'elaborate.' Out of the corner of her eye, she could see Uncle James hide a smile.

Her father turned his serviette over in his hands. 'You want your children to have the best start in life. I thought that Nicole not being there would give you that. I wish there were a way to see into a parallel universe where we could see what would have happened if I hadn't left her,' he added. 'But I suppose that's for God to know and for the rest of us to guess.'

Ariel supposed so too. She could tell by his posture that Seb agreed.

'I don't think this changes anything,' Seb said quietly. 'I can't come back here without thinking of what you've done. Both of you,' he added quickly. 'You and Mum.'

'Me neither,' Ariel said. 'That's why I'm going to live with Seb.'

'What?' Their father flinched badly, and glanced at Grandpa and the uncles.

'I'm moving to Southend. This weekend, before term starts. Seb's got a flat, and I'll finish my GCSEs at one of the schools there.'

'You can't,' their father said. 'You can't just make that decision—'

'You made the decision to lie to us for years. You made the decision to let us think our mother was *dead* instead of admitting that her illness made her a terrible person and helping us to navigate that as a family.' Ariel's voice was acid. 'You no longer make decisions regarding me.'

'How are you going to look after Rocket?'

'She's coming with us,' Seb said. 'Our landlord's been really good about it as long as we pay for a professional cleaner when we move out.'

'She destroys things,' their father said. 'That'll come out of your deposit.'

Seb shrugged. 'You destroy things too.'

Their father looked at Grandpa, and the uncles, at Aunt June.

'Actually, I think it's a good idea,' Uncle James said eventually. Uncle Chris and Aunt June and Grandpa nodded too. 'That's why we all helped Ariel move her things while you were at that conference in Cardiff.'

'You all knew?' their father demanded of his in-laws.

'We owed them, Peter,' Uncle Chris said. He was a quiet, bespectacled accountant Ariel had only ever heard speak when he really needed to. This meant they had exchanged approximately twenty words in fifteen years. 'We kept your secret because we saw how much damage Nicole was doing to your family and we respected your decision. But we probably shouldn't have done.' He drummed his fingers on the table. 'The least we can all do for Seb and Ariel now is help them get a fresh start.'

Peter did not look remotely as though he agreed.

'Now you know what it feels like,' Seb said, 'to have your loved ones avoid telling you something.'

'Some space will do you all good,' Aunt June said hastily. 'But we'll miss you. We *all* will.'

'I'll visit,' Ariel said. There was a lump in her throat. 'Sophey wants to see the Christmas market. And I'll come for your birthday, Grandpa, always.'

'That's because you don't think I've got many left,' Grandpa replied, but he reached over and hugged his granddaughter. Ariel could smell tobacco, and his woollen cardigan, and moisturising cream. She really would miss him.

'How will you afford it?' their father demanded. 'If you want independence from me, you'll get it.'

'I'll work,' Ariel said. 'Ernest Bezzina's offered me a job. Not many hours because it's the law and that, but enough to help Seb.'

'And I'm going to pause my degree,' Seb said. 'I'll work for a bit.'

'What?' Ariel asked. This part was not in their plan. 'Don't drop out because of me.'

'I don't have the head for studying right now, little miss.' He shrugged. 'Too much going on. My boss has offered me a full-time position for a year. It's cleared with the university. Preparing for the workplace and whatnot. I'm not dropping out. I'm... taking a gap year in the middle of the course, for work experience purposes.'

'You'd do that for me?'

'Of course.'

The lump in Ariel's throat got bigger. 'It'll be worth it,' she said. 'I'm going to try harder in school. My GCSEs will be great. I promise. Then you can go back to your degree and *that* will be great.'

'You don't ever have to try harder for me,' Seb said, but he reached out and squeezed her hand.

Their food arrived. It was delicious, although no one drank the wine the waiter recommended. Peter Scarlet paid the bill.

Now Ariel and Seb had this conversation with their father, there was only one more person to speak to before they both left Bath for good.

Chapter Forty-Nine

Gift number three was a meeting in a café next to the Abbey, on a day when autumn blew through the city with a bite. The café hadn't been there last time Nicole was in Bath, which was why the Scarlet children chose it.

The arranged meeting time was one o'clock in the afternoon, and Ariel did not sleep the night before. She managed a spoonful of cereal for breakfast and spent the morning drifting around the shops. Seb did the same. They arrived early, early enough to get a seat under the awning, facing the crowd outside, watching the world go by.

Neither of them recognised Nicole Scarlet.

She looked seventy. Her skin was terrible, with spider web-like splotches across her face. Her hair, which Ariel remembered as being long and dark, was cut short and thinning. Ariel had thought alcoholics were skinny, but Nicole was overweight and puffy, and she moved unsteadily on swollen legs. Ariel did not know if bad balance was a side effect of the drinking, or if Nicole was going through withdrawal. She had researched symptoms of alcoholism, made it through the first page and turned the laptop off.

It was Seb who said something first. 'Hi, Mum.'

'Hello Sebby.' Her voice was shy, but Ariel caught the intensity in her gaze, like it hurt to look at him. It hurt to look at Nicole, too. Her mother turned to Ariel and smiled. 'Hello, Ariel.' Ariel did not remember her mother's teeth being disgusting.

'Hello, Nicole.'

Nicole's smile faltered. 'Can I sit?' They nodded. She perched on the chair opposite and hunched into her cardigan. It was cheap and badly made, and Nicole's thumbs wore holes in the sleeves as she fidgeted.

A server came to the table. All three of them ordered tap water.

'I'm sorry. I'm sorryI'msorryI'msorry.' Nicole coughed out the words, like they were eating her throat. 'I don't expect you to forgive me for leaving. But please let me explain.'

'Go on,' Seb said. He was twisting his bracelets again. Ariel couldn't stop herself from folding a paper napkin, over and over.

'I'm ill,' Nicole said. 'I've been ill since you two were small. But I'm getting better. I *am*,' she said, tapping a hand on the table to emphasise her point. Seb recoiled and Nicole drew her hand back. She looked at both her children, searching for something in their faces. For Ariel's part, she did not recognise Nicole from photographs, her memories or family stories. 'Please let me be part of your lives,' Nicole whispered. Her eyes—had her eyes always been that shade of green?—were watery.

Seb and Ariel looked at each other. 'I don't think I can do that yet,' Seb said slowly. 'Can you?' he asked Ariel. She shook her head.

'Dad said he sent you our school reports,' Ariel said. 'And some of the shit we made as children. Do you still have it?'

'All of it,' Nicole said.

That's because none of it was valuable enough to sell, Ariel thought. She did not say that. Instead she said, 'You could write to me if you like. Grandpa can forward us your post.'

'I could write direct—'

'No. But if you'd like, we can correspond sometimes.' It sounded formal, like something Sophey would say. 'I can't do more than that.'

'I'm not even sure I can do that,' Seb said. The skin around his eyes was tight. 'But I'll be in touch if I ever change my mind.'

'All right,' Nicole said slowly. 'That's what we'll do.' She took a deep breath and blinked up at the café, at the Abbey, at the tourists. Next to the café, a lady in her twenties stopped pushing a buggy to stoop down and pick up her daughter's stuffed toy duck. As soon as the child had the duck back in her hands, she threw it aside, and giggled as her mother bent back down to collect it. The mother tried to hide a smile as she told her off.

'Would you like to get lunch?' Nicole asked. She glanced around and her gaze snagged on a chalkboard menu of sourdough sandwiches and vegan salad. Her eyes widened, ever so slightly, at the prices.

'No, thank you.' Ariel said. 'We both have things to be getting on with.' What she really meant was, *I don't know how I feel about you yet and I think I am overwhelmed.* Seb, she knew from a glance, was thinking the same thing.

'Thanks for meeting us,' Seb said as the siblings rose to leave.

'I've wanted to for years,' Nicole said immediately. 'But I thought it might damage... your father was right. You've done better without me.'

Now Ariel really was overwhelmed. She did not know how to express this, so she held out her hand. Nicole shook it, and her hands were sweaty and shaking. So were Ariel's. Seb shook Nicole's hand, too, and then he and Ariel skirted around the table towards the exit. Nicole watched them go.

Should they have hugged? Stayed longer? Made small talk? Ariel wondered if she should have wanted to embrace Nicole, to cry or excitedly catch up on the missing years. But the woman in the café was not the woman she remembered raising her.

Grandpa was hovering nearby, waiting, smoking.

'Do you understand your father now?' he asked when they approached.

Ariel had no idea when she would understand what she was feeling, but Seb said. 'I think the curse got her anyway.'

'Statistically,' Ariel said as she and Seb walked through town, leaving Grandpa with his remaining daughter, 'alcohol will be the thing that kills Nicole Scarlet.'

Seb took her hand.

Winter

Chapter Fifty

'Are you comfortable discussing your childhood with me?' Mirella Prescott asked. 'I may ask questions you find upsetting or confusing.'

'I'm all right with that,' Ariel said. She had brought a little squishy ball to the session with her, and now she passed it between both hands. 'The person I spoke to when I applied said that therapy can make things worse before it can make things better.'

'That can be the case,' Mirella acknowledged. She wore three gold earrings in each ear and three gold rings on each hand, and had hair so red that Ariel found it distracting. What was that Disney film? *Brave*? Mirella's hair was like the girl's hair in *Brave*. 'Your notes say you wanted to unpack the last eighteen months?' Mirella was asking. 'They mention family upheaval.'

'Just a smidge. There's a fair bit to discuss.' Ariel had initially hoped for a counsellor who wasn't white, so they could tell Ariel if she was full of shit. But then she thought, I shouldn't need anyone to hold me to account when I can do it myself. 'There's a lot to talk about, actually. Loads.'

Mirella sat forward in her chair. 'Then let's get started.'

Chapter Fifty-One

Ariel liked her new bedroom. The flat was a rental, so she couldn't paint the walls, but Sophey helped her pick out some floral prints from a local artist at a craft fair. The duvet cover and rug were new because she'd wanted a fresh start, and she'd added fairy lights to the headboard. LED battery powered fairy lights, of course. Her bedside cabinet held a drinks coaster and a journal for jotting down her dreams and anything else that bothered her. A plastic wallet in one of the drawers held letters from Grace. They were sharing book recommendations, and writing 'reviews' for the other person.

She'd given the medical dictionary to a charity shop.

Ariel liked the new garden, too. It was long and thin, separated from the upstairs flat's garden by a low fence. Rocket loved it, because there was enough grass and trees to provide entertainment. Seb found a bird bath at a boot sale and brought it home on the bus. Together the siblings scrubbed it clean and set it up on the tiny patio, just far enough from the garden chairs that if you sat very, very still the birds would come close enough that you could pick out the colours on their plumage.

She did not like the new kitchen because it was extremely ugly, but a handful of strategically placed utensil holders hid the worst of the outdated tiles, and it smelt like apple-scented cleaner soon enough.

There was a little desk in the corner of the kitchen. If they were being honest, it was a kitchenette. A stovetop and oven with some chairs, a table and the desk. It didn't matter that there was limited space for guests and no television to speak of: Ariel's job while she lived there was to pass her GCSEs and decide if she wanted to go to college or do A Levels. Seb's job while he lived there was to help Ariel through her GCSEs. So the desk lived where everyone could help Ariel with her homework.

Their upstairs neighbour was their landlord: Sharon, an accountant in her fifties who'd bought the downstairs flat when the previous owner died to rent exclusively to mature students and young families. Seb convinced her that he and Ariel fit into the latter category ('young family is always taken to mean a couple with a baby. It's time we reconsidered the definition to fit siblings, don't you think?').

It worked, because Ariel knew that Sharon wouldn't let the building fall into disrepair as long as she lived in it, and because it was a ten-minute walk to the nearest park and a twenty-minute walk to school. Also, Sharon liked dogs.

It was the first place in which Ariel enjoyed more than five consecutive hours of undrugged sleep for the best part of a decade.

Her dreams were still strange and vivid. The decaying tree was often there, but Ariel was used to it now. Rocket still got into trouble in her dreams, but Ariel was getting better at giving her subconscious a firm talking to when that happened. Besides, she fell asleep around midnight and woke up around five thirty. She would take that over thirty minutes a night, no questions asked.

Some questions were asked.

'I suspect it's a combination of a change of scene and a change of mindset,' Ernest said over tea. 'That and your emotional luggage is somewhat lighter these days.'

Once she knew she could approach her insomnia like a long-term project, Ariel felt a lot better about its existence. Going to school was a long-term project, she supposed. So was learning on the job at Bezzina's Emporium. So was ensuring Seb went back to university to finish his degree.

'Go part time at work after this year if your boss at the office wants to keep you on,' she told him over fish and chips on a Friday evening, at the end of a week in which he was so busy that she'd twice taken the train to his office to bring him dinner. 'And do uni part time. You're killing yourself to work all the hours here and they can just fire you whenever they like. So you need your degree to have other options.'

'When did you get so ruthlessly pragmatic?'

'When we opened a joint bank account for our bills and rent,' she replied. She didn't love how much time she spent looking at spreadsheets these days, working out how much money was left after they paid for essentials, although she liked that she could colour code different cells. All her Bezzina's money went to the joint account, until Seb found out and insisted she keep some for herself (the money wasn't much, but she and Sophey knew Ernest paid them far more than he needed to pay two teenagers). She was saving up for driving lessons, so she could take Rocket on adventures and not worry about hauling shopping home on the bus. She still liked to read fashion magazines in the bath, of course, but Sophey had persuaded her to try more vintage and second-hand shops. As long as all garments were fully washed to avoid any previous-owner germs, Ariel was willing to give it a go. She was a bit tired of looking like Madge and Chloe.

Settling into her new school was tough, but with the adrenaline of meeting Nicole and settling into the new flat and working on Josephine's project, the experience didn't stress her out as much as it might have done. It was hard, but so were all the other things. She did feel bad that she'd left Amanda back in Bath to give a presentation on *Aristotle and Dante Discover the Secrets of the Universe*, but she had finished her half of the report. On the first day of the new school year, Ariel received a text from Chloe, apologising for her behaviour at her dad's retirement party (and for that unsolicited phone call). Ariel thanked her for apologising and wished her good luck with year eleven.

Nicole Scarlet had written twice to Ariel, care of Grandpa. The first letter, in September, was actually a handmade birthday card, with diamantes and glitter glued to the front. The second letter, in October, was a proper letter, written across several pages and with multiple crossings-out, giving a brief account of Nicole's whereabouts and mental state over the previous decade. Ariel responded to the first—she always wrote thank you notes, a habit Nicole herself had encouraged since the children were old enough to write—but had not replied to the second.

She suspected she would respond to the letters, in time. Maybe after the new year, when the days were growing longer and she'd done enough therapy to feel more anchored in the sea of feelings Nicole's name induced. She still could not reconcile the Nicole from the Abbey with the Nicole from her memories, and she was not sure if she was ready for both Nicoles to exist. In their sessions, Mirella emphasised that there were no 'wrong' emotions, but that there were healthy and less-healthy ways of dealing with them. Ariel's preferred way, at present, was to stay as busy as possible and, when it felt a bit much, take Rocket for a walk. Some days she felt so many emotions that she thought she might explode. Mirella was helping her identify that they were mostly just variations of anger and sadness, pointed in several directions. She wondered if anyone had ever died from a surge in feeling. It would be an interesting addition to the McLean Women Death List.

She was always grateful to have Bezzina's Emporium. Ariel only worked a few evenings and weekends, but between them she and Sophey had sold five grand's worth of products since she moved to Southend. Granted, most of that was on a black military suit, to a goth on a late-night Halloween opening, but the girls took Rocket to Belfairs Woods with a picnic to celebrate. Rocket weed up a tree and then again on the picnic blanket. This is what Ariel got for training her dog to have personality. And for attempting a picnic in November.

As Christmas loomed large and Ariel settled into a school-and-work routine, she felt the same way about the shop now as she had when she mixed DIY potpourri, even if it was freezing on frosty mornings, she still hadn't quite figured out how the till worked. As for that lacquered cabinet... Ernest had gone over how it worked when he gave Ariel her door key. She wouldn't go near it unless under duress, or unless the carpet really needed a vacuum. She and Sophey had yet to see it in action, so to speak, but had a bet going about the eventuality. Sophey thought a group of teens would set it off, on a busy Saturday when they thought the staff's backs were turned. Ariel assumed it would be when a middle-aged woman wanted a refund on something she had already used.

Ariel took Rocket for a walk as the sun began to rise one Saturday morning in mid-December, stopping at a shop for tea and coffee for the weeks ahead, then arrived at Bezzina's Emporium and let them both in with her new door key. Rocket curled up on her cushion and annihilated a carrot as Ariel turned on the radiators and switched on the radio to a local station. It was playing Christmas tunes, of course. As Ariel filled the till with change, the door tinged.

'Weather's cold today,' Sophey said, 'But town's already busy. We're going to have a good day, I think.'

'Isn't that woman with the green hair coming in today?' Ariel asked. 'Her books have been ready since Monday.'

'I'll call her,' Sophey said. 'But first... coffee?'

'Please.'

Chapter Fifty-Two

2016 was close enough to hear it breathing. Ariel hummed with anticipation at the thought of a year that didn't involve moving house or uncovering family secrets. But before she could party on until the ball dropped (or hang out with Seb, Sophey and Karishma in the flat playing board games until the ball dropped) she had a final scale to balance.

Ariel wished it was a scale she could see, or at least close her hands around to feel its weights and components.

But she also wished she could play a musical instrument, understand algebra and persuade Rocket to stop chasing squirrels.

Back in November, Alexandria visited the shop every day for a week and left behind a stack of papers and three empty biros. Ariel read the papers slowly with a dictionary to hand. Sophey read them quickly but stuck around to help Ariel. Then, between them, they narrated it into a recorder and fed it through a transcription programme. Ariel used a graphics website to play around with cover designs, using the old books in the shop for reference. Sophey phoned a few suppliers. On the day of the winter solstice, Bezzina's Emporium of Magical Artefacts and Antiquities unveiled a shelf containing, for the first time in its existence, a brand-new book.

A Collection of Essays on the Ethics of the Everyday, by Dr John Ingram, with a foreword by Seb and Ariel Scarlet. It sold for five pounds, to cover the printing costs, and every library and school in Southend received a copy.

Ariel had mailed Grace an advance copy. She responded with a selfie of her reading it, glasses on, with several book emojis. Ariel mailed Grandpa one, too, but didn't expect him to let her know his thoughts straightaway.

That evening, they threw a book launch party. Ernest helped, mostly with the procuring of alcoholic beverages for guests. Sophey contacted everyone in the borough she thought might be interested, while Ariel designed and distributed posters to local businesses. Ernest took the excuse of an event to go through the shop's inventory and hoover behind some cupboards.

Or more accurately, he took the excuse to tell Sophey and Ariel to go through the shop's inventory and hoover behind some cupboards.

Not a lot of people turned up to the launch, but that was okay; there wasn't a lot of space. Ariel read her and Seb's forward to the guests, because neither of them wanted to speak for John.

In a corner of the shop, secure in a locked glass case with a label reading *Not for Sale* sat Henrietta's necklace, polished to perfection. Next to it perched a stack of John's books.

'Are you sure you want us to look after it?' Ernest asked when Ariel and Seb proposed their idea of moving the necklace into the shop.

'I think it should leave the family home,' Ariel said honestly. 'And it's glittery. It'll catch people's eye when they walk in.'

'You're happy to tell people about Josephine's curse?' Sophey asked.

'Within reason,' Ariel replied. 'It's like the website. We don't need to go into detail.'

'Tell people the necklace has a sad history,' Seb said. 'And tell them that they should read John's book to make it a bit less sad.'

Their father, of course, had been furious when he saw Ariel carrying it out of the house when she took her final journey to Southend. 'It's not your decision to make,' she said shortly. Something about her face stopped him arguing with her.

It was hard to tell in real time, but Sophey and Ariel thought the evening went well. People kept coming and going, anyway. David was there, and Alexandria too, mingling with customers as though book launches for the long dead were how they spent every evening. Ernest sold half a dozen Christmas presents—including some snow globes—and took down several email addresses for a newsletter Sophey and Ariel wanted to start in the new year.

As Sophey served customers and Ariel tidied a stack of John's books, the door creaked open and a petite Black woman with teal box braids stepped through. 'Is this the book launch for John Ingram?' she asked, catching Ariel's eye.

'It is indeed,' Ariel said, and held out a copy.

'This might sound a bit weird,' the woman said, taking the book cautiously. 'But, um, I think he was my great uncle. *Great* great times something uncle,' she corrected herself.

Ariel took her in (shorter than Sophey, excellent cashmere scarf, eyeliner Ariel would sell a couple of toes to learn to do). 'Welcome to Bezzina's Emporium,' she said after a moment. 'I... what's your name?'

'Rosie,' the woman replied. 'Are you—I'm sorry, I know this sounds weird, but is there someone called Ariel Scarlet here? Or Seb Scarlet?'

'I'm Ariel,' Ariel said. 'I'm, er, I'm John's fiancée's great-great-something niece.'

Rosie beamed. 'I was hoping I'd meet you!'

'Not to sound a bit stranger danger,' Ariel said slowly, 'because I think something quite cool is happening, but how do you know us?'

'My parents always talked about our Uncle John who died,' Rosie said, turning the book over in her hands. 'It really impacted his sisters, and I guess they passed the story down? I've been putting together our family tree, and I popped John's name into one of those search alerts in case it helped figure out our roots. I always thought we were from the Caribbean, but when I started digging I realised it was a bit more complex. Anyway, I poked around on those genealogy sites, and it turns out my mum's mother's side changed their name when they moved to London from Malta in the eighteen thirties. Ingram was anglicised from Ibrahim.'

'Malta?' Ariel had not been expecting John to be from anywhere in Europe.

'Mm. As far as I can tell, his family was originally from Egypt. Or Syria. It's taking forever to look into. But I saw your advert for the book launch on the search alert and I found your website, and I'm only in Bow, so I thought I'd come today.' She fidgeted with one of her braids.

Rosie, Ariel realised, was nervous. She had to be a good ten years older than Ariel, and a few months ago Ariel would have assumed that anyone with such good dress sense could walk into any room with ease.

'This is weird,' Ariel said out loud, and Rosie laughed. 'I should have said earlier,' Ariel continued, 'welcome to Bezzina's Emporium. Thank you for coming. Please grab a drink and look around, and... there's no pressure, but if you'd like to swap details, Seb and I would love to read what you've found on John. We've been looking, but we didn't know his family was from North Africa. And in the meantime, we can tell you about Josephine. Only if you want,' she added hastily.

'That would be great,' Rosie said. She looked around, taking in the shop's clutter as David and Alexandria pulled tarot cards with a customer. 'This shop really is magical, then.'

'Very,' Ariel said. She wondered if she should say what she was thinking, then went for it. 'That's how we learnt enough about John and Josephine to set up the website and uncover the book, actually. If you want, we could use some magic to help you look into your family tree and find out where John's family was from before Malta?'

'That would be fantastic,' Rosie said. 'Are those real silk scarves?'

'They are indeed...'

John's book sold ten, thirty, fifty copies. Mostly to academics and historians, pulled out of the woodwork by Ernest's long memory, but also to local schoolteachers and more students than Ariel could have hoped. Some were undergraduates, some were doing their PhD, some were in secondary school. It made Ariel feel like a computer programme to think like this, but she was fairly sure that the crowd of visitors was as diverse as you could hope to find on a chilly winter evening on the Essex coast. Rosie stayed for hours chatting to Ernest, and then to Seb when he came out of the stock room, where he and Karishma were checking the traffic page of Ariel's website.

Seb and Karishma had spent the past few weeks reaching out to bloggers and social media influencers to see who would be interested in reviewing *The Ethics of the Everyday* to coincide with the launch, and were eager to watch the results. Traffic was booming, Seb reported happily, and they were keeping an eye on it in real time in the back of the shop because that's where the internet worked best.

Well, checking site traffic was what they were meant to be doing.

'So *this* is where you work,' a voice said as Ariel bent over the ledger, and Ariel almost stabbed a hole in the page with the pen.

'Grace!'

'Evening,' Grace smiled. 'I'd like to buy, er, something magical. And a copy of John's book for Carrie, because I turned up this morning after I remembered it was launch day expecting to stay on her sofa but I forgot to ask first.'

'Been there,' Ariel said sagely. She selected a key charm from the counter, designed to imbue the holder with good cheer, and put both items through the ledger as on the house. 'Want to catch up while you're here?'

'Absolutely. The last book review you sent me needs translating.'

'It was a cartoon strip.'

'Exactly. Oh, hello, Liberty Print Girl. It's nice to see you again.'

'You too,' Sophey said cheerfully, balancing a tray of drinks. 'Have a lemonade. Don't lean on those snow globes.'

After Grace had gone home to her sister, Ariel went to sit on the curb outside the shop. She was wearing her big coat, so wasn't worried about messing up her jeans. She flexed her wrists under her gloves. The dog bite still ached sometimes, and there were a few yoga positions that were harder than they used to be. Ariel didn't mind. She felt like she and Rocket matched.

The door tinged as Sophey came out and Ariel shuffled over so Sophey could sit on the curb beside her. They sat quietly for a few moments, breathing in the cold, petrol-tinged air.

'The granddaughter clock sold,' Sophey said. 'To the art historian who looks like Prince Charles. He collects timepieces, apparently.' Ariel wondered how many clocks was too many clocks. 'How do you think this evening went?' Sophey asked.

'It feels like a beginning,' Ariel said. 'Good call on the libraries.'

'That's where the change will start,' Sophey said. 'Seb and Karishma said that those bloggers might want to visit in the new year and talk to us about John and Josephine.'

'Internet people in our shop? The marketing possibilities dazzle,' Ariel said. Then she thought about it. 'Actually, they do. We have the opportunity to make Bezzina's more than just...'

'An occulty antiques shop?' Sophey suggested. 'I was thinking that. We might have to make some updates if we're going to survive an influx of customers.'

'Like an electrical version of the ledger?'

'I was thinking of a fixed set of opening times.'

Ariel laughed. 'Want to hang out tomorrow and go over ideas? I'm meeting Grace for brunch before she goes back to Bath with Carrie for Christmas, but I can do any time after three. Or, wait.' Ariel dug her phone out of her pocket, tapped a message to Grace and continued, 'do you want to come to brunch before we talk shop? If Grace wants to hang out?'

'Sure. Want to go over that maths homework while we're in work mode?'

'Shit. I forgot—wait, you've already done it, haven't you?'

'Yeah, but I'm sure it's wrong. I don't know what algebra does. Let's have a study afternoon. A study-and-shop afternoon. Nan's said you're welcome to come to mine if you want. She thinks you're great. Obviously because you never say no to her cake. She's made Christmas cake.'

'That sounds good to me,' Ariel said. She meant it.

Epilogue

Tristan Oldfield Matthews liked his new front room. His wife, who had not worked since a gap year in France, spent the best part of two months carefully curating the space. It was the sort of tidy that made you loathe to sit down in case the couch told you off for slouching. Tristan sat anyway, leaning on the cushions he had purchased from Ernest Bezzina, then dug his phone from his blazer pocket and dialled a phone number.

'It's me. No, he won't sell. What do you think of making the shop a too hot to handle?' He listened to the voice on the other end. 'That sounds promising.' As the voice kept talking, Tristan gazed at the box of notelets his wife had arranged next to a pen on a side table containing the landline telephone. It was a chrome rotary phone, quite old fashioned these days, polished to a shine. Tristan kept a landline phone and made all his mundane, legitimate calls on it because at least two groups of people had tapped the line. At least, he assumed at least two groups of people had tapped the line. If he'd earned any respect in his line of work, he should be on *at least* two different organisations' persons-of-interest lists. He'd be disappointed in himself if this house, his family and the cleaning staff weren't under surveillance.

The phone he used for work, of course, was a burner.

'This group. Are they the ones who've been making noises already? Campaigners for... yeah, that's it. They're a safe bet. Set it up.' He listened again. 'Two years? Maybe three. 2019, tops. He's a stubborn bastard. But even if he won't sell... he won't live forever.'

Tristan ended the call, put his feet up on a pouffe and settled back on the sofa. These cushions were excellent value for money. He really did feel good.

At Bezzina's Emporium of Magical Artefacts and Antiquities, the evil eye above the shop door cracked in two.

McLean Family Tree 2016

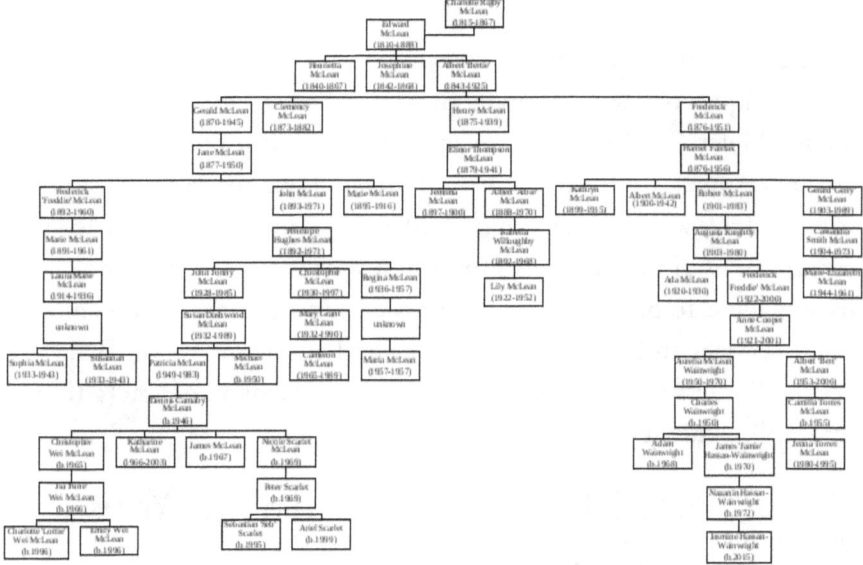

Acknowledgements

Magical charms and thank yous to Bel, Ruth, Jengo, Lindsay and May for your critiques of the early drafts of *Rotting Trees*, and to Debz Hobbs-Wyatt and Helen Gould for editing and sensitivity reading respectively. Free enchanted trinkets for life to the No. 1 Readers' Club on Patreon for joining the *Rotting Trees* weekly read along in 2024, and for your support for the earliest iterations of the Bezzina's Emporium stories. Finally, this book could not have made it to publication without the support of the Bath Centre for Fatigue Services and various professional and academic staff at Bath Spa University. Endless magical artefacts and antiquities for all of you (although better funding might be more helpful).

No. 1 Readers' Club Thank Yous

Ely, Grant, Ellen, Melody, JH, Sonia Marie, Natalie, Jackie, Bel, Lisa, Will.

About the Author

Born in Rochford in 1995, Francesca Astraea decided at an early age that the worlds inside books and television were infinitely preferable to the real one. Initially put off the idea of being a writer because it requires one to sit alone and ignore people, she now finds sitting alone and ignoring people to be the most satisfying parts of the job. She has one foot in Southend-on-Sea and one in the city of Bath. You can find her work at FrancescasWords.com[1] and support her work by joining the No. 1 Readers' Club at Patreon.com/FrancescasWords[2].

---

1.   https://francescaswords.com/

2.   https://www.patreon.com/FrancescasWords

Also by Francesca Astraea

Bezzina's Emporium of Magical Artefacts and Antiquities
Rotting Trees

Standalone
The Princess and the Dragon and Other Stories About Unlikely Heroes

Watch for more at https://francescaswords.com/.